A NIKKI PAGE MYSTERY
BOOK 3

Page Three Girls

SHERYL STEINES

NIKKI PAGE MYSTERIES

A coming of middle age story

CHAPTER 1

The phone jingled, jarring me awake and breaking the morning silence. I rolled over, glanced at the alarm, and swiped it off. It was still early; the sun was barely above the horizon, and the kids were asleep. I could have taken the lazy way and roll over for another hour of sleep, but I didn't.

Even though I had no place I needed to be this week, I couldn't stop waking at my regular time, partially to stay on schedule should that elusive job be found, but also, it seemed wasteful to ignore a perfectly good summer morning.

I rolled to my side, felt the empty space beside me where my boyfriend, Will Mann, had slept the night before. He was extremely busy in his small law practice and left for work earlier than normal. Partially to get caught up on his work but also to make an early meeting with his ex-wife, Janelle.

I'm Nikki Page. Once upon a time, shortly after my divorce, having my boyfriend run off to see his ex-wife might have left me in a cold sweat with a stomachache. But today, after all I had been through, especially in the last year, I was only mildly annoyed for Will, because I knew he didn't want to see Janelle. But she had been adamant.

Throwing off the thin summer blankets, I stepped onto the wood floor feeling the coolness against my bare feet. Steadying myself, I made my way in the semi darkness and prepared myself for a morning run.

Slipping on a t-shirt and running shorts, I thought of what I'd be doing if I had a job to go to. Not that I disliked spending summer days with my kids, but I hadn't had a job in weeks, making my only priority for this summer to find a new one. Honestly, I sometimes missed that stable, well-paying job at Able, Able, and Munch, but my perfect job had become a nightmare, and after eight months, I was still shaken from the murders, embezzlement, and money laundering. Oh, and almost losing my life was pretty much the kicker that often kept me awake at night.

Once I was dressed, I realized I wasn't in the mood for an early run. Instead, I brushed my teeth, ignored the dark circles under my eyes and went downstairs to rummage for breakfast.

With my waffle heating in the toaster, I turned on the coffee machine, and as it heated up, I opened my computer and pulled up the hundreds of emails that appeared in my email overnight, still feeling hopeful for a job interview request.

There were no new requests. I sighed, poured the coffee and switched to looking for other opportunities.

My coffee tasted bitter, and I pushed it aside as I found another job to apply for. After the initial questions, I sent my updated resume to the human resources department and hoped it wouldn't die with the hiring manager.

My phone rang as I pulled up the next job. It was too early in the morning for a call from a job inquiry.

"Isn't it early?" I asked my mom.

"I have a busy day. Any news on a job?" she asked.

I bit my tongue as I scrolled through new listings looking for well-experienced paralegals that also paid well.

"No new job yet, Mom. I'm sure I'll tell you when I find one." I took a sip of coffee. The second sip wasn't any better than the first. "Can I help you with something? I'm in the middle of my job search."

"Will should have hired you and not that other woman," Mom said. She had been saying it for weeks even though I've explained why, more than once.

"Mom. Will and I wanted to stay friends not employee/employer and now we're dating, so it doesn't matter." I sighed silently as I made a correction on my resume, though I'm not sure one word was going to make a difference. With thirty years of experience behind me, I thought it would have been easier to find something. I was sadly mistaken.

"You can still work together. You have more experience than that other woman," she said rather huffy.

I rolled my eyes. "No. Wilma and I worked together at Able, Able, and Munch. She has just as much experience as me. Besides, I'm happy for her. She's good at what she does and Will's happy with the arrangement." It felt like déjà vu. I know I had explained this all to her once, twice, or three times before.

"What about money? Do you have any of your severance package left?"

I sighed again. "Yes. I have money. Jack pays more than he needs to for child support, the college funds are robust, and Will insists on paying for our dates."

After saving the resume, I dumped the coffee and made myself a cup of tea.

"Anything else?" I asked.

I returned to the computer as Mom told me about my brother's new job.

"Allen loves his job. His company's hiring."

"I'm looking as we speak Mom," I said feeling harassed. It was definitely too early in the morning for this.

I moved the papers around my kitchen island and found the pile of documents I've collected regarding becoming a private investigator. I didn't tell Mom I was planning on expanding my level of offerings to a law firm.

"Listen. I need to go. I have several resumes I need to send out and get the kids up. Can we talk later?" I asked, even though I had no intention of waking the kids.

"Okay, Nics. You do that, I'll talk to you tomorrow."

"Sure."

After hanging up I sent the rest of the resumes from my list and opened several legal databases. While the kids continued to sleep their summer break away, I dug around my work bag, pulling out the Avers file. It was the client work I was doing for Will, mostly because his client Wayne Avers was familiar with me and felt comfortable with me still handling the paralegal duties for him.

To help make the arguments in this case, I still needed another legal precedence. But I had read the first paragraph three time, and knew, I was just too antsy to complete the work. I pushed the work aside for my resume again, and more job searches.

Another job, another resume sent.

Being jobless for all these months, had been a weight around my neck, while the rest of my life was great since Will and I had started dating three months ago.

My head swirled between my love for Will and the stress of the job search. That led me to think about how low my severance package was getting. Which then made me think of my ex-husband Jack's guilt that helped me provide for the kids, and Will's generosity with everything else.

My thoughts didn't end there, as I thought about being dependent on either of them, and it left me feeling wary and out of sorts. By the time I had cycled through all of those thoughts again, I was as exhausted as I looked.

I stood at the bay window in the kitchen and stared into the yard. Really, I couldn't complain about much else in my life as I thought of Will. His smile alone could bring me out of my emotional spiral. He was everything I had thought I would never have again; a partnership filled with love, with a person who would catch me when I fell without judgment. Only lately, it felt as though I was falling more than I should.

I sighed as I spotted a hummingbird around the blooming flowers that edged the deck.

The phone rang and for a split second I hesitated to answer it, thinking it was Mom with more job-hunting advice. I wasn't in the mood. Thankfully, it was Will on the phone.

"Hey, Will. How's your morning going?" I asked as cheerfully as I could, unsure of how his conversation with Janelle had gone.

"It was painful," he said. The frustration was dripping from his voice.

"Are you okay?" I asked. I knew I shouldn't ask him to tell me. I didn't know if I really wanted to know.

"Not really. Janelle is struggling. She found out about you and me and she's off the charts upset. Claiming … no never mind. She's going through something and took it out on me."

Even knowing Janelle was struggling didn't ease my concern over her recent and very unusual behavior. Her anger could become dangerous and I started pacing to expel my growing anxiety.

"You can tell me what happened, if it would help," I prodded.

"I know. I know. I wasn't expecting her to be so … needy. She was always so confident and sure of herself, but something changed."

He sounded fatigued as if he had been in court all day. Defeated even.

"What happened? I asked.

"She blamed me for the infertility, she apologized for how it all turned out, she was mad at me for not trying enough to fix us. She's all mixed up and unfocused."

I had known Janelle for almost as long as Will had. We had been friends. I was at their wedding, we spent years socializing. When Will told me about the divorce, I was surprised. But you never know what happens in private. While I hadn't been exactly where he was right now, I understood how difficult the aftermath of a divorce could be.

"It doesn't sound like Janelle. Do you know what brought it on?" I was genuinely concerned for her.

"As much as she complained about you and me, maybe it set her off, but things have been so odd for about three years. I'm not sure what to make of it all," Will told me.

"Oh."

"I can't stop living my life because she's feeling guilty about what happened. She made a choice."

"Yeah. And we have to live with the consequences of that."

My ex-husband Jack was living proof of how someone else's choices could crash the lives of those around them.

"Are you okay?" Will asked. I sensed a twinge of worry in his voice. It was now my turn to be concerned that I would run him out of my life if I couldn't get myself straightened out.

"I empathize with her. Sometimes I feel like I'm all over the place. But right now, I'm fine. Working on resumes and Wayne's file. How's your morning otherwise?" I asked him.
"The morning's been busy, and I've been in a crappy mood because of Janelle. I wanted to check in on you. You seemed a bit preoccupied last night."

He was right about that. I had had an interview last week for a job that was perfect for me. The right job, the right pay, close to home. Yesterday I found out the job went to someone else.

"I'm sorry. This job search is getting to me." I picked up the PI brochure and the application for the classes.

"Do you want me to put out feelers?" he asked as he typed.

I didn't want to rely on that. I had the right experience to find a job on my own, but at this point, I was desperate.

"If you could, that would be helpful. I've already sent out ten resumes today and more will show up this afternoon. I'm also going to apply for the PI program, so I can take the test for licensure."

"I think that's perfect. Are you still on for tonight?"

"If you let me pay."

He was quiet for a moment, and he stopped typing. "How about this. I'll cover us until you get a job, and then we'll reevaluate."

"Spoken like a true lawyer."

Will chuckled. "I love you," he said.

"I love you. I promise, I'll be a little less preoccupied tonight."

"Then it's a date."

"Thank you. For everything," I said. I really wished I had the words to tell him just how much he meant to me. But the words always stuck in my throat.

"I'm happy to take over for a bit. And I'll check around to see if anyone's looking for a paralegal or a PI."

"Thanks," I said as footsteps descended the stairs. "I think the beasts have awaken. I'll talk to you tonight."

We hung up and I watched one by one, in various stages of wakefulness, my kids enter the kitchen to start their day. I left my work behind as I wondered what the afternoon would hold.

***

Oppressively hot and moist summer air engulfed and stifled us. The kids had the right idea splashing around in the pool. As much as they tried to convince me to join them, I found more jobs to send resumes to, and I had to finish that Avers file and the PI application.

I stared at my most recent resume before sending it off. Before temporarily working for Will, I had worked for the law firm Able, Able, and Munch. It had been a good job with great benefits and good pay. I hadn't chosen to find out the partners were embezzling money, but I had discovered it and almost lost my life because of it. If I could only list that as one of my experiences, I might just find that perfect job.

I had finished my resume for today, and put it aside for now to finish my private investigator's class application.

When I finished that, I sent it off. The rest of the work I'd save for tomorrow.

What else was I going to do tomorrow if not for those things?

Feeling less than thrilled with my accomplishments for the day, I grabbed my bag for a trip to the store. As I slipped on my shoes, I caught my reflection in the mirror beside the door. Again, it was a surprise to see how tired I looked, which in this moment, matched how exhausted I felt. I was in serious need of a way out of this slump, and it was increasingly causing me discomfort when I realized just how much my previous lack of a job search was affecting my job prospects. It might be time to find a headhunter.

I ignored my image and climbed into the car and drove to the store.

The phone rang and I answered without seeing the caller's name as I assumed it was Will. It wasn't. When I heard her voice, my heart skipped a beat. It was Susie on the other end of the call and I couldn't find my words.

"Hi, Nics," she said expectantly.

"Suz. Hi," I said flummoxed. I hadn't spoken to Susie in three months. The last big client situation I had worked on with Will had been a missing person's case that involved an old friend of Susie's. On the surface, it shouldn't have been an issue for us. But the reality of the situation was the investigation brought up a lot upsetting memories for her, some of which involved attempted sexual assault. I hadn't known these things at the time they happened, but the memories clouded our forty-year relationship. I wasn't sure if we'd ever get back to where we had been, before I worked on the case.

"Did I get you at a bad time?" Susie asked.

"No. Just surprised. I'm on my way to the store. What's up?" I asked but it came out stiff and formal, not warm and comforting.

"I'm sorry I haven't called. There were things," she said it so quietly, I could barely hear her.

"It's okay. I didn't reach out either. How's the family?" I asked.

"Everyone's good. Gary's working a big case with …" she stopped before she said his name.

I had dated Gary's partner, Andy Butcher for several weeks. I thought for a brief moment that it could have led to something, but it ended up going nowhere. I wasn't sad about that.

"It's okay. You can say his name."

"I'm sorry I took it out on you. I'm sorry I left the friendship because of what happened. I'm sorry I didn't reach out, and I'm sorry I haven't been there for you." Susie rattled off the list.

"Stop apologizing. It was a difficult thing to be forced back into those memories. I miss you but I always figured you'd reach out when you were ready."

I wasn't sure she'd ever be ready and that loss was sad for me. We had been friends since kindergarten.

"Can we go to lunch this week. Maybe tomorrow?"

Surprised again. "I'm free tomorrow. We can meet at the café around noon?"

"Yes! That would be great. I miss you too, and I just want to get back to the way it was before I freaked out."

She hadn't freaked per se, and it wasn't right away. It happened slowly after the memories resurfaced for her. Last I heard she was in therapy to deal with what had happened twenty years ago. I had left her alone and hoped she and I would find our way back. But she ghosted me, and I went on. I'm glad she made contact now.

I pulled into the parking lot and found a spot. "I'm here now and need to pick up a few things. We'll talk tomorrow."

"Great. Thanks, Nics! I'll see you tomorrow."

After hanging up the phone, I took a breath and closed my eyes as I thought about Susie and how I missed talking to her. She didn't even know about Will and me.

Her call was a great surprise, and I was hopeful. Maybe things were looking up for me.

I opened the door; the heat enveloped me as I exited the car and rushed through the parking lot for the coolness of the grocery store. I grabbed a cart and backed into Andy Butcher.

CHAPTER 2

Andy and I hadn't spoken since I had solved his murder case for him. Well not exactly solved it, rather I was convinced his suspect wasn't the suspect he was after. I was right, he was wrong, and it pissed him off.

After going around and around with him on his murder case, I realized two things. One, he wasn't the right person for me, and two Will was. But as I stared up at him, and I remembered our time together, I was surprised how uncomfortable I was standing beside him holding my empty cart. He stared at me, just as surprised to see me.

"Hi," I finally said.

"Hi," Andy responded without emotion. His eyes darted around me, away from me, into the exciting produce section, as if he were looking for an escape.

"How are you?" I asked, realizing I wanted to be anywhere but here, just as much as him.

"I'm good… I'm… I need to go."

Andy swiftly skirted around me. Rather than taking the usual trip around the store starting at produce and snaking around the aisles toward the freezer section, he headed straight to the other side of the store. Bemused as he ran, I realized he hadn't taken a cart.

Weird and uncomfortable, I steered my cart inside the store and began filling it with necessary items. My phone rang and I dug into my purse for it. The call was from a law firm I didn't recognize but was sure I applied to.

"Nikki Page," I said.

"Mrs. Page. This is Samuel Ross with Grater and Ross. We received your application for a paralegal with our firm," he started.

"Yes. I remember," I said, but I really didn't. I had sent over fifty resumes in the last two weeks.

"I'm not sure if we're the right fit for you, but we are most interested in interviewing you."

My stomach dropped. Why weren't they right for me?

"Um. May I ask how you're not right for me?"

"I suspect we're smaller than you're accustomed to and we aren't able to pay what your experience says you're worth. But we saw your resume and knew your experience would be perfect for us. Would you be interested in coming for an interview tomorrow?"

It didn't sound promising if the partner didn't think it was right for me. But then, I was desperate and would take the first decent job that came my way. "I'm free tomorrow. What time shall I come for the interview?"

"Ten would be helpful. I can send the details to your email, if that's okay."

"Yes. Thank you. I'll see you tomorrow."

I hung up. It was a strange call to cap a strange shopping experience. But the last interview for a job that was perfect for me, ended with the job going to someone less qualified and essentially cheaper than me.

It still stung and now that the wrong job was calling for me, I was reassessing the idea that things were look up for me.

I continued through produce, picking vegetables and fruit before moving to bread, sandwich meats and milk. I couldn't shake the idea that something was so wrong with Grater and Ross that even they suspected the job wasn't suited for me.

Customers buzzed about the aisles, in and out, comparing prices, searching for the items on their list.

I felt disconnected to it, simply going through the motions as I filled my cart. Emotions whirling around me. I felt apprehension and my heart pounded. Tears threatened to fall.

Unsure why I was becoming so emotional, I knew I needed to leave. If I could, I'd leave the cart and run for my car, but my kids needed to be fed.

I wiped my eyes finished with my list and headed to checkout, nearly bumping into Andy, who at some point fetched a cart and filled it, with mostly chips and beer, though I think I saw hamburger meat in there next to the eggs.

Rather than standing behind him, I chose a longer line on the other side of the cashiers and kept my head down. I smiled when it was my turn, but tapped my foot against the floor anxious to be out of the store.

"I'm sorry, ma'am. The card didn't take. Can you reinsert it?" said the smiling cashier. I tapped the card on the reader again, watching as the computer took the payment. I breathed out stale air as the receipt printed.

As the last of the groceries were placed in my cart, I rushed from the store to the safety of my car.

It took all that I could to keep my speed steady as I made it home. I pulled into the garage and let the tears fall, unsure of how to stop my life from spinning out of control.

***

I wiped steam from my mirror, staring at my sad expression. After my tears, I put away groceries, and relaxed in a shower trying to wash the unexpected anxiety attack from my mind and clear my head. I was excited for my date with Will, and I didn't want to let my swirling emotions ruin it.

I thought of the interview request from Samuel Ross. I had never been told by a prospective employer that the job wasn't right for me. I reminded myself that it was just a job interview; I didn't have an offer, but if I were to get one, I didn't have to take it. Or, I could take it and continue to search for the right job when it presented itself. I still had the control.

It also occurred to me, in the oddest of times and places, that even without a job, I was in control. I didn't have to do anything that wasn't right for me. It was that realization, and the idea that if I just said, "Fuck it," I would be set free of the commotion in my head.

I smiled with that thought and proceeded to apply make-up, and then dry my wet mop of hair.

"Fuck it," I whispered to my reflection and fluffed up my straight, smooth hair.

It was hot, and I slipped into a sleeveless top and cute jeans; my earlier worry falling away.

The doorbell rang and Jacob beat me to the door.

Will and Jacob were chatting, laughing at something as I walked down the stairs.

Will gazed up at me, his smile wide. The conversation stopped and Jacob, when he glanced at me, seemed embarrassed.

I met Will at the door, kissed him gently. "I'm ready," I whispered in his ear. I felt him gently shudder.

I turned to Jacob, Julia, and Emily, watching us from the kitchen, smiling and yet it was uncomfortable with their eyes on us. "We'll be home around nine. There's money on the counter for dinner."

"Have fun," Emily called out.

Will led me to the car with a hand on the small of my back. The day began to wash away nicely.

"You seem in better spirits. Anything good happen?" He closed the car door after I took a seat.

"Yes and no. It was a weird afternoon."

"Weird? How so?" He backed out of my crooked driveway toward the restaurant.

"First, I saw Andy. It was awkward. Really weird." I watched Will as I told him about the encounter. Once it would have bothered him, but there were no funny faces or clenched jaws.

"There really wasn't closure for you two. I suppose that's normal. So, what else happened?" he asked and turned left out of the subdivision.

"I got a job interview for tomorrow, but it's also a weird thing. Do you know anything about Grater and Ross?"

His eyebrows raised. "Grater and Ross? I know them. I thought they were retiring soon." He stopped at the light and looked at me. "Did they mention that?"

I shook my head. "Samuel Ross said I was perfect for the job but they weren't right for me. I'm interviewing with them tomorrow, but I don't know what I'll do if I get an offer. You sure they're retiring?"

Will pulled away at the green light and continued down the road. "That's what I had heard. They're both in their sixties, not old by any means, but that's the talk of the legal water cooler."

I chuckled. "I'll ask them tomorrow. The problem is, I'm not getting interviews. I've had two interviews in three months. I'm a little concerned."

He held my hand as he drove on. "You're an amazing paralegal. You'll be a great asset to whichever firm you join. Even Grater and Ross would be lucky to have you." He stopped at the next light and turned toward me. "I know you've been feeling low because of the job hunt, but you'll get through it, and everything will work out."

The light turned green, and Will veered left toward the restaurant.

"I'm sorry. I know I've been out of sorts about the job search. But everything else has been great. The kids are doing well, they're speaking to Jack more or less, you and I are great and Susie called today. I'm having lunch with her tomorrow."

Will smiled. "I'm glad she called you. That's been a bit strained since we found Sabrina Crew." She had been our missing person, a former friend of Susie's.

He pulled into the restaurant parking lot. I waited for him to open my door. He seemed to like that. We walked toward the restaurant, my hand in his.

We were the only two in the restaurant and were seated immediately. Will ordered the wine, and I reached for the menu, hiding behind it as I searched for my dinner, though I knew I'd be having salmon.

"Do you need a reference for the interview tomorrow?" Will asked. I glanced up; he was chuckling.

I couldn't help but join him. "Do you think they'll ask?"

"I don't know. You don't seem happy about this interview," he said.

"Well, considering you've heard they're retiring soon; it seems like a bad option for me. But then, I haven't had the interview yet."

He took my hand. "I know you're worried about money, but maybe we can restructure our lives to make it easier."

I raised my eyebrows, confused and curious by what he had in mind. "Meaning?"

"Possibly cohabitation. If we moved in together, at your place, which is the logical location, with your kids and all, I'd pay rent to you for half, it'll ease up the finances a bit."

The suggestion surprised me because we had only been dating for three months. I bit my lip. "You want to move in with me and the kids?" I'm not sure why the suggestion flabbergasted me, since he spent many nights with me there. Besides, I was pretty sure our relationship was moving in that direction. And yet, there I was, at a loss for words.

"Yeah. Unless you want to move all of you into my two-bedroom house in a different school district."

I laughed. "Not what I meant. You sure you're ready to take us all on?"

"I love you, Nikki. You come as a package, and I'm very fond of your kids. I think they like me. They seem to encourage my staying over."

My hands fell to my lap. I was still shaking at his suggestion. I never thought I'd find myself here again, in a loving relationship. One that fit with me, with the kids. It was natural, easy, and didn't interfere with the life we had been living. The kids liked him. Hell, I was in love with him.

The wine arrived, and we watched as the bottle was opened, as Will tasted it and nodded. Two glasses were poured.

We ordered our meals, and when we were alone again, he said, "Think about it. But if you're unsure, we won't." He took a sip of the wine.

"I don't want you to move in with me to help me save money. This has to be the next step in our relationship because we want it to be," I said.

He nodded. "I'm ready for the next step. I've known it for weeks."

"It's not that I'm not ready. Can you give me time to talk to the kids? Make sure they're okay with the changes that come with it? It's a huge step."

He nodded. "I wouldn't expect anything less. I'm ready for the next step. I'll pull back if you're not or if they're not."

"Thanks for the patience. And about the job interview, if they were to offer me a job, do you think I'd be wrong to take it?"

He shook his head. "I think if it's something that works for you in your life now, take it. I can tell the search is getting to you. And maybe if they offer it to you and you take it, you work there until something better comes along."

"Can I pay for dinner tonight?"

He looked at me as if he was studying my face. "I'd say no because of everything else, but if it means you'll feel better about your situation, I won't say no."

"Thanks."

***

We made love when we came home. I lay beside Will, curled against me, asleep with ease. I, on the other hand, couldn't settle enough to sleep. It was 1:15 a.m. and I stared at the black hole of a ceiling with my thoughts racing through my emotional day tomorrow, or actually later today. The not right job interview, my lunch with Susie, each emotional in their own way. I was feeling nerves, and it was all I could think about.

I slipped out of bed and headed downstairs where I found a notebook and began to scribble: suit, resume, bag. I sighed. Still unsettled, I made myself a chamomile tea in hopes it would help me sleep. I took it to the sofa, turning on the television. I heard footsteps and turned, expecting Will. It was Jacob.

"What are you doing awake?" I asked him.

"I was gonna ask you the same thing."

He joined me on the sofa.

"I have a job interview tomorrow and I'm uncharacteristically nervous about it," I admitted.

"You'll do fine," he said and lay his head back on the sofa.

"And why are you awake?"

He shrugged. "Dad wants to take us away for the weekend."

My heart sped up. I knew this was a good thing, and yet it added to my restlessness. "Where does he want to take you?"

"He thought the Dells."

"That's good that he's planning time away with you."

Jacob shrugged again. "He probably won't be able to go. You know?" He looked at me, a pointed question because of Jack's wife Amber who seemingly still didn't like mine and Jack's kids.

I remembered my new motto, "Fuck it," and I felt my muscles relax. Only if it was that simple for my kids.

"Well, think positively and believe it will happen because he wants to do it." I knew I didn't believe it as Jack hadn't been the most reliable in the last three years. I'm pretty sure Jacob didn't believe it either.

"Maybe." Jacob yawned; his eyes closed.

"Go to sleep," I said.

"You too," he said lazily.

"Can I ask you something?"

Jacob opened his eyes and turned to face me. He had a twinkle in his eye that unnerved me as if he knew what was coming. "Sure. What's up?"

"What if Will moved in with us?" I asked.

Jacob smiled. "It's about time. He's here all the time anyway."

"Do you think Em and Jules will be okay with it?" I asked.

"Yeah. We like him, Mom. He's a good man. It'll be nice to have another guy in the house. Now that that's settled, you should go to sleep so you can stay awake for your interview."

He patted my shoulder and stood, walking out of the room as if he knew I needed him for the moment and that moment was gone.

I yawned, put my mug in the sink, shut off the lights, and headed to bed.

I snuggled beside Will, his arm found its way around me. "Everything okay?" Will mumbled.

"Yeah. I think I'm overthinking things."

Will's hand comfortably rested on my hip. I put my hand over his and leaned into him. "Probably." He kissed my shoulder.

"Jacob's on board with you moving in."

"Uh huh."

"He thinks the girls will be good with it too. I'll talk to them tomorrow."

"Hmmm."

"I love you."

"Love you," he said with a sigh.

As I decided to stop worrying about the things I couldn't change, I felt sleep creeping up on me. Everything that was coming my way tomorrow was just one step in the bigger picture and I suddenly had hope things would be better than okay.

CHAPTER 3

The alarm beeped so softly as not to wake me. Will desperately tried to sneak out of bed. I stretched and rolled over as the water from the shower sounded like a summer rain. I lay there until he was finished, still in awe by where our friendship journey had taken us. Will and I had gone from friends to lovers, in such an organic way and we were still getting used to the change.

But it had been a good change. Our days and nights together were more than I had expected from this stage in my life. I was finally feeling settled, not because I had a boyfriend, but because I learned to forgive, and to open up to all things.

Will finished in the bathroom and rushed to the closet, closing the door behind him. The walk-in had been half empty since the divorce and in the short three months we had been together, his side was filling up like his things belonged.

I curled inside the blanket, not quite sleepy, not quite ready to jump out of bed. Will left the walk-in, and I rolled over, catching his eye. He was fully dressed in a suit with his tie still loosely around his neck.

"Sorry to wake you."

He sat on the edge of the bed.

"You didn't."

He leaned over and kissed my cheek. "Good luck with everything today. Keep me posted."

"Thanks. I will. Have a good day."

Our hands touched even as he stood. I watched him leave the room and though I could have slept another hour, I climbed out of bed.

Still invigorated by my new motto, I showered, and dressed for my interview, ignoring any reservations that lingered in the back of my head.

I hadn't dressed up in months. It felt odd as I slipped on dress pants, a collared shirt, a blazer, and my heels.

When I finished my makeup and fluffed up my hair, I made my way downstairs in my usual work costume that I had worn for almost thirty years. But after being laid off, the outfit felt stifling.

Was it because the job wasn't right for me, and I really didn't want it or was this the time to make a change?

I pulled out a bagel and cream cheese and took small bites but my stomach roiled. Even my morning coffee had a funky taste to it. I chucked it up to nerves, and was surprised by them. I pushed emotions aside and packed my resume and references in my bag, and realized if I left now, I'd be early but not overly early, and headed to my interview.

Even in rush hour, the drive was short, and I was at my destination in ten minutes.

I could get used to this.

Pulling into the lot, I easily found an empty parking spot and turned off my car. The building had once been a small family home, now turned into a commercial property. The once single-family home was blue, neatly painted, well maintained, with the law firm name on wooden sign sticking up from the lawn beside the door.

Would I be happy working here?

As much as I tried, I couldn't forget my conversation with Samuel Ross that was only yesterday.

The job isn't right for you.

It had been weird and now that I was here, this place felt miles away from my life's experience. No more plush offices, or a team of lawyers and paralegals. No more bustling work environments that were both invigorating and exhausting at the same time. Was I ready for something so much folksier and quieter?

I sighed, pulled down the mirror and checked my makeup, fluffed my hair and laughed at the ritual.

"Fuck it," I whispered to myself. I closed the mirror, grabbed my bag, and stepped out of the car.

It was warm and glorious. As much as I needed a job, I'd miss the daily freedom of hanging out with kids and enjoying the summer. It really had been a great summer.

I climbed the three steps to a small deck, and walked to the front door entering the building. I wondered how long the house had been an office.

The receptionist's desk was in the center of what had been a large foyer, the front room was now a waiting room. I walked in, and the receptionist looked up and smiled.

"You must be Nikki," she said. "I'm Carey." She stood and held out her hand to shake mine.

"I am, and I know I'm a bit early. Habit, I suppose."

"No worries. I'll let the partners know you're here. Why don't you take a seat in the waiting area."

I followed her instructions and entered the front room where the walls were covered in old photos from the history of Lake Zurich interspersed with photos of the Grater and Ross families. There were oil paintings and colored pencil drawings. Every inch of three walls were covered in beloved pictures.

I sat in one of the two dark green leather sofas, that were well-worn and surprisingly comfortable. I leaned back as Carey entered one of the two offices on the other side of the foyer. While I couldn't hear what she was saying, her cadence was warm and soft. When she exited, she came to me in the waiting area.

"They're ready for you," she said and I followed her to the office.

What surprised me right away was how small the partner's office was. A large partner's desk sat at the center of the room. The perimeter of the room was covered with bookshelves, fully packed with legal books, pictures, and other prized possessions. Clearly, one of the partners was a baseball fan, the other had pictures of several local actors I recognized, which made sense considering Grater and Ross was an entertainment law firm.

The shorter of the two men came to me, his hand extended. I shook it as he introduced himself. "It's nice to meet you, Mrs. Page. I'm Samuel Ross and this is my partner, Ethan Grater." I turned and shook the hand of the taller of the two men, though he couldn't be more than 5'9" or 5'10".

"It's nice to meet you. Thank you for the opportunity," I said.

Samuel offered me a seat on a rusted folding chair.

"Before we start with the formalities, I was wondering if you were related to Jack Page. We've worked with him before."

I held my breath and slowly let out air. "Ex-husband," I said.

"Oh well, then I won't ask anything more about that," Samuel said, embarrassed. "Shall we begin?"

I nodded.

"We see you worked for Able, Able, and Munch until it closed. Such horrible business," Samuel said. "It's family law and you did what for them?"

"It was pretty horrific to find myself in the middle of an embezzlement and money laundry scheme. Unfortunately, several people I cared about lost their lives because of it." My breath hitched.

"I'm so sorry you experienced that. And my condolences."

"Thank you," I began. I shifted on the hard seat. "Before it all happened, I wrote briefs, documents, managed client accounts, billed, reported. Pretty much the standard work for a paralegal. I worked mostly for Justin Able." I hadn't thought of him for many months, and in that moment, I was overcome with sadness and anger. He was such an idiot for the mess he created for his family. Unfortunately, he paid for those mistakes with his life.

"And you worked for Will Mann. How come for only three months?" Ethan asked.

"He and I are friends. He needed a temporary administrative assistant as his was on maternity leave. I handled all of that work plus paralegal work for him. Same thing, client calls, briefs, documents, research," I said.

"Your experience is impressive. We did call the number for Able, Able, and Munch to speak with the former HR department reps that are still handling severance issues and health insurance claims. They had very nice things to say about you."

I felt my cheeks warm. "It was a good job until it wasn't."

"Yes. They did say you were the one to discover the money laundering and embezzlement. That's quite amazing. You worked with the police?"

I nodded. "Yes. I helped find and collect much of the information they needed in order to go after the partners."

"We are excited about that. You are able to transition and adjust to whatever comes your way," Samuel said.

I glanced at Ethan, he seemed to nod frequently. "With Will Mann. Did anything exciting happen there?"

"I worked on all manner of family law issues. I'm still helping with one case, but it's small and just really me trying to keep all the pieces in order. We did have a missing person's case that took up a lot of my last few weeks."

"That does sound interesting. And were you able to find this missing person?" Ethan asked genuinely interested.

"I did find her. She had been missing for a long time, so it was pure luck I found the one thing that led me to her. A PI had searched for her and her daughter almost twenty years ago, but was unsuccessful. Both missing women are safe and back in hiding as they wished."

"You helped solve several crimes if I remember all the gossip that surrounded that case," Samuel said.

I nodded. "In the course of finding the missing person, I discovered a potential cold case murder that led to the murderer. I suppose there's nothing more exciting than that." I had started to relax in the course of the discussion and felt the tightness in my shoulders ease.

"Don't sell yourself short, Mrs. Page. We like that you are willing to go beyond your experience to help our clients. I'm not sure if you had heard in legal circles, but we're planning on remaining open for the next two years. We have clients with a variety of issues, and we need someone we don't have to hold hands to get through the work. We'll be sending some clients to other lawyers and working with other clients until we close shop. We need someone who is smart and self-sufficient," Samuel said. He smiled at me like an elderly grandfather might with his grandchild. Thinking of the task that would be ahead of me if offered the job, it didn't seem horrible, and rather something I'd be able to do and a lot less stress than I had experienced in my last two jobs.

"Thank you for saying so. I love being a paralegal and helping those sometimes at their most vulnerable. It sounds like a fascinating proposition."

"Do you have any questions for us?" Ethan asked.

I looked at him. He looked younger than Samuel, more fit, leaner, less gray hair. He seemed affable. "How many people applied for this job?"

The partners shared a glance. I tensed a bit.

"We've only had two. I fear our retirement plans have kept applicants away," Samuel said.

I nodded as I thought about that. It could be true and again, insecurity threatened to rear its ugly head.

"We also think you're probably overqualified for what we need, but we're finding ourselves desperate for assistance. We really need someone to help with the remaining clients and the closing of the office. Two years is all we ask," Ethan said and I could hear the desperation in his voice.

"Why did your last paralegal leave?"

Again, the partners shared a look.

"She wanted more money than we could pay her. She was young, and in the end, it worked out well. I don't think she was organized enough to help us with what we'll need," Samuel said.

We looked at each other for the longest two minutes of

my life, when Samuel stood. "Well, I think we have what we need. We'll call you when we make a decision." He smiled.

I stood and Samuel walked me to the foyer.

"It was nice to meet you," Carey called to me.

"Thanks. It was nice to meet you too," I responded and let Samuel lead me to the front porch.

There Samuel closed the door behind us and stood beside me for a moment.

"Thank you, Mrs. Page, for coming in. Now do you see why we think this job is wrong for you?" he offered a smile.

"Yes. I can see why you had said so. But shouldn't that be up to me to decide that?" I asked him.

He chuckled. "I suppose I underestimated you. We really do think you can help us move forward with our plans and not have to worry about our clients. So, Ethan and I will meet and discuss. We'll get back to you this week. Thank you again."

I shook his hand. "Thank you for interviewing me. It's a bit different than I expected."

He nodded but didn't go back inside. He watched me enter my car and continued to observe me as I settled in and backed out of the spot.

I glanced at the clock. It was 9:44 in the morning and my stomach lurched as I thought of the oddest interview I had ever been on. I had the feeling I'd be offered the job. I wondered if I could handle the weirdness of it all.

I had paced and changed three times before meeting Susie at our agreed upon time and place. I was edgy. We hadn't spoken in almost three months, and we had never gone that long without either seeing each other or talking on the phone.

I walked into the café and glanced around restaurant searching for Susie's familiar face. My belly churned. First the weird interview this morning and now Susie. It shouldn't be like this.

When I didn't see her, I wondered if she was still planning on coming. I followed the hostess to my table beside the large window, which overlooked the small courtyard. I took a seat and pulled out the menu for something to do.

Susie still didn't show, and I glanced at my phone. She was only five minutes late, and it wasn't abnormal for her. She had a toddler after all. But in the next breath, I noticed her, standing at the foyer, her eyes darting across the room looking just as nervous as me. When our gazes met, she smiled, and my muscles relaxed, though my stomach was still raw. Possibly for this, maybe for the interview I still hadn't processed yet.

I stood as she walked toward me, and in an instant, time melted away and she reached around me, enveloping me in a wide hug.

"I missed you so much," Susie said as she held on, just like we would do for each other after breakups, or setbacks in school. It was as if no time had passed.

"I missed you too," I said as I pulled away and stared at my friend. She looked different and I was surprised by that. By the additional gray that flecked her hair, by the dark circles under her eyes.

"You look great!" she said a little too loud, causing stares in our direction.

"Thanks. So do you," I said as we sat.

"Thanks for saying so, but no I really don't. The last several months have been difficult for me."

I was about to say something but the waitress arrived and took our drink orders. Susie and I had been here so often that we asked to order as well. When the waitress left, Susie looked away as she stared at the pictures on the wall, I glanced around the room wondering who I might know.

"I'm sorry," Susie said again.

"Don't apologize any more. We're passed that. Just tell me how the kids are," I said and took a sip of water.

"They're good. Busy with everything at the high school, middle school, and elementary school. The baby starts pre-school in the fall."

I was amazed by that. It was hard to believe the baby was now old enough for school. "Wow," I said.

"And you. What are you doing now? Job, boyfriend, new hobbies?" Susie asked. When she was excited, she spoke quickly. But beneath her excitement, I could hear her nerves in her speech.

"The kids are good. They're enjoying their summer, working, getting ready for the new school year and I've been enjoying hanging with them. So, the usual," I said.

"I'm so glad. And they're getting along with Jack?"

I nodded. "They seem to be working it out." I took another sip of water as my tea arrived and Susie's lemonade was placed in front of her.

"You're not upset about Andy?" she asked.

"No. I'm really not. Will and I started dating," I said.

Susie's eyes bulged open; her smile grew wide. "No way! Seriously?"

I laughed. We had missed so much. "Yes. Seriously. And the biggest thing. He wants to move in together. Live with me and the kids."

Again, her eyes widened. "Nics, that's great. I'm so happy for you. I'm so happy it's going well."

Susie grew quiet and contemplative after that.

"Are you okay?"

"I missed so much," she said.

"You were haunted by horrible memories and needed time to deal with them. I understand. And now we're here having lunch. We'll get back to where we were. I know it."

Susie nodded. "I'm sorry I couldn't be there for you at the beginning of your relationship with Will. Wow… Will. That's so great." She smiled at me, it reached her eyes, and I relaxed knowing she was happy for me or more importantly, we were speaking again.

Our food arrived, and we dug into our sandwiches, mine tuna salad, hers, turkey. I glanced around the restaurant as we ate, and noticed a familiar face across the room. It looked as though my former babysitter, Penelope Pinkerton was sitting alone, reading a magazine. She put it down, wiped away tears and picked it up again. She stared at it again and slammed it shut. The young woman pushed herself away from the table and left without eating her meal.

My first inclination was to follow, but it had been years since I last saw her, and I shouldn't interfere. "Susie, I need to check something. I'll be right back."

Susie looked at me, confused. I went to Penelope's table and picked up the magazine. It was a publication I didn't recognize, and I thumbed through the volume and caught sight of the semi-nude picture of a model named Penelope Pink on page three of the magazine.

"Oh," I murmured. Page three? I thought of the old term, Page Three Girls. I couldn't recall where I had learned about page three girls, young models and actresses who posed nude and their pictures published on page three of the magazine, just like this. It was big in the 1970's but not as much today. I rolled up the magazine and brought it with me.

"What was that about?" Susie asked.

"That was my former babysitter. She seemed upset. I might reach out and see if she's okay." I shoved the magazine in my bag.

"Do I smell a case on the horizon?" Susie joked.

"Maybe. But I hope not. I liked Penelope. She was a good babysitter and a nice, responsible teenager. But the other news, I hadn't shared."

Susie looked up, a crooked smile on her lips. "Oooh."

"I applied for Private Investigator classes. I'd like to test for a license."

"I did miss a lot. That's remarkable. I'm so happy for you," Susie said as she reached for my hand and squeezing it.

"I'm pretty pleased myself," I said and took a bite of my sandwich.

"We have to do this more often," she said.

"Well, if I get this job, I'll be in the area. Piece of cake then."

Susie raised her half full glass of lemonade. "Then we will."

***

I hugged Susie as we stood outside our cars.

43

"And you're really good?" I asked Susie.

"I'm good. I needed to deal with the past. Really deal with it. I'm just sorry I pushed you away when I went through it. No more though."

"No more." I hugged her again, and we entered our cars.

I watched as she pulled away, and I dug out my phone finding Penelope's phone number. I dialed and waited but the call went to voicemail.

"Hi, Penelope. It's Mrs. Page. Nikki Page. I saw you at the Cracked Egg Café and I wanted to say hi and catch up a bit. You seemed upset. I hope all is well, but if you ever need help, please don't hesitate to call me." I left my phone number and hung up.

I pulled out the magazine and opened it to page three and glanced at the other models on the page. None of them seemed particularly happy in the pictures, not even remotely sexy as I would have expected. But I had a feeling this might be what had Penelope so upset.

I searched for the name of a photographer and saw that it was a man named Jon Jaime Ray. I pulled him up on my phone and saw he had a legitimate website, sleek and well-designed with a model list that had to be over one hundred models.

I stared back at the magazine, thumbed through the pages, realizing it wasn't porn, but rather, an updated version of an entertainment magazine.

Without knowing details, I would leave this alone, unless Penelope reached out to me. I took one last look at the unhappy models, shoved the magazine in my bag and headed for home, wondering what had happened to Penelope Pinkerton.

CHAPTER 4

My phone never rang today, and yet, I kept glancing at the screen, waiting, hoping Penelope would return my message.

It didn't seem probable that she would call me back, because I hadn't seen her in years and whatever was troubling her was none of my business.

Why was I purposely sticking my nose in it?

I put away the dishes, and washed down the counters. I thought of a different time, when my children were younger, when their problems were small, when we had a happy little family. There was Penelope, the favorite babysitter, the one Jacob had a crush on, the one that Emily tried to emulate, to be a bigger girl, the babysitter that made Julia laugh and snort milk through her nose.

Even though I hadn't seen Penelope in eight years, I remembered the feelings for the young woman who was so helpful in so many ways. Seeing her, particularly distressed as she was, and believing I knew why, left me feeling slightly apprehensive and really confused as to why I was overreacting this way.

I continued to wash down the kitchen, but sounds of summer grabbed my attention, and I glanced outside where the kids splashed each other in the blow-up pool they insisted on getting this year. It appeared to have been a great idea.

Still work had to be done as I turned to the laundry, pulling it from the dryer putting the clean clothes away. My thoughts floated in my head as I worked through the menial tasks. I supposed I could have been feeling this way because of the job interview, or my lunch with Susie, or the countless worries that seemed to fill my time.

When my phone buzzed, I yanked it from my pocket and stared at the screen.

It was Susie sending a quick text about her baby and her oldest daughter. This was the type of texts that stopped three months ago. I chuckled at the familiarity of it, relieved Susie and I had reconnected.

I texted back and let out a breath. I looked around my spotless kitchen and determined there was nothing left to do.

I opened my computer, and read my emails. I clicked on the approval for the application for the PI classes and reviewed the email, noting my next steps.

The phone buzzed again. I glanced at the screen. My stomach churned; my hands shook as I answered the phone. "Penelope, hi. How are you?" I said breathlessly and a bit surprised.

"Did you mean it when you said you could help me?" her voice was soft, yet she squeaked out her question. I thought she might have been crying.

"I did mean it, Penelope. I saw you at the café. You looked upset. Do you want to tell me what happened?"

"I need help, and I don't know where to go," she said.

She sounded desperate and clingy, so different than the babysitter I used to know. But then, I understood the predicament more than she knew.

"Does it have something to do with page three girls?" I asked.

"Can we meet at the coffee shop? In an hour?" Penelope asked.

"Of course. I'll meet you there," I said, even though Penelope wasn't forthcoming with the nature of her problem.

"Thanks, Mrs. Page. I really appreciate it," she said and hung up without saying goodbye.

The kids were still pruning themselves in the pool when I packed my bag, notebook, phone charger, wallet, phone, and the magazine into my tote bag. In a way, I was envious of their free time, their kid time, without work, school, or other commitments that filled their lives to the absolute brim.

I joined them outside.

"Hey, Mom. Come in, the water's great," Emily said.

"I can't. I'm meeting someone in about forty-five minutes. I wanted to ask you and Julia something."

The kids stopped their splashing and looked at me, grins on their faces. I glanced at Jacob, and he shrugged.

"It's okay. Jacob told us Will's moving in," Julia said.

"Are you okay if he moves in?" I asked.

"Yeah. Duh?" Julia said.

"It's about time," Emily added and ducked herself under the water. When she came up, she whipped her hair up and away, reminding me of a video I may have seen once or twice.

"You're really okay with it?" I asked again. I didn't want them to come back three months later, angry because there was no hot water, or they ran out of cereal because Will finished it before they could eat their breakfast. It wasn't only me taking a major life step.

"Mom, we're good with it," Jacob said as Julia splashed him. He returned the splash. I walked away before getting drenched and finished getting ready to meet Penelope.

50

While I hadn't met Susie in the coffee shop, walking in and looking around left me with a feeling of déjà vu.

The restaurant was nearly empty as I walked to the counter and ordered my drink. I didn't feel confident that Penelope would show but I ordered my drink anyway and took it to the window where I had a great view of anyone coming or going from the café.

I took out the magazine but didn't open it, I wasn't sure if it was a good idea for Penelope to face the trouble right away. There wasn't any time to debate with myself as she walked in. Her eyes seemed to dart across the empty store until she finally caught my gaze. She looked away, and sat across from me. She didn't say anything but wrung her hands.

"Can I buy you a coffee, a tea? Hot chocolate, maybe?" I asked her.

Penelope shook her head and stood up. For a minute, I thought she was going to leave, but she ordered at the counter and came back quickly with her own drink.

Penelope didn't say anything as she played with her cup.

"Is this related to what happened at the restaurant? Related to this?" I asked, and slid the magazine to her.

Her skin blanched when she saw the magazine and pushed it away. She nodded, and didn't look at me.

She took a sip of her drink and continued to rub her hands together.

"I can't help you if you don't tell me what happened. Take your time, but please let me know how I can help."

Penelope nodded again, pushed her drink away.

"It's…" She was nervous as she began to tap her fingers on the table. "It's bad. It's… you saw the magazine." She sighed. "It wasn't supposed to happen like this."

"How about you start at the beginning," I said.

She tapped the magazine cover, but didn't open it. "I wanted to do some modeling. I got this recommendation for a photographer, producer type. He was supposed to be this big hot shot guy. I saw the pics he took, and watched some videos. He was good. So, I called and went to meet him. It just happened so fast."

Penelope lifted the cup and put it to her lips but didn't drink. She held it mid-air. "He said he could make me famous, and rich and I was getting so excited. Head shots, magazine covers, it all sounded great. And then, before I knew it, I had no shirt on and pictures were being taken and I don't know how it all got that way."

She pulled out a pile of photos from her tote bag and placed them on the table. I waited for her to push them over. "I didn't agree to take nude shots. I didn't agree to take pictures at all. He made it sound like it was just procedure. Let's take a few and see how it goes. And then I realized what was happening."

Penelope pushed the pictures toward me. I glanced down, and shuffled through five pictures; they were similar in tone, in coloring, in pose. I pulled out the picture published in the magazine.

"How did you get these prints?" I asked her.

"He sent them to me." She pulled out the envelope and the letter.

Can't wait to work with you again. Jon Jaime Ray.

I shuddered. "Did you sign any paperwork? He can't use the photos without a model release," I explained. Without that contract, Penelope had options. If this Jon Jaime Ray had a signed agreement, there wasn't much recourse for her.

"I swear, Mrs. Page. I didn't sign anything. I went over there to talk to him about what he could do for my career. Just a discussion. How the process works." With each spoken thought, her voice rose. Her stress palpable.

"What happened that day?" I asked.

"I don't remember. I don't remember how I went from talking to him in his office to how I was on that bed with my shirt off. It happened so fast." Penelope wiped tears from her eyes. "I grabbed my things and ran out of the studio. I never signed anything." She shook as she told me about that day.

I thought about the how. How did she go from the office to the bed and not remember? I could only think of one thing. Did he drug her?

I was presuming and jumping forward too fast. One step at a time.

"The first step, we need to get a copy of the signed model release. If Mr. Ray can't produce one, then you have options. But…"

"If he can provide one, I'm fucked." She wiped tears from her eyes.

It would be hard to prove a signature was forged. All we could hope for was he didn't have one.

"I know this is scary, and you're probably feeling vulnerable and violated but you still have options. If you say you didn't sign anything, and he provides a signed contract, you can have a lawyer look into a forged signature. Let's take a step back first. I suggest for now, I'll ask a lawyer friend of mine if he could send a letter to this photographer requesting the signed release. What he tells us after that, will give you a direction in which to proceed."

"I swear. There won't be one. I never signed anything," she said, visibly more upset the longer we sat here.

"Penelope, while I believe you, I'm concerned about what happened in that studio. How was he able to get you from chatting to a seminude photo session. Is there anything you can tell me about that meeting?"

Penelope shook her head. "I remember him suggesting a test shot. It was just so subtle. Move here, look over here, open a button, and another."

I still wondered how he convinced her to take the nudes, but for now, I'd let that go. "I'll talk to Will Mann. He's a great lawyer and I'm sure with a letter we can get you an answer."

"What if there is a model release?" she asked softly.

"Then Will should be able to recommend a lawyer who can offer you sound advice. I'm legally unable to offer you advice, but I can talk to Will on your behalf. I'll let you know if he's willing to send the letter, and when it'll go out."

"Thank you, Mrs. Page. I didn't know what to do and your call made me feel like it might not be so bad."

Penelope collected the photos and the note, and placed them back into her bag. "Thank you." She stood up and smiled before leaving me alone in the coffee shop, without having finished her drink.

I sat back in the chair as I contemplated what she had told me. I wanted to know how she ended up taking nude photos. Based on her story, she didn't realize she was taking them. Did she drink something, was she drugged? If she was drugged, that was an additional level of disturbing.

I knew I was inserting myself where I didn't belong, but for now, focusing on Penelope and her problems took my mind off of my own.

CHAPTER 5

JR Productions, a sleek, slick website where videos flashed with strobing lights, and nearly naked bodies grinded against each other in frenzied movements. The music thumped; I could almost feel the beat through me.

There was so much movement and stimulation on the home page, I wasn't sure what to look at first.

I scrolled down the page, past the videos to the pictures of beautiful young models, sexy poses, smiling, or wistful stares for the camera. The photos took place at a variety of locations across Chicagoland; the beach, forest, a sunset boat ride on Lake Michigan. I scrolled through the visually stunning images.

After my first glance at the website, I could see why Penelope would be so interested in working with the talented man.

That is if he actually took these pictures and produced the videos.

I continued to click through the website, and found the page with a comprehensive list of models. Mostly women, some men as I examined the thumbnail pictures next to each name.

"There must be hundreds on this site," I said to myself.

I clicked on links beside the names and was taken to individual model pages. Again, models posed in beautiful positions and locations beside their biographies. However, there were other models, whose photo shoot appeared makeshift, and published quickly. Those models seemingly looked unhappy to be there.

A bad feeling sat in the pit of my stomach as I continued through the website, yet I couldn't put a finger on why I felt this way.

I picked up my mug and sipped lukewarm tea as I clicked on a few more of the model bios.

The list of models was long, and if I had the time, I'd look through each model's webpage but as it was, I only had time to review the names, searching for anyone I might have known. That's when I found Penelope Pink; Penelope's stage name and pulled up her bio.

The information given was pretty much a standard bio, where she was born and raised, her interests, reading, painting, rock climbing, singing, dancing, and acting. All of the information was familiar to the Penelope I knew years ago.

I returned to the home page and clicked on a few more links. But the more I had clicked through the site, the less I wanted to be there. The sexy pictures gave way to something that appeared closer to porn, and I was far from being a prude. Though I felt the need for a shower to wash away the vibes I was getting from the site.

But it was the last link at the bottom of what had seemed like an endless page that caught my attention. I hovered over the link before clicking and found myself on a sign in page.

Hmmm…

Based on what was easily accessible on the page, I had a feeling if I signed up for this website, I'd find full-blown porn I didn't want to pay for or have in my search history.

I had enough to convince me there was something more going on. I returned to the letter for Penelope.

While I knew I should speak with Will before writing the letter, he was unavailable, due to a court case early in the morning. I ignored the fact I hadn't spoken to him about it yet either. It was a simple request, and if he really didn't want to sign on the letter, I'm sure he'd recommend a lawyer for Penelope. At least I hoped so, and I began to craft the letter, requesting a copy of the model's release signed by Penelope Pinkerton.

I re-read my carefully worded request and modified a sentence and rewrote the final paragraph. When I had what I wanted, I printed off the letter, put it with the magazine and the growing pile of information I had started to print off.

I re-heated my tea and sat back on the sofa wondering if what I was doing was appropriate. After all, I had inserted myself into someone else's problem where I probably didn't belong. Did I really want to take up my time investigating Jon Jaime Ray?

The problem was, I knew I wanted to because I didn't trust the man whom I didn't know and I believed that he may have drugged Penelope to get her to take those pictures. If he did it to her, how many others did he do this to? He needed to be stopped.

So many people longed for fame, fortune, an exciting career in the entertainment industry. I could see how it was enticing, and I'm sure most of the models didn't think it would end up like this, missing their dream.

When it came down to the list, there were over two hundred models on the website, each with bios, pictures, videos, each one in different stages of undress or sadness in their eyes. I was developing a picture in my mind that Penelope wasn't the only one unhappy with the outcome of their meeting with Jon Jaime Ray.

I glanced out the window. The swimming pool stood empty as the kids moved their party to the fire pit. While it was summer, it was early in the season, and the Midwest nights were still cool. Jacob stoked the fire as Emily and Julia made smores. I could hear the laughter through open windows. I was about to join them, when Will walked in, a little rumpled from a long day.

"Hi, babe," I said. I grabbed his bag and kissed his cheek, and in my head thought of how to separate him from his day. I reached around his neck pulling him closer. It had been such a long time since I had the desire to welcome someone home.

I didn't even care that he was bedraggled, and missing his tie, or smelled of heat and hard work. "Hungry?"

He nodded and kissed me. "I could get used to this," he whispered and pulled away when the kids raced into the house.

"I'm famished actually," he said.

"Will, you missed a great game today," Jacob said. Will joined the kids at the kitchen table as Jacob proceeded to tell him how the Cubs won in the tenth inning by one run with two outs.

I left them to their chatter and pulled together a plate for Will; the leftover ginger chicken, rice, and vegetables we all had made the night before. As it microwaved the full plate, I watched my kids interact with him, asking about his day, and him asking about theirs. There was something easy about their conversation, and thoughts of Jack popped into my head. Usually, I had nothing but contempt for the man who blew up our family, but tonight an underlying sense of sadness filled me, though realistically, it was Jack who chose to miss out on his older children's lives.

"When are you moving in?" Jacob asked. "I mean, you practically live here anyway."

Will glanced back at me as I pulled his dinner out of the microwave.

"I guess that means they're good with it," Will said.

"Apparently they've been expecting it," I commented. Expertly, like I had done most of my adult life, I balanced the plate, grabbed silverware, and a napkin, and walked the food to Will.

He grabbed the plate and dug in. Seeing it was eight at night, I wasn't surprised.

"Mom, are you around tomorrow?" Jacob asked.

"As far as I know. You need something?"

"Maybe you can join us in the pool," Jacob teased.

"You're a funny, funny boy," I said.

Giving us space, the kids walked away, talking amongst themselves, and I joined Will at the table, something that has recently become habit. I was looking forward to the eventual conclusion to his client's case so dinner didn't have to be so late.

"Are you ready for tomorrow?" I asked. It was hopefully the final court case for the Micky Kern custody battle. I had worked on that with Will three months ago. Not only was I glad it would soon be over, but I was sure all parties involved wanted a resolution. It had been a heartbreaking custody battle.

"I'm ready. It's just a formality, but I wanted to make sure I had all the I's dotted and the t's crossed. Just in case." He took a bite of his dinner.

I couldn't help watching the marvel of this man sitting next to me. He entered my house that would become his home too. He was tired, and bedraggled and just fit with the rest of us.

All I could think was, damn, he was still a handsome man.

He looked at me. "What?"

I shook my head. "Nothing. Well, that's not true. I just feel at peace right now."

He smiled. "I'm glad. The interview went well then?"

It seemed like another lifetime since I sat with Ethan Grater and Samuel Ross. "It was fine. Though it had to be the oddest interview I've ever been on."

He raised an eyebrow. "Odd would sum up the partners."

"They told me more than once that the job was wrong for me, but I was right for them."

Will took another large bite and chewed.

We sat in silence as he ate a bit more. He rested after his last bite, reached for my hand and interlaced our fingers together. My stomach fluttered when our gazes found each other. As he rubbed his thumb against my hand, it felt electric.

"If they offer, you'll take it, then?" he asked.

It wasn't the job I wanted. It was too small, the salary was the least amount I had made in the last ten years, but I had been sending out resumes for weeks and was ghosted on the only other job interview I had had. I needed a job and to work. It was the only thing that could get me out of the jobless funk I found myself in. I needed this job, or at least I believed I needed it as a way to avoid my dwindling severance package. "I think I'll take it, that is, if they offer it."

"They'll offer," Will said and took another bite. When he swallowed, he looked at me, a serious expression on his face. "Remember, you have all the control. You can take the job and keep searching for something better… or you decline the offer and continue to search for the right job for you."

I knew he was right. I didn't have to take the job. I had enough money to last a few more months. But the idea of not working unnerved me. The last time I was out of a job for this long, I was on maternity leave. And I had Jack's salary to get us more than just by.

I toyed with his water glass, wiping water droplets from the kitchen table. "I haven't had any other offers."

"Please don't take something that's gonna make you miserable. You're so much more capable than you give yourself credit for."

He squeezed my hand, took a few more bites of his dinner and glanced out into the backyard, a contemplative expression on his face.

"I appreciate the vote of confidence, but I really need to have a job."

He turned toward me. "I'd like to start moving in. I'll pay half of your mortgage. It'll ease up for you. So please consider holding off."

The idea of his moving in, paying half the mortgage stopped me in my tracks.

Was he moving in to help me financially or because it was the next step in our relationship. For a moment, it felt as though he was trying to control something that wasn't his to control.

"Why?" I asked. This was odd for Will, and it made me rethink and assess, and I was feeling cautious.

He met my gaze. "Because I love you, and I want you to find fulfillment in your job. But if you really want to take it, should they offer, I'll support you."

"As long as you're not moving in just to help me financially," I finally said.

"I wouldn't do that to you. I won't come at our relationship as anything but honest."

He stood and took his plate to the dishwasher and found a spot for it. It was pretty full, so he filled the container with soap and turned on the cycle.

"So, tell me about the lawyers," I said.

He chuckled. "There's no other way to explain it besides saying they're odd birds. Nice enough, good lawyers, a little old-fashioned."

"So that's all?"

"It's all." He grimaced. "You were worried about my concern?"

I grimaced. "It's odd for you. You're usually not so demanding of things like that."

"I've been out of sorts for days. It's as if I don't help to protect you, something bad is gonna happen." He sat back in his seat.

My muscles tensed. "Protect me from what? What happened today?" I reached for his hand. "I don't need pro-tection. Just a partner. So why the extra worry?"

"Janelle."

"She called again?"

He laughed a tired laugh of a person who'd had enough. The smile didn't reach his eyes, and it definitely wasn't happy. "Janelle came to the office today. She's trying to convince me we should give it another chance. That she still loves me."

I thought back to her earlier phone call to Will. I hadn't given it much thought at the time. But her interaction with him was increasing. This time she had come to the office, with others around, to tell him this. I'd been around enough people stuck in an idea they couldn't drop. It was troublesome.

And then, it hit me like a load of bricks. "Is that why you want to move in with me?"

It was an unwelcome question for Will as well. He shook his head. "No. No, Nikki. Please don't think that."

There was more strain on his face as he tried to convince me that the two events were completely unrelated.

"I promise you. I love you, and I want to take the next step."

I nodded. "Okay. Is she gonna be a problem?"

He rubbed the stubble on his chin. "I don't know. I can't help but draw the conclusion that our relationship was the catalyst for her behavior." He reached for my hands. "I'll figure it out. I promise."

"Have you ever thought to get back with her?"

"No. She divorced me. I accepted it and moved on. I'm with you, and I plan to stay with you."

We both stood. He touched my cheeks with both hands and kissed me. I wrapped my arms around him, moved closer to him, to feel his warmth against my skin.

"It's you and me." He glanced at the ceiling. "And the kids. I don't want to jeopardize this. I'll figure out what Janelle's playing at. In the meantime, did you have a good lunch with Susie?" he asked.

I wasn't sure if he was being purposely evasive to hide something from me or he wanted me to not worry about this wrinkle and wanted to ease my mind. "Lunch was good. We're good, I think." I walked from Will and found my bag, pulling out the magazine and the letter. I stood at the island. "There was something unusual at lunch." I placed my work on the table, the letter on behalf of Penelope on top. "I saw an old babysitter at the café. She looked distracted. Crying. She left before her food arrived. And me being curious, I noticed she had left a magazine on the table. I went over and took it."

Will pulled the letter toward him and read. He didn't say anything when he had finished, but opened the magazine to the page I marked and stared at the pictures on page three.

"The babysitter is Penelope Pinkerton. Pretty, smart, talented singer." I pointed to her pictures. "Have you ever heard of page three girls?"

He looked at me and shook his head, confused. "No. I don't think so."

I explained how nude pictures of actresses and models found their way to page three in certain magazines. Mostly a popular culture event in the seventies and that gave it its name.

Will nodded. "So, this is Penelope Pinkerton, page three girl? She doesn't look particularly happy to be shooting these." He pointed to her picture.

"She wasn't. She claims she didn't meet with the photographer to shoot nude pictures and she's adamant she never signed a model release."

Will stared at the letter again. "Do you believe her?"

"I haven't seen or spoken to Penelope in six or seven years. I couldn't say for sure if she would sign a form and deny it. What bothers me is how she could have gone from discussing the photo shoot, to actually taking the pictures. Without signing a form. She swore she signed nothing."

"What did you find out about the photographer?" he asked.

"Only what was on the website. It's slick and beautifully put together if not laden with questionable content; both pictures and video. Something doesn't feel right to me about the whole thing. There are over two hundred models listed on his website. Each with a link and a bio and nude shots, soft core porn videos. It's disturbing," I admitted.

"She was probably promised fame and fortune and felt guilty after she took the pictures," Will said.

"That would be the logical explanation for what happened. The only thing I can do for her is get a copy of the signed model release form. If there isn't a signed release, she has recourse. If there is a signed release, did she sign it or was it forged? I just want to help where I can."

"I agree with this. I can sign it." He glanced at his watch. It was nearly ten. "Can you call her? I ought to talk to her before I sign that letter."

I nodded and dialed my phone.

"Hello?" Penelope asked. She sounded as though I had woken her, or maybe she was still crying. Either way, she sounded unlike the girl I used to know.

"Hi, Penelope. It's Nikki Page. I have Will Mann here with me. He'd like to speak with you before he signs off on the letter to the photographer. Is that okay with you?"

"Yeah. Yeah. That's okay," she said.

"Hi, Penelope. I'm Will Mann. Nikki tells me you didn't sign permission for Jon Jaime Ray to use any pictures. Is that correct?"

"Yes. I went there to talk to him. We talked. He wanted to take sample pictures. Next thing I know…"

"You sure you didn't sign anything without reading it first? Maybe he wanted permission for test shots or he had you write out your name and address?" Will asked her.

"I swear, Mr. Mann. I didn't sign a model release form. It wasn't what the meeting was supposed to be about. He was talking, telling me what he could do for me. Promised he'd make me a star." She hiccupped. "I'm sorry. I didn't do that. I wouldn't do those pictures." Penelope was crying, and I could hear the frustration in her voice.

"Nikki and I will walk through a simple request letter and have it sent to the photographer. We'll ask for the form and see what he has. Okay, Penelope?" Will asked.

"Thank you. Thank you. I was so worried."

"We'll help however we can. Try and get some sleep," I said.

"Thanks, Mrs. Page."

After we hung up Will glanced at me.

"What do you think?" I asked.

"I think we'll get the answer, but it won't be what Penelope wants."

"I think you're right."

CHAPTER 6

Early morning, and a light breeze blew through the windows as I continued to edit a document I was working on for Will. Probate and property theft seemed to go hand in hand as I noted the next precedent in the almost completed document.

I leaned back in my chair and sipped my coffee as I reveled in the early morning quiet that would end as soon as the kids woke. It was the best time of the day to get work done.

At eight, the doorbell rang out, but I had expected it. I dropped what I was doing and ran for the door. I opened it at the same time I grabbed the envelope that needed delivered.

"Mrs. Page?" the young courier asked.

"Yes." I handed him the envelope and a five-dollar bill.

He mock saluted and returned to his car. I watched him leave with the formal legal letter requesting the signed model release from Jon Jaime Ray. The photographer was in the area, and he'd have it within the hour.

Still silent in the house, I returned to the Avers file, and reviewed the last of the document. It wasn't the most exciting or challenging work, but it was something. I didn't enjoy the contention between brothers, but sometimes that was the job. I made a final adjustment to the document and saved it before sending it off to Will for his review.

Like every other summer morning, the kids rolled down stairs, sleep in their eyes, pajamas hanging off of them, wild bed hair. A herd of footsteps came down stairs.

"Morning," I chirped and watched the grimaces. Emily turned on the coffee maker, Jacob pulled down bowls. Julia grabbed their cereal. It's as if they had it all worked out as they made their breakfast and shuffled themselves to the tv in the den.

"So, what's on the schedule for today?" I asked and sat on the edge of the sofa.

Julia glanced at me. "Swimming and stuff this afternoon."

Of course, the typical summer day. That was something I thought of quite a bit this summer as I promised myself, I would join in, yet I hadn't been able to make the time. There was always something that needed to be done.

"You should come in with us," Emily said.

I glanced out the window and then back to the pile of work. It could wait.

"I just might do that," I said.

When the kids were sufficiently sugared up, caffeinated, and awake, they bounded out of the house for the pool. It was an unusually warm late morning and today I joined them. I pulled the lounge chair beside the pool, dropped my towel and book on it and enjoyed the sun heating my skin.

I climbed inside the blow up, above ground pool. The water was bath warm. I closed my eyes, knelt down covering myself with water. For the first time in months, there was a calm over me and nothing to interrupt it.

Around me, the kids swam underwater, retrieving weighted toys, splashing, and simply playing. Even now, their laughter was a thing of amazement. My eyes sprung open, and I stood, watching them. "Don't you have dinner tonight with your dad?" I asked. Their expressions, frowns, and downturned lips told me otherwise. "What happened now?" I asked.

"He had to cancel. Something about staying home with Amber and the baby. Someone's sick or tired or both," Emily said. Her voice was curt and that surprised me. She usually stuck up for her father, or was at least the less angry of the three of them.

"Sorry. I didn't know. I'm sure he'll reschedule when he can," I said. I hoped that would be the case and for Jack's sake, he wouldn't return to his old bad behaviors.

"Really, Mom. Even you know better than that. Amber's been a nightmare. She doesn't like this new version of the dad who spends time with his kids from the first marriage," Jacob said.

"It's an adjustment for him, for them. Give him time," I said, though based on Jack's past I wasn't sure how that would happen. I kept my mouth shut.

"We'll see," Julia said and she dove under the water, pulling on Jacob's leg. They began to splash, putting their father behind them.

I did the same and floated on my raft letting myself relax.

***

I showered off the pool water before fixing lunch and ate outside with the kids. We were finishing sandwiches when my phone rang.

It was Wilma Haynes, my friend from Able, Able, and Munch, who was now working as Will's paralegal. It had been a tough decision three months ago when I walked away from a great boss, and fabulous job, but Will and I were headed down a different path together; working for him wasn't an option.

"Hi, Wilma. How are you?" I asked and stepped away from the table.

"Doing well. I hear things are well with you," she said cheekily.

"Did he tell you he's moving in?" I asked.

"He did. That's great! I'm so happy for you. And the job search?" Wilma asked.

In an instant, that question hit me, and was a cloud over my nearly perfect life. "It's slow but I had an interview this week. We'll see."

"Good job?" she asked.

"Not on the scale of Able, Able, and Munch, and definitely not as good as Will's, but it's something. If I get it, I'll probably take it." I glanced at my phone. It had been over four hours since the letter was delivered to Jon Jaime Ray, and I was pretty sure that's why Wilma was calling.

"I wanted to let you know Jon Jaime Ray called the office. He faxed the signed model release form to us."

"I figured as much." I was disappointed but not surprised. Even if Penelope was adamant she hadn't signed anything, clearly, she did, or there was a slim possibility that the photographer signed it for her.

"There is an issue though. It's hard to tell without the original, if the signature is legitimate. I can send it to you and maybe you can see if it's Penelope's signature."

"Sure. I'll call her and let her know."

"It's on the way."

***

It was déjà vu as I sat in the coffee shop waiting for Penelope to arrive.

After printing off the model release, I understood what Wilma had noticed on the signature. It didn't quite look right as if whoever signed the form, hesitated, stopped, and started again. She could have been drugged; Jon Jaime Ray could have signed it.

I sipped my drink as I spied each customer, looking for a friendly, familiar face. I knew no one here. I took out my phone as Penelope walked in. She glanced around, and I waved her over.

She joined me. Her demeanor seemed happier, more confident than she had when she came to see me yesterday. I regretted what I had to tell her.

"Hi, Mrs. Page," she said and sat down. "I can't believe you heard back so soon."

"I put together the letter for Will. We simply asked him to produce the model release. It was couriered to him this morning. I'm sure he was anxious to resolve it quickly." I pushed the model release toward Penelope. I didn't want to tell her it was in Jon Jaime Ray's best interest to get that taken care of as soon as possible in order to keep Penelope from suing him.

She picked up the agreement, her eyes widened. "I didn't sign this," she shouted. Patrons turned toward us; I felt my cheeks flush.

Realizing her loud voice, Penelope glanced down. "I didn't sign this," she was nearly whispering.

I pulled out a notebook. "Sign here." I pushed the paper and pen toward her.

Penelope looked at me, confusion on her face until recognition. She signed her legal name. I glanced at the two signatures. As much as I wanted to believe Penelope, I wasn't an expert. The signatures were similar yet different.

"If you didn't sign this, someone did. You'll need a handwriting expert. If you signed it but don't remember, is there any way that you were incapacitated? Could you have been drugged?"

Penelope shrugged. "I don't remember. It happened so fast. I don't remember how it all happened."

I was frustrated. Not so much at Penelope, but at the situation. If she wasn't lying to me, then something happened that day. I had lots of thoughts about what that could have been and none of them were good.

"If you didn't sign it, maybe he signed it for you," I suggested.

She shook her head. "I don't know. I don't know." Penelope stood up and grabbed the copy of the model release.

I stood and handed her the name and number of a lawyer. "Lorraine Skyler. She's really good, and she can help determine if your signature was forged. She can advise you on the next steps."

Penelope stared at the paper, grabbed it. "Thank you," she said cooly, and she stormed off.

I had never felt more useless in my life, and I worried that she might do something rash and irreparable.

CHAPTER 7

The interview was almost forgotten as I dug at the weeds growing in the garden beneath the sunroom window. Cleaning the tangled mess was hard work. I dug, cut, and pulled at them, slowly releasing the roots from the dirt. I was hoping the hard work would take my mind off of Penelope's predicament and the mess I contributed to.

Unfortunately, the hard labor did little to ease my mind. Penelope maintained her innocence, even after finding a signed copy of the model release form. It appeared to be her signature.

Was it buyers' remorse or did Jon Jaime Ray forge her signature? Either way, Penelope's only hope was a handwriting expert to prove she didn't sign it.

My phone rang as I yanked a bedraggled yet hard weed that refused to surrender. I pulled off my glove, looked at the screen and was immediately reminded of the interview.

"This is Nikki," I answered breathlessly.

"Hi, Mrs. Page. It's Samuel Ross. Did I get you at a bad time?" Samuel's soft and calming voice was already so familiar.

"No. Just pulling weeds. How are you?" I asked.

"I'm good. I'm calling to offer you the paralegal position," he said. His voice was pleasant, possibly happy.

For the last two days, I'd thought of this job and what I would say if I received an offer. I couldn't shake my disappointment over not finding a job in all these months. But I couldn't let that stop me from accepting an offer. I needed to work if not just for the paycheck but for the need to have something useful to do.

"Thank you for the offer. I'd be happy to take it."

Would I regret it?

"That's great. Great, Nikki. We were concerned you wouldn't be interested, and we can use you." He sounded relieved. "I'll send you the complete offer. But we have a request."

My stomach roiled as I waited for his request.

"Is there any way you can come in for a few hours tomorrow so we can hit the ground running?" he asked.

I was surprised by that. I was hoping to get through the weekend and prepare myself for the start of working again.

"Um, sure. I can make that work."

"Good. Great. We'll see you tomorrow. Around ten?"

"Sure. I'll see you then.

***

Half pulled weeds lay where I left them as I rushed around the house, pulling laundry out of the dryer, adding a load from the washer, and running the dried clothes back upstairs. I sorted, folded, put away.

When I had a handle on the laundry, I ran to the store for food.

It was five thirty by the time I came home with a full trunk and enough food to get me through the first two weeks of work. Always the hardest days to get used to.

"We'll get those, Mom," Jacob said and I gratefully watched the kids put everything away.

Emily stood at the stove stirring noodles. Even dinner was nearly ready.

I pulled out my identification documentation, found my work bag, added some notepads. I looked around the house. I was ready, if not excited, to start tomorrow. But mostly, I was exhausted.

My phone rang. I felt flushed as I answered Will's call. "Hi, sweetie."

"Hi. How was your day?" he said.

"Well, I got the job. I start tomorrow."

"That's fast," he said surprised.

"Yeah. I should be more excited." I sighed.

"You can always keep looking if you really want to. For now, this can be a helpful bridge until then."

Possibly.

"Always so positive," I said to him.

"I try."

"Are you heading here soon?" I asked hopefully.

"I'll be there in about forty minutes. I wanted to let you know there's been a little hitch in the Penelope Pinkerton case."

My stomach churned. "What happened?"

"The police just left the office. Jon Jamie Ray was found murdered in his office. They found the request letter on his desk and wanted additional information."

I started to shake and felt my mouth go dry. "I… I'm not sure what to say. I just gave Penelope the letter yesterday. What… do they know what happened?"

"The police wanted to know about the letter. I could only tell them so much, obviously."

"They'll go after her," I said.

"Not necessarily. You know how these things go. They'll look at everyone," he reminded me. Though I had been on the end of insistent detectives who only wanted to look at me.

"I'm sorry I got you involved," I managed to say.

"It's not your fault. I was happy to assist. It was only asking for the model release, and I could only tell the police what was in the letter. Client attorney privilege and all."

"Did you tell them I gave Penelope the letter and another attorney's name?"

"I did tell them that. I suspect Andy and Gary will be by at some point to ask you what you know."

"Great. Just what I need before the job starts." Worry filled me. "I'll call Penelope and see what she knows."

"Be careful, love. This seems to be getting out of hand very quickly."

"I'll be careful. I'll see you when you get here."

In an instant, I was anxious, and hoped he'd be home soon. I didn't want to face Andy again, especially alone. It was too awkward.

I dialed Penelope. The phone rang until voicemail picked up and my worry grew.

***

The doorbell rang, an hour after dinner, an hour and half after Will told me about Jon Jaime Ray's murder. I had tried to reach Penelope twice more; she still didn't answer.

I opened the door, and grimaced seeing my ex-boyfriend, if you could call Andy Butcher that, standing there with my best friend Susie's husband Gary Ponder waiting for me to let them in. I didn't have to ask what they wanted as I held the door and motioned them inside.

They followed me to the front room and awkwardly sat across from me on the second sofa. Andy could barely look me in the eyes. I concentrated on Gary.

"What can I tell you?" I asked when we sat.

"How did you get involved with Penelope Pinkerton?" Gary asked.

"Penelope is a former babysitter. I happened to see her at the café on Tuesday. I tried to get her attention but she ran off, clearly upset. She didn't even wait for her food," I began.

I counted to ten to keep my emotions from running away from me. Gary waited patiently, while Andy's leg bounced up and down.

"I called her to ask if she was okay and to call me if I could help. Several hours later, she did call, and we met."

There wasn't much more I could tell them. I took a breath and let it out slowly as the detectives waited.

"You know I can't tell you more. She's a client of Will's. You'll need to reach out to her," I said.

"Nikki. Did you give her the model release form?" Gary asked.

I glanced at Andy; his gaze was elsewhere.

"Yes. I gave her the signed form and a lawyer's name to help her with whatever questions she might have."

"Did she sign the form?" Gary asked.

While I wasn't a lawyer, I couldn't speak on the case. She was, in this situation, Will's client, and I had acted as the paralegal. "There was a signature on the form," I said.

"What else can you tell us?" Gary asked.

"I acted as the paralegal for Will. I can't tell you anything else about Penelope. What I can tell you is, the website for JJR Productions has over two hundred other models listed on it. There's something not right about it or the situation. I have reservations about the innocence of the photographer."

I was feeling worked up about the questioning, partially because of Andy. But mostly because I walked myself into this situation and made it worse for everyone involved.

"Do you think Penelope is capable of murder?" Andy asked.

I thought of the young girl I once hired to take care of my children when they were younger. Did I see it but missed it? I couldn't say for sure.

"Again. I can't answer that. I know Penelope as a smart, capable babysitter with real ambition. I trusted her with my children for years."

"When was the last time you saw Penelope, before Tuesday?" Andy asked.

"I haven't seen her in seven years."

Will walked into the front room, his eyes found my gaze. Before either detective could ask me anything else, Will took a seat beside me and put his arm around my back.

Andy's jaw clenched.

"Stay out of police business, Nikki. I mean it. Don't interfere," Andy growled.

"I think that's unnecessary, detective. Nikki knows her legal responsibility. I think it's time you and Detective Ponder leave," Will said.

Andy stood and walked away, letting himself out and slamming the door behind him. Gary stood at the door.

"I'm glad you and Susie are talking again. She missed you," Gary said. I was surprised that was what he decided to tell me.

"I missed her too." I reached over and gave him a side hug.

"Having said that, please don't take this on. Unless Ms. Pinkerton's lawyer hires you, stay away. Okay." Gary was far gentler than Andy had been. He let himself out the door. I closed it behind him.

"Thanks," I said to Will.

"What were the police doing here?" Jacob asked.

I jumped at his voice. I hadn't realized he was anywhere near us or the conversation.

"I was helping Penelope with an issue. And the issue was murdered last night."

Will enveloped me in his arms. He kissed my temple. I glanced at Jacob; he didn't seem uncomfortable, but I did sense worry.

"They think Penelope killed someone?" Jacob asked.

"They're following leads. A clue led them to Will and that led them to me," I explained. I couldn't tell him anything more. "It's fine. It's the natural process of an investigation."

Jacob looked at Will and then me. "Okay. Seems like a lot of trouble to help an old friend," Jacob said. He crossed his arms against his chest. In that instant, I realized he'd taken on a more adult look. Not just wider shoulders, or a thin beard growing on his chin, but something in his eyes as he studied us.

"The police need to cover all angles. The timing of the evidence they found may seem suspicious in light of a murder," Will said. "If Penelope needs other options for lawyers I can provide names."

I nodded. "I'm going to call her again. I'm worried."

I stepped aside as Will and Jacob talked about other things. Again, I let the phone ring until it reached a full voicemail. I returned to my guys.

"She's still not answering, and her voicemail is full." I pulled out my phone and searched for her address. "I'm going to run over there. I'd like to see how she's doing and give her that lawyer's name. I think she's gonna need it."

"I'm coming with you," Will said without me asking.

"You just got home. You eat. I can…"

He held up his hand. "Let's go. I'll drive."

"Don't get arrested," Jacob said.

"Very funny," I said and followed Will outside. It was a hot evening, more so than what I'd expect on a June night outside of Chicago. I climbed inside his car. He pulled out of the driveway, and we headed toward Penlope's house.

"You could have stayed and had dinner," I said.

"And let you walk into something big, without backup. This is fine." Will turned right and continued along the street.

I leaned against the headrest. "I'm sorry I got you involved. Hell, I'm sorry I got involved." I rubbed my temples. A headache was quickly forming as I examined my recent life choices.

"You were trying to help someone you cared about. Don't let that deter you from helping."

"I have to start work tomorrow. Ugh. This is gonna be a long night."

Penelope didn't stray too far from home, living within two miles from her former high school. We pulled into her driveway; the house was dark.

We left the car and walked to the front door. The sun was still out, enough I could see through windows. I glanced inside the dark and empty house.

"If she's home, she's not in this part of the house."

"Let's go this way," Will said. He took my hand as we trudged across the lawn and around the townhouse. The ground sloped upward toward the stairs to the deck. We climbed. The first window gave me a view to the kitchen. Another vacant room.

The long, narrow deck spanned the back of townhouse. I walked around two large flower pots filled with summer flowers and stopped at the bedroom window. The sun was lower, harder to see inside, but what I could see was the bed, neatly made with clothes scattered across the comforter. A half full suitcase lay on the edge of the bed.

"It looks like she thought about leaving. I can't determine if she changed her mind or not," I said. I pulled out my phone and called her mother.

"Hi, Mrs. Pinkerton, it's Nikki Page."

"Nikki Page. Wow. How are you? I haven't talked to you in years."

"I know. It's been a while, and I'm sorry for calling now. I was helping Penelope with a project, and I can't seem to find her. Have you seen her?"

I hated asking the question and leaving her mother worried, but I was hoping maybe Penelope was there. Or at least her mom would know where she was.

"I… I haven't. Should I be concerned?" Mrs. Pinkerton asked. I could hear the fear through the phone.

"No. Not at all. Like I said, I was helping her with something, and I needed to give her the results of the search I had done. That's all. No worries."

I hated lying, but I didn't think at this point there was a reason to worry her mother.

"Okay. If you think so. If she calls, I'll tell her to call you. You sure my baby's, okay?"

"Yes, I'm sure. Please have a good evening. Sorry to bother you." I pocketed my phone and glanced at Will. "That didn't go well."

"She's hiding, and it doesn't look good for her. She needs to go to the police and discuss what happened," Will said.

"I know. Let's go home. Hopefully she'll call me back soon."

***

It was after nine by the time we got home. The kids were watching a movie in the basement. I was glad for that, since all I wanted to do was climb into bed. I, after all, had a new job starting tomorrow morning.

Will and I readied for bed in silence, alone with our own thoughts. I climbed into bed after him. He pulled me near and kissed my cheek.

"I'm sorry for getting you involved. It's not even your specialty." I leaned against his shoulder. He kissed my forehead.

"First, stop apologizing. Second, all I did was sign a letter asking for a signed contract. I was happy to help. We got what we asked for and the rest..."

"The rest is unbelievably bad timing," I said. "I hope she didn't do something that will ruin the rest of her life. It's not worth it."

"Since I was the lawyer of record for the letter, I'll call tomorrow and see what the police have for evidence and suspects."

"Thanks. I feel so awful. If I hadn't interjected myself in her problems, she wouldn't be in this situation either."

"But she was in a situation. It still might have turned out the same whether you helped or not. You can't blame yourself. And you can't assume she killed the man."

I was about to answer when my phone rang. "Penelope!" I said, louder than I expected. "Where are you?"

"It doesn't matter. I didn't kill him. I hated him, but I didn't kill him." She was crying, and I didn't blame her for that.

"Did you speak to the police yet?" I asked.

"No. I went there to confront him. He was already dead. I didn't do this. I ran because I needed to think."

"You need to call a lawyer and voluntarily speak with the police. Otherwise, it will look like you're evading and that will draw suspicion," I told her.

Will took the phone. "Hi, Penelope, it's Will Mann. I'm advising you to take the name of a lawyer who can help you. Nikki is right. You need to talk to the police."

"I didn't do this. I didn't agree to the photos. This isn't what was supposed to happen." Her crying became harder, louder. We waited for her to calm.

"I know this is hard, but I'll text you the name and number of a lawyer who can help you through this. Please take it," he said.

"I… fine. I'll take it."

"And call him," he said.

"I will. I'm sorry you both got involved in this. All I wanted was him to admit he twisted the situation and get the original pictures back. Thank you for your help." She hung up.

Will used my phone and texted her the information, and I snuggled back into him. "I'd like to investigate this on my own."

"Are you sure?"

"I haven't seen her in so long but what I do know about her is she was capable, ambitious, and could find her way out of problems. I don't think she did this. I think it's an incredible coincidence, and I want to make sure that other suspects are investigated."

"I'll support you however I can. But be careful. Andy isn't happy you're involved." Will kissed me. "Now go to sleep. You have work in the morning."

CHAPTER 8

Why am I doing this?

Having doubts on my first day of a new job probably wasn't a great start to the job. At five minutes before ten on Friday morning, I was wearing the third outfit I had tried on that morning; it had been that kind of day already. I took one last look in the rear-view mirror. I fluffed my hair and added a little lip gloss.

"For what?" I said to myself as I stepped out of the car with my purse and lunch and walked the short steps to the front door.

A deep breath, and I let myself in. Carey looked up and smiled.

"Nikki. So glad you're joining us." She glanced at the partner's closed door, and turned back to her desk and a neat pile of papers. "Sam and Ethan are on a conference call, so I have a bunch of things for you to fill out." She held up the pile.

"Thanks. I'm glad to be here. I figured it would be that kind of day," I said and pointed to the large stack of papers.

"Follow me." Carey stood and walked me past the partners' office to a small room beside it. She opened the door.

It was more like a large closet rather than an office. The desk was neat and tidy with pads of papers, pens, pencils, a stapler, a calculator. It looked like I would be all set. I even had a credenza with shelves above it.

"Thanks." I took a step inside. Carey placed the pile on the desk top.

"The instructions to get into the systems are in this pile. How to log in and such. It's a pretty simple system because the boys aren't too tech savvy. Follow me with your lunch," she added.

I followed to the back of the office where a once small kitchen was turned into a small kitchenette. "You can use the refrigerator or whatever else you might need. There's coffee, tea, sugar, and creamer in the fridge. Every once in a while, we'll order lunch together. The boys like to buy lunch every so often. It's pretty casual and oftentimes slow, but you'll pick up on how things are done. I know they were anxious to have you start today so you can become familiar with the admin stuff. They also want you to meet one of their clients. You'll be working closely with Myles Landry."

"Oh. Samuel hadn't said anything about meeting a client."

"I'm not surprised. Anyway, you'll be fine, I'm sure. If you need anything else, let me know."

Carey smiled and walked away. I placed my lunch in the fridge and returned to the small office.

The walls were thin, I could hear what I thought was Samuel laughing and Ethan talking. I sat at the desk and dug into the pile. There was the W2 forms, the health insurance, the 401K. I sighed as I began to complete them. They didn't take much time.

I turned on the computer and followed the instructions, created an account, changed my password. I was done before the lawyers were finished with their meeting. It took me all of forty-five minutes.

Unsure of what was next, I went out to find Carey.

"Do you want all of these papers?" I ask her.

"I'll take them. We have a bookkeeping firm that also administers the 401K and other HR items for us." She took the pile. "Oh. This is for you."

She handed me a thick folder with Myles Landry's name across the label.

"Myles will be in at one this afternoon. He's a really good client, a little different than you'd expect. He's suing his landlord for wrongful eviction and for keeping his property."

"Is there anything I should know about the lawyers?"

"They're good men. They expect to retire in about two years. They need help winding down clients and transferring them to other lawyers. They liked your experience because they thought you'd be organized and knowledgeable to help transition the clients to other firms. There are a handful of clients who will be kept on the books for two years, and you'll be responsible for them as your job goes."

I nodded. It seemed straightforward.

"Why now? Why did they decide now? I didn't think they were that old."

Carey's smile faded. "Ethan never married or had children. He was very close to his brother and his brother's family. Wife, three kids. His niece Mara died five months ago, and it devastated the family. He just doesn't have it in him anymore and really wanted to do this now. Samuel convinced him to do a full transition and take the time to do it right."

I glanced at the door. "That's sad. I'm sorry to hear it."

The door to the partner's office opened, Samuel walked out. "Ah, Nikki. Good, good. I'm glad you're here. Finding everything you need?"

"Yes. I'm logged in, and paperwork is finished."

"Good. Carey, we'll be in here updating Nikki on all things client related." He motioned for me to come in.

I entered the office; nothing had changed since I was there on Tuesday. Piles still covered the partner's desk; the shelves were still stuffed. Ethan was sitting at his desk, scribbling notes. He glanced up, smiled, and pointed to the empty chair beside him. I took a seat.

"As you know," Samuel began, "our concentration is entertainment law and intellectual property law. Your first case you'll be sitting in on is with Myles Landry. He's also known as Lola Langston. He's been our client for years. He's a drag queen working at many theaters across Chicagoland." Samuel slid a legal filing to me. I picked it up and scanned the document. Myles was indeed suing his landlord.

"His current situation is this. His landlord threw him out of the house in breach of their lease, and is holding Myles' workwear hostage."

I looked around the desk for a paper and pencil, not having expected this.

"No worries. It's all in the folder you're holding," Ethan said.

I glanced back at the notes in my hand.

"Myles asked us to sue the landlord for breach of the lease. We need you to review, make changes, format the documents in the folder. He'll be in at one."

I nodded. "Is there anything else I should know?"

I looked from Ethan to Samuel. Both shook their heads. "If you have any questions, let us know."

And with that, I was dismissed to begin working on my first client for Grater and Ross.

Pulling up my favorite databases, I researched landlord and rental laws. With the digital document on my screen, I began the process of making any necessary changes.

Even though I needed to add a few pieces for clarity, and ended up reformatting two documents, the work was easy. Or maybe I had just done the same things so often, it was just familiar. I printed off what I had and stuck it in the folder.

Unsure what to do next, I brought Samuel the documents.

Samuel glanced at me. "That was fast."

I resisted the urge to shrug. "It didn't need much. Let me know if you have any other changes. Or if you have something else you need me to do.

"Enter your time in the system, look around the computer and the files. I'll let you know if there's anything else."

I nodded and went back to my solitary office. Even at Will's office in the front entry, away from others, I never felt so alone and hoped the feeling would pass. I entered the time it took to review and update the documents into the client tracking system.

While I waited for document changes from Samuel, I pulled up the internet, specifically JJR Productions. I reviewed the model list. In my gut, I knew the murderer was on that list, but I wasn't sure how to go about investigating who that might be. I had no doubt Penelope wasn't his only victim. The timing of the murder was just a coincidence.

I copied the list of models into an Excel spreadsheet and began my first search, finding myself engrossed in the life and times of Amy Abbott, until a knock on my office door.

"Oh. Hi, Ethan," I said as I clicked off the search page and put my hand over the list. Who was I kidding, Ethan saw the move.

"Hi. I reviewed the documents. They look good." He glanced at the paper resting under my hand. "What's that?"

I felt my heart pounding in my throat.

"Sorry. I've been helping a friend with a problem and printed off what I think contains the name of a murder suspect. I hope that doesn't change your opinion of me."

His smile was wickedly funny, wide yet crooked and it reached his eyes, one raised one looking directly at me. He shook his head. "No. Not at all. We asked you in today to meet with Myles, and it was a bit of a surprise. We also don't have anything else for you today. So no, do what you need to do today." He began to turn but stopped. "That doesn't have to do with that grizzly business about that photographer Jon Jaime Ray, does it?"

It had become big news over the last twenty-four hours. I wasn't surprised he had heard, especially in the entertainment law field. But why did Ethan immediately think what I'm doing has to do with that?

"Good guess. I know one of Jon Jaime Ray's models. I was assisting her with an issue she was having."

"I'm not surprised. That man. That man was an awful human being. Unfortunately, we've come across him several times over the years." He scowled.

His reaction told me his exchanges with the victim were bad.

"Not that it's my business, but I suspect he was difficult to work with."

"That's putting it nicely. He wasn't a nice man. We had to sue him on several occasions on behalf of our clients. I'm not sure about everything that man was into, but he was unethical and a pain in my ass." He pursed his lips. "I'd say look through the files to see what I mean, but you can't use what you find in the investigation."

I nodded. "Knowing what you just told me, I'm sure the internet will provide information that's legal for me to use."

He smiled. "Please use your time today. At least until Myles arrives." He walked from my office door, and I looked into the public records for anything related to Jon Jaime Ray.

I sat in the partners' office as we waited for Myles Landry and wasn't expecting it when Lola Langston walked through the door; a long flowing caftan floating behind her.

"Hello, boys and oh, a girl," she said as she seemed to float through the partner's door.

"I'm Lola Langston." She held out her hand, and I shook it. Her confidence and assuredness left me awestruck as she took a seat beside me.

"I'm Nikki Page," I said, sheepishly.

"Well, it's a pleasure, Nikki, dear. So glad you're on my team. From what I've heard, you're the best at what you do," she said.

I was surprised the partners would have said anything at all but I went with it. "Thanks. It's nice to meet you too."

Lola clapped her hands together. "So, what news do you have for me today?" she asked.

"Nikki reviewed the documents and added a great catch of legal precedence. We will file this with the court on Monday," Samuel said and slid the document to Lola.

"I do love a good catch." She caught my gaze and winked.

I shrugged and offered a smile.

"Nikki, what can you tell Lola about the case?" Samuel said.

I'm glad I had read the entire file, forward and backward.

"The case is straight forward. Lola, your landlord evicted you for non-payment, though he endorsed the check made out to him. If his bank didn't add the funds to his account, that's between him and the bank. I didn't see any subpoena for the bank," I said.

"It's in the system," Samuel said.

"No. It's on my computer," Ethan corrected. "I'll forward that to you today."

"Sometimes, they're two halves of one brain," Lola whispered in my ear.

I couldn't help but laugh.

"Anything else you noticed, Nikki?" Samuel asked.

"I did a quick look online as I was working on the documents. The list of items the landlord is holding, which from the pictures in the folder, cost more than what he claims you and your partner owe him. I didn't see anything in the documents that were sent to you that lists how he wants you to make restitution. It really feels like he's throwing stuff out there to see what sticks. I don't think he has a case. But you never know how a jury will swing it." I looked at the partners.

Samuel glanced up, his eyebrows raised and his smile widening. "That's correct in every way. We think there's a case for discrimination, and we'll add on as we produce more evidence."

"Do you really think that's it?" I asked Lola.

She shook her head. "I don't. At least I didn't. My landlord was always chill, easy to get along with. Something happened to him or with him at the time we paid our rent check. I suspect he's taking it out on us."

"If he needed money, bringing a lawsuit down on himself seems like a waste of money and time. Why would he need you out of the house?" I asked.

Lola shrugged. "It could be his great niece. She seems to like the house. I suspect he wants us out so she could live there rent free. He doesn't have legal recourse, as you've seen, to evict us otherwise," Lola said.

"And you've never had trouble with him before?" I asked. I felt like I was getting into an easy groove with this case, and it felt right.

"Never. He had us over for the holidays and other times. We always got on well."

I looked at the partners. "I might be able to ask around. There might be someone who knows something," I suggested.

The look on Ethan's face told me that wasn't a good suggestion.

"No. No. I think we have a good enough case here, Nikki. No need to worry yourself over his reasons."

Just when I thought I had found my groove, I was dragged back into the monotony of it all.

Lola, feeling my tension, said, "I'm on board with this, if this is why you wanted me in today," Lola said.

"That and for you to meet our new paralegal. I wanted you to know you're in good hands," Samuel said.

Lola smiled at me. "I'm sure that's the case. I can see it on her face."

I offered a confused look, and Lola laughed. "If that's everything, boys, I'll head out and look forward to getting this asshole to give me back my property."

She stood; I joined her. "Nikki, dear, walk me out, would ya'?" she asked.

Lola said her goodbyes, shook hands with each lawyer and led me outside.

"It's a pleasure meeting you, Nikki. I'm surprised a woman of your experience took a job like this," Lola said.

She was definitely open, blunt, and observant.

"I lost my job months ago and have been working part-time or temporary positions since. I needed something permanent. Kids aren't cheap you know," I said trying to match Lola's humor. I didn't think I was naturally funny, and yet she laughed.

"I'm a pretty good judge of character. But I think you're too good for the boys." She winked. "Just don't tell them I said that."

"I have to ask. And you can tell me to mind my own business, but…"

She held up her hand. "Why do I dress like this when I'm not working?"

"Well, for the job I understand. But every day? You also go by Myles, correct?"

She smiled. "Consider me gender fluid. I live as whoever I feel in the moment or the situation feels right. Today I'm dealing with my landlord and Lola's items, so I felt like Lola." She leaned against the car, not interested in leaving yet. "Does this make you uncomfortable?"

I shook my head. "Not at all. It was more curiosity on my part and being a little nosy, which sometimes I am. You might be right that your landlord is dealing with something and hoping you won't fight the eviction, give you more money for your work clothes. He's clearly in the wrong. I'm glad I can help."

I held out my hand. Lola took it and shook it firmly. Even being just Nikki, I never felt as confident as Lola appeared.

"It was nice meeting you. I look forward to working with you on this." She smiled a flashy smile and got into the car, an innocuous beige sedan. Before she closed the door, she said, "Be you, Nikki. Whatever that feels like." She closed the door.

I watched Lola pull away and out of the small parking lot. I walked inside when I couldn't see her car anymore.

Samuel stood at Carey's desk.

"How did you like our Lola?" he asked.

"I like her very much. A great deal of confidence. It's something to admire."

"You'll be working on this very closely. Ethan put the documents into the shared folder on the computer. Look at the subpoena and the other documents we've already collected. That should get you to three p.m. and then head out. You can start for real on Monday. We arrive at nine, Carey is here at eight." He smiled and backed himself into his office, closing the door behind himself. I headed back to mine, left the door open and perused the computer until Penelope had other ideas.

"Hi, Penelope," I said as I answered her call. "What's happening?"

"I didn't kill that asshole. He was dead when I got to his office. I called the police," she said.

"Did you tell this to the police?"

"They're looking at me for the murder!" She was hysterical. "I didn't kill him."

"Did you call the lawyer Will recommended? You need legal representation," I reminded her.

"No. That will make me look guilty!" she screeched.

"No. It will make sure you're not wrongfully arrested." I was flustered and upset she hadn't taken Will's advice. "Call the lawyer."

"You offered to help me," Penelope whined.

"I will help you any way I can. I'm not a lawyer, though. You need to call one. If not Will's recommendation, find your own. Call a criminal lawyer." My voice was gruff and my heart sped up.

"I'll call. But I didn't do this."

"I didn't say you did. I want you to have representation. It will help you through this process. Please call him now. And I will help you with what I can. I promise." I saw Ethan standing outside my door. "I need to go. I'll call you this weekend."

I hung up, my cheeks flushed. "Sorry. My friend is having difficulties with the case."

"From what I heard, your friend is in trouble, even if she didn't kill Jon Jaime Ray."

"I hope she heeds my recommendation."

"Yes. I hope so too. He was trouble in life, and I'm sure he'll be causing trouble even in death."

He didn't wait for me to respond as he quietly walked away.

***

I spent most of the rest of the afternoon looking through the subpoena and other documents in the digital files on the computer for everything related to Myles Landry. When there was nothing left, I spent the last twenty-five minutes, researching lawsuits against Jon Jaime Ray. They included sexual harassment, non-payment, breach of contract, and fraudulent contracts.

With a list of plaintiffs, I compared the fourteen lawsuits to the list of models. Ten names matched. I was convinced I was on the right track.

Samuel poked his head in my office. "It's three. You can head out. We'll see you on Monday." He glanced at my desk. "Ethan told me you were working on something for a friend who got caught up with Jon Jaime Ray. I hope your friend is okay."

"I'm not sure. I'm sorry for working on it this afternoon."

He waved it away. "We had nothing for you today. Put it all away and have a wonderful weekend."

He smiled and walked off.

I cleaned up the little work that I had for my first day and put all of my notes on Jon Jaime Ray's murder in my bag. I glanced inside the partners' office. Samuel was deep inside a folder; Carey was finishing up her work for the day. Ethan was nowhere in sight.

"Good night, Samuel," I said.

He looked up and smiled. "We really wanted you here to meet Myles. And you did. Go home and enjoy your weekend. We'll start fresh on Monday."

"I know it's none of my business, but is Ethan, okay? He seemed distracted."

Samuel appeared surprised by my question and cleared his throat waving the question away. "He's fine. It's just been a long week. Go on home." Samuel smiled.

I nodded. "Have a good night." I turned to Carey. "Have a good weekend."

"Good weekend to you too," she said with a wide smile.

I had an uneasy feeling as I entered my car and drove home.

Images of Jon Jaime Ray, Penelope Pinkerton, and the other models floated in my head as I tried to figure out where they all fit. If Jon Jaime Ray did something to Penelope to get her to sign away her rights, I could only think she was she drugged. If she was, did he forge her signature? And what about all of those models on the website? How many of them were caught up in the mess?

By the time I got home, I was exhausted, and couldn't shake the idea that taking this job wasn't the best option for me. Even Lola Langston thought it was odd. But it was only two years. I could make it until their retirement. Couldn't I?

I dropped my bag in the mud room, dragged myself inside. The kids were nowhere to be seen, and I changed into a t-shirt and shorts.

It was a glorious afternoon, the last I'd spend at home on a weekday for the foreseeable future. The sun's pull was strong, and I found myself outside on the deck, my computer on the table, my legs up on lounger. I stared into the back yard, the old wood swing set still at the property line, the swings blowing in the breeze. The fire pit was cold but filled with ash from last night's fire, summer flowers were in full bloom.

I glanced at the computer beside me and pulled it close. I continued to the next name on my model list.

While the computer churned out the search results, I stared back into the yard. I closed my eyes, felt the breeze against my skin and reveled in the feel of it.

When I glanced through the results, nothing was jarring or suspicious or made we want to dig further into the model's life and career. I moved on to the next one.

I continued through the list and made it through the first thirty names and nothing in the names gave me a tingle until I pulled up the name Ericka Mason. As I read about her life, there was something about her story that gave me a bad feeling.

The young model/actress, Ericka Mason had committed suicide several months after working with Jon Jaime Ray. I pulled up the photo spread from the same magazine that Penelope had been in. Same pose, same empty gaze at the camera. I dug deeper, found her family, noted her brother's name, her parent's names and that her mother had died five years prior, her agent's name and an old address. I rechecked my list of lawsuits. No one in the family, including Ericka, had sued the photographer.

I looked for any police investigations into her death. It was an open and shut case from the police perspective. The family didn't pursue it any further.

Was her suicide a result of her interactions with Jon Jaime Ray? And if it was related, did the family exact revenge?

I marked Ericka Mason's name on my list.

After another hour of searching for models and anything that felt unusual in their lives, I put the computer back on the table. While I hadn't found anything else in the search, I was forming a picture that there would be more than one suspect in Jon Jaime Ray's murder, and if I could prove to the police that they needed to be investigated, maybe Penelope could be saved from this turmoil.

I yawned and closed my eyes. The sliding door opened with its familiar squeak and gait crossed the deck. I turned toward Will and smiled. He leaned over, and I wrapped my arms around his neck and kissed him.

"Hmmm," he said.

"Welcome home," I said.

"Nice way to come home."

"It is."

He sat at the edge of the lounger, studied me a moment before noticing the computer on the table. "That much work today?" He pointed to the computer.

"No. I was looking into Jon Jaime Ray's murder. I found another possible suspect."

"And your first day. How was it?" he asked.

"Weird. Met an interesting client – a drag queen. She dressed as her persona for the meeting. Tells me she dresses either as Lola Langston or Myles Landry as the mood fits." I leaned against the lounger. "She's gender fluid. I was amazed by her confidence and how sure of herself she is."

"You're not so sure of yourself?" He took my hand but his focus remained on me.

"Between the divorce and my job, I'm not so sure of myself these days."

"Divorce can mess with you, for sure." He looked at his hands.

"Did Janelle call or stop by the office today?"

Will looked at me.

I thought I saw tears in his eyes and my stomach dropped. "What happened?"

He wiped at his eyes. "I'm sorry. I'm not so sure about myself lately either. Janelle is being relentless. Our relationship was definitely the catalyst for her behavior."

"She's angry we're together?"

"She's angry and thinks we've had an ongoing affair over the years."

I opened my mouth to spout my righteous indignation, but promptly closed it. Will was upset enough.

"It's ridiculous. I know. If she calls you, can you let me know?"

"Of course. She's becoming a problem."

Will nodded. "I know what set her off, but I don't know why. She had the affair, and she asked for the divorce."

I touched his hand. "We'll get through this. Maybe she just needs time to adjust," I said hopefully. It was the third time in a week Janelle had reached out to him. It sounded like each contact was growing more intense. I didn't want to let him know I was worried about it.

"I ask a lot. But are you okay?" he asked.

I reached around him, lay my head on his shoulder. "Mostly perfect."

"I do have some news for you. I received a copy of the security recording outside Ray's office the night he was murdered. It shows the murderer coming in and leaving the office."

I raised my eyebrows. "How'd you get it?"

"Penelope called my recommendation, and he got it from the police. I asked to view it."

"Can I see it?" I asked, a little more excited than I should have been.

He nodded and motioned for me to join him inside.

At the kitchen island, he pulled his computer out of his bag and set it up. I waited anxiously for him to find the recording and start it.

"The murderer comes in at 4:13 a.m. and leaves at 4:27 a.m. Here."

I watched as it played out. The nondescript person entered the JJR Productions office and by the posture and movement, whoever it was, knew where the cameras were. Their face was obscure from all camera angles. Not only that, it was early morning, dark outside, and whoever this was took that into consideration. Clothes were dark and baggy, leaving it difficult to make out the body type and sex and with the hunch in their back, there was no easy way to get a good height description.

"Can't tell if it's male or female or how tall they are. Whoever did this knew the office and planned for it," I said. "How did they know he'd be there at that time?"

"The same people who knew about the cameras. I'm guessing they were watching him closely. He must have worked odd hours all the time," Will said. He sped up the recording several hours stopping at 8:08 a.m. when Penelope was seen walking into the office. She walked with confidence but quickly stopped as if she changed her mind and was about to turn back. Instead, she took a deep breath and at 8:10 a.m. she marched into the office. She came running out at 8:12 a.m.

She was pacing, as she took out her phone and dialed. It took her several tries and you could see her hands shaking as she did.

"Penelope doesn't look like she's faking it. That looks like genuine shock," I noted.

"They'll continue to look into her if the evidence seems solid."

"I've been researching the list from the website. I have another possibility. A young woman killed herself after working with Jon Jaime Ray. If she had a similar experience to Penelope's, it's a possibility the family went after him. I bet if I keep at it, I'll find others."

"Any other evidence about the woman's death?" Will said as he shut down his computer.

"Nothing else jumped out at me about it. I'm still looking, and I'll still work on it when I can. I promised Penelope I'd help if I could and there are things I can do," I said.

"All that I ask is that you be careful. There's a murderer out there who doesn't want to be found."

"I'll be careful. I promise," I said as I wondered if I was doing the right thing.

CHAPTER 9

He did it again," Jacob grumbled. He sulked as he walked through the forest preserve. We were heading for the dam, the bait shop, and most importantly ice cream. Will was up ahead with Emily and Julia. They were off the path by a few feet, looking into the weeds.

"What did who do?" I knew the answer to that question but asked it anyway. Jacob's look of disgust let me know I shouldn't have asked that.

He kicked a rock.

"He rescheduled. He didn't cancel," I reminded him. "He'll come get you for dinner tomorrow."

"She did it," Jacob said. He stopped and looked out into the creek overflowing from a recent heavy rain. I joined him and spotted several ducks swimming by.

"Jacob. He's trying." I put my hand on his shoulder.

"Stop defending him."

"I'm not. Not really."

He glanced at me. "He's not trying hard enough."

It wasn't worth fighting with Jacob. His father was trying but he was brow beaten, trying to balance an infant, wife, and older children. He was failing miserably, probably at all three. Jacob was having the most issues with Jack. Julia and Emily were adjusting far better than he was.

I gently pushed him forward as we sped up to catch up with the others when my phone rang.

It seemed awfully loud in the quiet forest.

Will looked back at me. I looked at my phone, held up a finger to wait. "Penelope, hi. What's happening?"

"They questioned me again. I was at the station for three hours!" she screeched into the phone.

"Was the lawyer with you?" I asked.

"Yes, but what good did it do? Three hours, Nikki!" She was hysterical again.

"Do you know any of the other models who worked with him?" I asked.

"I didn't do this, and I know other models he did this to. But they're focused on me because of the letter you convinced me would make this go away."

I didn't think that's what I said to her, and I was feeling my heart race. She was blaming me for this.

I stopped walking and looked out into the prairie. "The recording showed you walking into the office," I said.

"He was already dead."

"I realize that, Penelope. I also saw the murderer enter and exit the office. I've already discovered additional persons of interest. I'll send them to the police and your lawyer when I get some more information. What did your lawyer say about the signature on the model release form?"

I heard footsteps through the phone. She was pacing.

"He's hiring a handwriting expert to look at the signature and compare it to mine. Nikki. Help me. I didn't do this!"

Her voice was filled with frustration and fear. I was feeling it myself. But I was also very surprised after seemingly blaming me that she would continue to ask for help.

"Did you know Ericka Mason?" I asked.

The pacing stopped. "Yes. I knew her. Why?"

"How well did you know her?"

"Very well. We were roommates in college. I saw her for at least six years after we graduated but lost touch. And then out of nowhere, she calls and tells me about this photographer who was helping her. But she didn't tell me who. I didn't make the connection until this happened to me."

"Do you think she killed herself because of what Jon Jaime Ray did to her?"

She snorted an angry laugh. "No. I'm betting she pushed back and that's why he killed her. She never would have killed herself. She wasn't that type of person."

What type of person kills themselves? It could have been underlying depression, or the events that shaped her life. For now, I'd trust that Penelope knew her and asserted that. It put an additional spin on the likelihood someone in her family wanted to get back at the photographer. I made a mental note.

"Does the family think so as well?"

"They were upset as you'd imagine. But they blamed the photographer. They never said anything about who he was. I didn't put it together. I didn't know."

"I'm sorry this is happening to you. I promise if I find anything useful, I'll let your lawyer know."

"I'm sorry I yelled, Nikki. I'm so…"

"I understand. I promise, I will help you. Anyway, I can."

"Thanks," she said and the line went dead.

Will was watching me. They all were. "She was questioned for three hours. She blames me because of the letter, and yet, she still wants my help."

"She's desperate and lashing out. And you'll do what you always do. Research and dig until you have useful information to send to the police. Did you tell her about the model who committed suicide?"

"I told her. She said it wasn't possible. That Ericka wouldn't have done that."

"Does she think Ericka was murdered?" Will asked.

"She does."

"That's motive for the family," Jacob said.

Will took my hand, and we followed the kids around a bend in the path. We were getting closer to our favorite part of the trip, the bait shop and the ice cream.

My kids walked along, whispering to each other, stopping periodically to look at flowers, birds, or the garter snake that slithered across the path.

While they were pissed for their canceled plans, they hadn't been surprised and made the best of the rest of our time in the woods. They had expected very little when it came to their father and that saddened me.

***

I dreamt of Penelope, Ericka, and Emily, so similar to the other girls. Had her life choices taken her down a different path, could she have ended up like these young women?

The dream ended with me jolted awake. My eyes adjusted to the darkness, the only light from the beside clock that said two in the morning, and the bright moon outside my window.

I was shaking, thinking of the dreams and faces that haunted me. The broken families, and the list I hadn't gone through last night because I chose to eat pizza with the kids and watch a movie. While it didn't make up for their dad cancelling on them, it was something.

Not wanting to wake up Will, I moved to the chair beside my bed, but my movement woke him anyway.

"Nikki? Is everything okay?"

"I can't get them out of my head. I want to check a few more names, and then I'll come back to bed."

"You know, you have all day tomorrow. It's Sunday."

He rolled on his back.

"Just give me a few minutes. I promise I'll be back to bed soon."

But I wasn't back soon. I dug through twenty more names on the list and found that three of them sued Jon Jaime Ray; sexual harassment, fraudulently signing the agreement, theft. Another four had him charged with rape. One rape case was still open, the other three discharged and settled out of court. Other lawsuits were still pending.

But there was something I hadn't expected in a totally unrelated lawsuit, the one against Jon Jaime Ray, filed by Ethan Grater.

I supposed if Ethan and Samuel had bad business

dealings with him, it was possible the business ended in a lawsuit. More fraud, more embezzlement, more theft.

Jon Jaime Ray filed a countersuit, both were still ongoing.

It occurred to me that maybe, if Jon Jaime Ray was that deplorable of a human being, someone else, not on the model list had it in for him.

By three thirty in the morning, I was barely staying awake and shut down my computer. When I climbed back into bed, Will rolled closer to me, wrapped his arm around me.

"Find anything new?"

I yawned. "Jon Jaime Ray was not a good man. He has open lawsuits against him including one filed by Ethan Grater."

"That opens the suspect list quite a bit," Will murmured in the darkness.

"Yeah. It does."

We both settled and as tired as I was, I was also energized by the idea that Penelope wasn't the only one who hated the man, and there was hope I could help get her out of trouble.

***

I had every intention of working on Sunday but as it turned out, my computer sat on the island, unopened for the entire day.

But for now, I stared at the phone in my hand completely taken back by what I had just heard.

"You're kidding," I finally said.

"What do I do?" Jack asked sighed. There was a whine to his expectant question, a sigh at the end as if he was emotionally battered by the choices he had made. At least that's how I imagined what he was going through.

It was the moment I finally hit my limit with Jack Page.

"Fuck it," I murmured to myself. I released the anger, and fear that I'd held onto since the divorce. I knew I was done with letting Jack get to me and for being a victim in what he had done to all of us.

"I don't care," I said with an eerily calm voice.

"Nikki?" He seemed confused by that.

"I don't care what it's doing to you. You've made the wrong choices in the last three years, and you need to live with the consequences."

Again, I remained cool. He was no longer worth the energy.

"I need your help," Jack pleaded.

"Your wife is being irrational. You've made adjustments, you're doing what you're supposed to be doing. Just because she doesn't like it doesn't make it my problem."

Jack sighed heavily. "Nikki. Please tell the kids what I'm dealing with. She's losing her mind when I go over there. She doesn't want me to see you."

"She doesn't want you to see your kids. She doesn't want you to pay child support, or alimony. I don't give a fuck anymore."

I leaned against the island and stared into the backyard. Again, the kids were splashing in the pool, Will enjoying his day off. The scene made me smile until I thought of the phone call I was still on. There was no way I'd be telling the kids about their father's trouble. They didn't need to know his wife threatened him with a divorce he couldn't afford.

"Can I see the kids this afternoon?"

"Yes. You either tell them the truth or you find a way to see them. I'll stay out of the way so you don't have to see me and lie about it to your wife."

"I think she has post-partum depression. She says she doesn't and won't get help."

"I don't care. Do what you're supposed to do and stop calling me." I was going to hang up but stopped before clicking the button. "By the way. Will's moving in with us."

There was silence on the phone. I was anxious to get this call over and join the kids and Will outside. But for this Jack needed to know.

Finally, Jack said, "Oh."

"No other comments. No rules for my dating and who they can see?" I was teasing, egging him on, forcing him to say something. I'm not sure why I was being so mean.

Whatever my reason, it felt fun, and I should have felt ashamed. I didn't.

"Are you going to get married?"

"Probably and then, Amber will get her way. No alimony for me."

"Nikki. You seem especially bitchy today. I'm sorry."

I ignored the bitchy comment because I was purposely laying it on thick. I wanted to wrap myself in that emotion and protect myself from Jack. Maybe it would spur him forward to figure out his situation.

"You need to do more than apologize. Come over as soon as you can. I need to go." This time I clicked to end the conversation, grabbed my towel and joined my family outside in the pool. For the first time in a long time, I felt like I had everything under control.

***

My personal bag was filled with my computer and my notes. I wasn't sure how much work I'd have on my second day. I wanted to be prepared.

In my work bag, I placed my work computer, my notes on Myles Landry's case, and zipped it up. The bags on my shoulder were heavy and bulky as I walked downstairs to Will pouring coffee in his thermos.

"How did you sleep?" Will asked, now screwing on the cap.

"Pretty good. I said what I needed to say to Jack. He understands me fully now. What's on your plate today?"

"Calling my lawyer about Janelle. I took what you had on the Avers case, and I'll get that filed. I think Wayne will have his say, and we can get this resolved. Otherwise, just more lawyering." He put the thermos in his bag.

"Do you think going to your lawyer will help with Janelle?"

Will shrugged. "I don't know. I'll let her sort it out. Janelle is just so unlike herself and I get the feeling there's more to her unusual behavior. Did Jack act weird when we started dating?"

I thought about that. He seemed a little irked by the idea. But then, I turned a new leaf and really didn't care. "I don't know. I find it funny that the ones who asked for the divorce can't deal with us moving on."

"I suppose Jack just assumed you'd lay down and not move forward. But then, I think he finally realized what he did, and he's having trouble with the consequences of his actions."

"Janelle never liked me." I was surprised I mentioned it to Will. But it had been obvious over the years. I'm not sure if it was jealousy or she just didn't like me.

"I know."

I was surprised by his honesty.

"She never believed that we hadn't slept together at any point in our relationship. She may have been jealous because of your kids. I'm really not sure."

With his bag across his shoulder, he said, "By the way, I have a free afternoon today. I thought I'd kick out early. You're done at 4 ish?" Will asked.

I nodded.

"When do you think you'll start the PI classes?"

"I can start the certification process next week. I need to complete the rest of the forms and pay for the program. The good news, I already have the degree and work experience in a law firm. I thought I would check with Stan Marley and see if he could recommend a PI that might take on apprentices. I'll need that for licensure."

"Are you excited about it?" he asked.

"I am. It's strange to me that everything else in my life is falling into a happy place. The kids are in a better place, Susie and I are good, I have you, and I'm happy. But there's that side in my life that's a mess. I just want the equilibrium of both sides being in sync. The PI stuff is new and exciting, it's the law stuff I'm struggling with."

"If you need to leave this firm, then you will. And you'll find the right place for you." He glanced at his watch. "I need to go. Morning's busy, afternoon not. I'll talk to you this afternoon." He kissed me.

"I love you," I said as he whisked himself away.

"I love you more," he responded and headed out.

I watched him leave and reluctantly cleaned up and headed to work.

CHAPTER 10

The office was dark. Even Carey wasn't this early. Without a key, I sat in my car and perused my email. I saw it, the email of acceptance to the PI program. I was in and could start as early as today.

The possibilities floated around my head. There was a sense of freedom, of new beginnings, of good changes. I glanced up when I saw something from the corner of my eye and saw Carey pull in. I left my car and followed her.

"I should get you a key," she said as she let me inside.

"It would help. I like coming in early. It's quiet, and I tend to get a lot done."

"I'll get that for you. I think the partners left some emails for both of us. They'll be in around ten."

Carey turned on her computer. "Oh, and Ethan told me to tell you if you need to work on the project for your friend until they get you up to speed, he said do what you need and use whatever systems you need."

"Thanks." I entered my office, turned on the computer and gave myself a minute to collect my thoughts.

I dug into my work email. For my first day, the partners had sent a few emails with requests and instructions. After printing them off, I began to pull up the documents they requested I look into. I did what I needed to do, reading and reviewing, looking up law precedence as I updated and adjusted the documents. There had been three documents they requested from me but the work was easy. When I finished, it was only 9:30 and the partners wouldn't be in for another half hour.

I tossed my folders into the inbox and pulled up my list of models, reviewing my notes and marking the models that I thought warranted another look.

In a half hour, I only found one more story that looked promising, or at least odd. It was another model who had done several photo shoots for Jon Jaime Ray. Her story was upsetting. She was currently completing a second stint in rehab, according to the article. Granted, she could have become an addict on her own. It didn't mean the photographer had anything to do with it. But then, from the pictures I had seen, I thought there was a strong possibility the experience led to the videos that led to the drugs. It was a gut feeling.

I found her family and made a note to contact Natalia and her parents Stefan and Nya Blankman. I circled it and jumped at the knock on the door.

"Sorry. I didn't hear you come in," I said to Ethan as he stood at the entrance.

"It's okay. Did you find what we left for you?"

"I did." I stood and walked the folder to him. "I finished these so I was doing a little research on the models that worked with Jon Jaime Ray."

"Any possible suspects?" he asked without emotion.

"There are plenty of models affected after working for him, but nothing concrete. I'm not finding that connection yet."

"I'm sure you will."

I thought of what Ethan's relationship was to Jon Jaime Ray. I wanted to ask him about it, about the lawsuit, but I left it alone, for now.

"There's something about Jon Jaime Ray that's unsettling to me. The pictures, the videos and the stories I'm finding, it seems like he was taking more than sexy pictures. Nudes and sexually explicit. Based on what I do know, he probably took them without the model's consent or drugging the models for their signatures. I'm hoping when I give the police what I found, they'll start down that line of questioning."

I watched Ethan's reaction. His face remained calm, though he let out a sigh. "That would explain a lot, actually. We stopped doing business with that asshole because our clients who had dealt with him, or the work we had with him, seemed questionable at best."

"You knew about the work he was doing and lawsuits against him?"

I thought I saw Ethan squirm for a moment, but he was able to gather his composure. "We were aware." He cleared his throat. "All reasons why we severed ties with him."

Nervously perhaps, he tapped on the door jamb. "If you need to use anything, please do. We won't be ready for you until after lunch. We would like you to join us." He tried to smile, but the news about what I had learned seemed to bother him. For that I felt badly, especially on my first real day.

"Thanks. I will."

He took the folder and left me alone to retreat to his own office. I heard the door close. It was going to be a long morning.

***

I brought my lunch into the conference room. Samuel was already there, carefully taking out all of his lunch items.

When they were neatly in front of him, he unwrapped his sandwich and took a bite.

"Oh, Nikki. Good. Please sit."

I took the seat across from him and took out my own sandwich.

"Ethan told me you're looking into that ghastly Jon Jaime Ray murder. You have a friend involved?"

"She's a person of interest. But yes. I think there are about 200 or so possible suspects. I think a lot of models had a bad experience with him."

I took a bite of my sandwich. It was dry.

Ethan soon joined us but had no lunch. "Have you found anything else?" he asked when he sat.

"No. I figure every model on the website should be interviewed as a possible witness or suspect." I took another bite.

Ethan slid the folder to me. "Good work. I only made a few notes. Nothing that changes much of anything."

He glanced out the window that led to a small side yard. There wasn't much out there.

"I'll work on this when I finish lunch. You said you had something for me this afternoon?"

Ethan glanced at Samuel. "Nothing difficult. Could you please pull a list of all clients in the system who have outstanding balances, and another list of clients without balances. We'll be looking at those, first to collect money, the second list to start passing them off to other lawyers if they haven't worked with us in over two years. We'll have to determine the best fit if they haven't already found another lawyer."

Ethan's voice was emotionless, cold, remote. I shuddered and wondered what the change in his demeanor meant. Had I done something wrong, or was he reacting to closing the office and retiring?

"I'll pull those lists. Do you have a letter you'd like me to send to the outstanding balance list?"

Samuel nodded. "It's in the system. We sent one out about four months ago. You can use that. Make any necessary updates."

I watched Samuel eat very methodically, one item at a time before moving on to the next. When he finished his sandwich, he worked his way through the carrots.

Ethan scowled as he slowly sipped on his pop.

Odd as it was, I finally stood and threw away my lunch bag. "I'll start on those lists now."

The system was exactly like Will's and the one I used at Able, Able, and Munch. I easily pulled the list of clients that hadn't worked with the partners in two years or more. I printed the list. It was substantial.

I moved on to the outstanding balances, downloaded the list, imported it into the email system. I found the email they wanted me to send. After adjusting dates and wording, I tested the email. It worked fine, and I sent the outstanding balance email to the clients that fit the criteria.

It was three by the time I finished sending the first group of emails and corrected the documents Ethan had reviewed.

I decided it was time to ask the other models what happened between them and the photographer.

To determine a pattern of abuse, I looked up Ericka Mason's family and found contact information for her brother. I dialed Allan Mason.

"Hello?" he asked with a tinge of confusion in his voice. I'm assuming Grater and Ross on the caller ID would be unnerving.

"Is this Allan Mason?" I asked.

"Who is this?"

I explained who I was and why I was calling. "I'm calling about Jon Jaime Ray's murder," I finally said.

"Who are you again?" he asked. There was a twinge of annoyance and possibly anger in his voice.

"I'm Nikki Page. I'm looking into some things about Jon Jaime Ray's death. Specifically, I'm trying to determine the extent of abuse toward his models."

He was quiet for a moment. I glanced at my phone to verify he was still on. "Mr. Mason?"

"Yeah, I'm still here. That's the producer. The one that died the other day."

"It is."

"Why are you talking to me? I didn't know him." He was tense as he spoke.

"I was reviewing the list of models who had worked with him. I discovered Ericka Mason was one. She was your sister?"

"Yeah. So. What does this have to do with me?"

"Her suicide. It was after she had worked with him. I saw some of the pictures."

"He was a lech. He drugged her or something to get her to take those filthy pictures. She wouldn't have done that. He did it. He killed her because she was gonna report him to the police."

It was just as Penelope had assumed as well. "What did the police say to that? I saw her death was ruled a suicide."

"Why do you care? Police didn't care then. Let the murderer go. She didn't deserve it."

"I have a friend who's being questioned in Jon Jaime Ray's death. She didn't do it. I'm trying to prove there was a pattern of abuse with his models and not just with my friend."

"You're calling because you think I killed that ass?" His anger was palpable. How did this conversation go so wrong so fast?

"No. Not at all, Mr. Mason. I just want to know if he abused your sister. Did she tell you what he did to her?"

"So, you can blame me for killing him? No. I didn't. And yes, he made her take those pictures. That... that video. I figure whoever did it, did the world a favor," he spat. I could feel his anger through the phone.

"All I want is to make sure the actual murderer ends up behind bars, rather than one of his victims. I'm really trying to find out if he had a pattern of abuse with his models or just my friend."

"Well, it wasn't me! That man, if you could call him that, was slime. He got Ericka to take those nudes. She didn't want to, but he did it anyway. She didn't agree. Never signed anything, but there it was, her signature on that form. She was so upset. Couldn't eat or sleep. Was depressed." His voice sped up the more upset he got.

"Is that why she killed herself?"

"I already told you. Are you an idiot? The police got it wrong! The papers got it wrong? She didn't kill herself. Jon Jaime Ray did that. She was gonna go to the police and tell them what he did."

"I have a friend who's a suspect. She claims the same thing Ericka claimed. I want to prove Jon Jaime Ray did this often, and it could be one of many models. If I get the police to agree to that approach, they'll ask you. Where were you two nights ago, the night Jon Jaime Ray died?"

He laughed. The laughter stopped as quickly as it started. "I didn't kill that bastard. He wasn't worth my time. Don't call here again!"

He hung up silently without the benefit of an old-fashioned wall phone and that sound of it slamming in my ear.

He told me plenty but refused to give me an alibi. I put notes in a small notebook I carried with me. It was worth looking into. He'd need an alibi for the night of the murder.

I plotted out my next phone call, the next model on my list, Natalia Blankman and her parents Stefan and Nya, but all I got was a phone that didn't stop ringing. Nor did I reach an answering machine or voicemail.

I stared at the list. After speaking with Allan Mason, I wasn't up for another bitter family or angry model. The victims deserved justice, as did their families, but I knew their feelings would still be raw so soon after Jon Jaime Ray's murder. Maybe questioning them right now wasn't the right path.

There were about ten others to consider, and I chose to find a different approach with my next computer search. Maybe it would be easier if I began pulling up business associates and let the police deal with the victims. After all, that's what they've been trained to do. I couldn't bear putting someone else in that much pain.

Today, the databases churned out data as I searched for the victim's business associates. I was desperate to find any other connection to his murder that would take the investigation away from Penelope and the other victims.

My first query found a new business name, JJ Enterprises, the photography and video business that 'employed', for a lack of a better term, all of the models. Here I found a list of the lawsuits, and I printed what I had found.

I searched for various versions of his name, and that's when I hit pay dirt. I didn't realize it at first glance, EG Entertainment was a connection to the photographer. I looked up the articles of incorporation. My heart sped up; my stomach roiled. Jon Jaime Ray was business partners with Ethan Grater.

CHAPTER 11

I printed off the public records and shoved them carelessly in my bag as I couldn't wait to leave the office for home.

I was planning on keeping the new knowledge to myself as I said goodbye to Carey. I peeked into the partners' empty office. The boys had already left.

The more I learned about Penelope and the other models, the more unsettled I was about the systematic abuse against them. But with Ethan's connection to the photographer, I couldn't help wonder how much Ethan knew or may have participated in.

Being home felt safe, away from the ick of Jon Jaime Ray and his murder. I opened the door and yummy scents wafted to me, beckoning me inside. The kids had started dinner, and I was surprised by the complexity of it; chicken, green beans, rice. I was also surprised they were home. They were supposed to see their dad tonight.

"I like coming home to this," I said as I put my bag down and ignored the fact they weren't out.

Jacob slammed down the pot on the stove. I figured he was angry at Jack. I wouldn't pry and let him cool off before pressuring him to tell me what happened.

"How's the new job," Emily asked as she checked the chicken in the oven.

"It's a little slow, but it's only the first official day. I'm sure it will pick up eventually."

I took out a spoon and tasted the rice. Julia smiled expectantly.

"Is it okay?" Julia asked.

"Really good. Thanks."

Emily took the chicken from the oven, and placed it on the counter. "How's Penelope's case going?" She took out a serving fork and placed it on the baking dish. I noticed there were five large breasts rather than our usual four.

The garage door opened, and Will entered. I looked at him. I couldn't help but smile.

"Hey. Perfect timing. That smells great." He walked over, patted Jacob's shoulder, smiled at Julia, and kissed me.

"This was a great surprise." I grabbed the plates Jacob handed me and dug in pulling my portion. "And answering your question, Em. My investigation into Penelope's situation is surprising and upsetting. I can't say more. Not yet."

Will looked at me, confusion on his face.

I shrugged, and we moved to the dining room and took our seats.

"How upsetting?" Will said when he sat.

"I'm not sure yet. But I have an uneasy feeling."

Will held my hand as we ate, and I kept an eye on the kids. Specifically on Jacob, still steaming.

"Did you do something fun today?" Will asked. He glanced at Jacob; I knew he saw what I had seen in my son.

"I sat outside and read and slept. It was great," Emily said.

"Minnie and I played video games," Julia said.

"That's because he cancelled on us," Jacob grumbled. Jacob's phone dinged. He glanced at the screen and placed his phone down.

"Did he…" I was about to ask what reason Jack had given this time, but I kept my mouth shut and took another bite.

"Does it matter what the reason is? He cancelled. I told him if he's not gonna honor his promises don't bother to come back. He didn't even have a legitimate reason to cancel." Jacob pushed his plate away, and looked at me. "Are you going to defend him?" he asked with an accusatory tone in his voice.

"No. I'm not gonna defend him. I have no words." I took a bite of food, much like my kids did when they didn't want to answer me.

The mood shifted. Emily picked at her food; Julia looked as though she might cry.

"Listen carefully," I began. "While, I still believe your dad wants to make it work, I'm disappointed he's not doing more to make it right," I said.

"Don't defend him," Jacob growled.

"Don't speak to me like that," I said. "I'm not defending him. As soon as you brought up your dad the whole atmosphere changed. Grew cold. Don't let your dad take up space in your head." I took a breath.

"He's having trouble with Amber. Dad seems really upset," Emily piped up.

"It's no excuse," Jacob said.

"I think we all need to calm down. Since you made dinner, Will and I will clean up," I said.

"No. We'll get it." Jacob grabbed his plate and took it to the kitchen. I watched the kids clear our plates. As if on cue, my phone rang.

I sighed. "Hi, Jack." I walked upstairs.

"Did the kids tell you I cancelled on them?"

"I noticed when I got home," I said without much emotion.

"You know how it is. Babies are hard and need everything."

"I raised three kids. Don't make excuses. Just work it out with Jacob." I felt a burning rage inside of me.

"Nikki. I need help. I can't do this. I have so much pressure here, and I need some understanding. Please tell them that." Jack was nearly begging.

"Unbelievable."

"Nikki."

"Jack. You cancelled. You can't do that. Amber should be able to handle one baby for an hour. It was dinner." I paced my bedroom. I couldn't believe I was having this conversation, again.

"I'm trying to work it out with Amber. For Brayden. But it's getting in the way of my time with our kids." He sounded dejected. I only cared for the sake of my kids. The rest, I couldn't give a shit.

"I don't give a damn about you and your marriage. All I care about is our kids. You have some choices to make then. Grow a pair and make some decisions." I felt like this conversation was on a loop. Over and over, and over again. I didn't want to have it again.

Will made a face. He seemed impressed.

Jack was silent for a moment. I glanced at my phone to see if he had hung up. Unfortunately, he hadn't.

"How are you?" he asked softly.

His question surprised me. He never asked.

"I'm fine. I started a new job." I rolled my eyes at Will. He chuckled and sat on the bed, leaning against the headboard.

"That's great. Where are you working?"

Something wasn't right with him. I couldn't figure out why he seemed so interested.

"With Grater and Ross."

"Oh," he said. "I'm surprised. I thought they were retiring."

"They are. I'll be helping them wrap things up," I said. I rested my head against the cool window to ease the tension headache that was forming.

"You are so much more talented than that. I can look around and help you find something better."

I sat in my chair, tucked my legs underneath myself. "Jack, what do you want?"

"I'm not sure how to ask."

Oh, man. "Just ask," I said with frustration in my voice. I was feeling it in my guts.

"When is Will moving in?" he asked.

I thought back to the divorce decree. There was nothing in the order that said I couldn't date or live with someone. I glanced at Will.

"You seemed fine with it when I told you this weekend. And there's nothing in our decree that says I can't live with someone."

"It's… I was surprised when you told me. I've had some time to think about it. It's so soon, don't you think?"

Bite me, I thought.

"Don't judge," I said, feeling angry.

"Are you getting married?" He sounded distressed, and it was my turn to be confused.

"It's none of your business. And if you're worried about your kids and their reaction to my relationship, don't be. They're fine." My voice rose. I was embarrassed by the highness, and my heart pounded. Will scooted over and sat on the ottoman beside me, holding my hand.

"Hang up with him," Will whispered.

I nodded.

"I'm hanging up, Jack. You're stepping out of bounds, and I don't owe you an explanation."

"Nikki, wait!" he said quickly.

"No."

I ended the conversation. When I looked up, past Will, Jacob was standing at the door. "You fought about me," I said with certainty, even though it was really a guess. Jack cancelling shouldn't have sent the kids into this much distress. I knew there had to be more.

Jacob nodded. "I told him Will spends more time with us than he has in the last three years. I told him we were really glad Will was moving in."

My heart pounded. "That explains the weird call." I held up my phone absently.

"Sorry, Mom. I shouldn't have told him anything. I hate what he's doing so much."

I walked to Jacob, still standing at the door, his arms crossed against his chest as if protecting himself. I put my hand on his shoulder.

"It's not on you. I told your dad Will was moving in. He canceled because the baby's a lot of work, and Amber might have postpartum depression. She's struggling, and he's trying to help."

Jacob rolled his eyes.

"On that, I understand, so don't roll your eyes. If she's really struggling your dad needs to step up and get her help. He was never good with the multi-tasking when it came to the family," I said.

"Sorry about rolling my eyes. I know it's serious. But it's unfair that dad gets away with all of it."

I didn't disagree. As always, it was Jacob who had the hardest time with what Jack wasn't doing for the kids.

"Your dad's not getting away with it. He's suffering in his own way."

This time I accepted Jacob's eye roll. "So, I shouldn't expect much?" Jacob asked.

"Don't let him take up space in your head. He's trying and

not succeeding. So don't expect too much."

Jacob grimaced but gave me a hug. When he pulled away, he slunk out, closing my door behind him.

I fell backward on my bed, and stared up at the ceiling. Dealing with Jack and the aftermath was becoming too much. I helped the kids as much as I could, even took them to therapy after the divorce. But now, it was the same old issues, in new and exciting packages, threatening everything.

"Are you gonna be, okay?" Will asked. He lay down beside me, falling in the opposite direction so our heads were together.

"I'll be fine." I rolled over and faced Will. "It's so much all at once. The new job, I already regret. The kids and their relationship with their father."

"Me moving in."

I shook my head. "No. That I feel good about."

"You shoulder the burden for the rest."

I have. Since the day I met Jack. I was responsible for everything. I've been on top of dates, schedules, the kids, running the household, and work. It's all been on me. He was just not the go-to parent. And it was still happening. Only now, I felt useless because I was unable to help my kids.

Will touched my cheek, stroked it gently.

"And?"

"Jack's bothered by you moving in," I said.

Will raised an eyebrow but retained composure. "Do you think he'll try to stop it?"

"No. He has no reason to."

He kissed me. I melted into him.

I lay beside Will face to face and he stroked my hair.

"You know he's been unhappy with his life, and now you're happy. It could be he's a bit jealous."

I laughed. "Karma's a bitch."

Will laughed. "You don't think that's possible?"

"He left me for his secretary, a younger secretary. He married her, had a baby and didn't see his older children regularly for three years. I don't see it."

Again, Will stroked my hair. "He left for what he thought was greener pastures. Didn't take into consideration she wanted nothing to do with his kids. She got pregnant and added another dimension to the situation. And now he's struggling with her, with the new baby and your new attitude toward him. His life is spinning out of control. Yours is looking up. Why wouldn't he be jealous."

"I still don't buy it."

"Give yourself a little credit. He realizes what he gave up. And now that you've moved on, he really sees it."

I shrugged.

"Okay. If you don't believe that, can you tell me what you learned today?"

I rolled up and pulled out my notes from my bag and handed them to Will. "Moving on, I learned that not only was Ethan suing Jon Jaime Ray, he also happens to be business partners with said dead guy in a company called GE Enterprises." I pointed to the articles of incorporation.

"Huh. Isn't that interesting."

***

Once I finally fell asleep, it was peaceful, and yet I woke exhausted. I changed and found myself on the treadmill earlier than normal. As I picked up speed, Will hopped on the elliptical beside me.

"Sleep, okay?" he asked as he started his workout.

"Finally. I kept thinking of Jack being jealous. It made me chuckle." I increased my speed.

He side-eyed me. "His difficult home life makes you chuckle?"

"No. His not liking that I'm happy makes me chuckle. It's like he was happier when I miserable."

"Did you ever think your relationship was toxic?"

I looked at him. It was a good question. I wouldn't have thought so, but now it seemed it might have been. "Not while we were married. Now, looking back on it, definitely." I clicked the speed button and began running.

Beside me, Will upped his speed. "What's your next step with the case?"

"I'll pull the list together and give it to Penelope's lawyer. If I have time, I'll call a few families to verify any abuse. I want the police to understand Jon Jaime Ray abused and angered a lot of people."

"Do you ever wonder how a good upstanding lawyer like Ethan Grater ended up being partners with a man like him?"

"You mean a soft-core porn producer?"

"Yeah. One of those."

"I don't know Ethan at all. It's definitely a twist I wasn't expecting. I would say he either didn't know, or Ethan's not who everyone thought he was." I glanced at my time. I had ten minutes left of this workout.

"Promise me you'll be careful."

"Always."

***

With my new key, I entered the office early, turned on the lights and walked to the partners' office. I knocked on their door, though I knew neither were here, and I opened the door. It was dark, the desk was covered in piles of papers and folders, and I pulled an envelope from my bag. I laid it on Ethan's side of the desk.

I stared at it, wondering if my better option was to hand it to him myself, but I thought surprising him face to face wasn't the answer. I left the envelope and closed the office door behind me.

I glanced through the foyer window; Carey was pulling into the parking lot, and I entered my office before she made it inside.

This hadn't been a stellar first week of work. Usually there was training on the system, getting familiar with the clients, and much more work to jump into. I was surprised when I opened my email to find five separate documents waiting for me to adjust, research, format, or write. I downloaded each document, opened all of my databases and reviewed each client and their individual needs.

I looked up when Carey knocked on my door.

"How's it going, Nikki?" she asked with a wide smile.

"It's going well. A little slow, but I suspect it will pick up." That seemed to be my go to answer. I didn't really believe it would happen.

She seemed to want to say something but didn't immediately. "Can I help you with something?" Everything about this job was awkward. I felt as though getting to know my co-workers wasn't worth the effort because there wasn't going to be a practice in the immediate future. It felt cumbersome to get to know even Carey, a nice woman as far as I could tell.

"I was wondering." She was wringing her hands, a serious expression on her face. "I heard you're looking into the murder of Jon Ray, that photographer."

I nodded. "I am. I'm trying to help a friend prove she had nothing to do with his murder."

"I know you want to help your friend, but Jon Jaime Ray isn't worth the effort. He was a horrible person."

"Be that as it may, the wrong person shouldn't be sent to jail for a murder she didn't commit."

Again, Carey seemed to be thinking of how to say something. "I suppose. I don't think anyone is going to miss him."

I couldn't help but wonder what *her* connection to Jon Jaime Ray was. Maybe Carey knew him from her work here. I pulled out the list from my bag. "I created a list of all the models on his website. I didn't see your name on it. Did you have pictures taken?"

She shook her head. "No. Thankfully I cancelled the appointment the day before. Something didn't feel right about it. He was a creep, and I felt it through the phone."

"How did you hear about him? It seems he had a healthy list of clients."

Carey stepped into the office and took a seat in the only visitor's chair. "Ethan's niece told me about this amazing photographer and videographer. Mara Grater was a friend of mine before she died. She told me about him. Raved about him. But I couldn't go through with it. He gave me the creeps, and it was just a phone call. I couldn't do it."

So, Mara Grater worked with Jon Jaime Ray. I looked down at the alphabetical list, but I knew I wouldn't find Mara Grater there. I would have made a note about it if I had. Did she know the photographer through Ethan?

"You were close to Mara?"

"We were close for a few years. I'm two years older than she was and only became friends when I started here. When Mara died, it was shocking. Devastating for everyone who knew her. She was so sweet and lovely. The police never found out what really happened to her."

"I'm so sorry for your loss."

"Thanks. I miss her all the time."

Ethan entered the office, far earlier than he had since I started last week. He stopped beside my office door.

My heart sped up as I thought of the envelope on his desk. I shouldn't have left it. I promised Will I'd be careful. I broke that promise.

"Any luck on the investigation?" he asked without much interest.

"I discovered something unsettling. But so far nothing concrete."

Ethan nodded once and returned to his office.

Carey stood. "I hope you can help your friend." She turned and returned to her desk.

I returned to the document I had started. Footsteps rushed toward my office. I looked up. Ethan was red in the face holding the open envelope I had left for him.

"Where did you get this?" he growled.

"Online."

The realization that his secret was actually available for public consumption hit him instantly. "It's not what you think," he pleaded.

"You didn't start a porn production company with a photographer who abused his models?"

"I didn't know what that man was into. It was supposed to be a real estate deal. Building a studio. I didn't know."

I found that dubious, and his tears appeared forced.

He entered my office and closed the door, leaving me alone and trapped in my office. He dropped the envelope on my desk.

"I didn't know what he was doing. All I knew was the man was an artist. Had a lot of models under his belt. He convinced me of the possibilities. The videos, the movies. We'd make a lot of money. I'd have my retirement wrapped up."

"What happened between the two of you?"

He sat in the visitor's chair, visibly shaking. "I'm so sorry you found out like this. I… when I found out he duped me,

I sued him. He took me for a lot of money. I was trying to secure my future." Ethan ran his hand across his chin. He couldn't make eye contact with me.

"Did you kill him?" I asked directly.

For that, he looked up and laughed. "No. I had a case against him. I would have won. With him dead, I won't see any of my money again."

"I'm sure you're not the only person who didn't like him. Can you think of anyone else who might have wanted him dead?"

He glanced at the list on my desk and pointed to it. "I'm sure you have all the names on that list."

"Did you know Mara connected Carey with him?"

He seemed surprised by that.

"Carey almost met with Jon Jaime Ray. Had a change of heart the day before the meeting. She said he gave her the creeps."

"I... I had no idea Mara knew him. And Carey." He glanced back at the closed door. "I'm so glad she didn't get caught up in that. But Mara. There's no way she could have known. Are you sure that's what Carey said?"

"She asked me about the case and admitted Mara told her about him. Mara liked him quite a bit, it sounded like."

Ethan shook his head. "I suppose Mara could have known him. She was beautiful, lovely, and wanted to be an actress."

He was shaky when he stood. He turned with a sadness on his face and returned to his own office, leaving the articles of incorporation for his company with Jon Jaime Ray on my desk.

I felt like I had killed his puppy or best friend. I got the information I wanted, but it didn't feel like a good win. It felt sad.

I looked back at the list and reviewed all two hundred names. Mara Grater wasn't among the many women and men.

But then I thought of the sign in link at the bottom of the Jon Jamie Ray's website page. I wondered if I might find Mara Grater beyond that link.

CHAPTER 12

Half way through investigating the list of models, I realized I wasn't making any progress with the list.

I sat back in my chair. It felt like an uphill battle, like there was no clear evidence in this direction. I was hesitant to check into the names of those who had filed lawsuits or criminal charges against him. I had been shaken after my call with Ericka Mason's brother. I was wondering if being a PI was really in the cards for me if I could let an interview rattle me so much.

But it was a good plan, because those were the models who had taken it further. Walked through their fear in the name of justice.

I was torn between wanting the right person sent to jail and knowing a victim may have killed him.

Always curious, quickly becoming a busy body, I pulled out the list of charges and lawsuits against Jon Jaime Ray.

I returned to Natalia Blankman and her parents, Stefan and Nya. Again, I tried Natalia, but the number had been disconnected. Her parents phone continued to ring.

I looked at the rest of the list. Who lost the case? I narrowed on Delinda Love. The charges in her case were dropped for insufficient evidence, and I wanted to know if the thirty-year old makeup artist and former model was mad enough to commit murder. I dialed her number.

"Hello?" Delinda asked with confusion in her voice.

"Hello. Is this Delinda Love?"

"Yes? Who's this?"

"I'm Nikki Page. I'm looking into the death of Jon Jaime Ray."

"Yeah and?"

"I know he was an ass, but I've been hired by a person of interest, who I believe had nothing to do with the photographer's death."

She snorted. "And you think I did it."

"I don't think anything. I'm merely trying to prove an existence of abuse against his models. The police seem to only be looking at one suspect," I said as anger boiled inside of me. Maybe it was my approach that sounded as if I was accusing everyone I called.

"I'm sorry, Ms. Page, but you call here telling me you're investigating that asshole's murder because your client didn't do it, makes it sound like you think I did it. Like any of us are guilty. He got away with what he did," she spat.

"I'm sorry. I didn't mean to accuse you. Really. I want to know his history of abuse. There's over two hundred people on his list of models who could be responsible. I only want the right person put away."

"I get that. I get your self-righteousness. The only person who should have been put away is dead. I have no sympathy for that bastard. But since you asked, he abused me. I never signed that model release even though it was signed. It wasn't my signature. And after that was faked, I came to full consciousness when I was naked and having my pictures taken. And the best part," she said as her voice rose and cracked with distress. "The best part of all of that, I went to the police. He either bought someone off or hid the evidence. The charges were dropped for insufficient evidence. The police didn't seem willing to keep investigating. I was a laughing stock, embarrassed, and the nightmares I couldn't stop. He ruined my career."

I looked at her physical stats. She was too tall to have been the murderer. But I asked anyway. "Where were you three nights ago at four in the morning?"

She laughed. "I was sleeping. My husband could attest to it. So could our video cameras. I never left the house. No matter how much I hated him, I didn't do it. But if you do find out who killed him, send them flowers, candy, money. Whoever did it saved someone else the trouble he put the rest of us through."

"I understand where you're coming from, but if you have any other information, please call me."

"Yeah. Sure. I was there once. Experienced that and never went back. But…"

"Anything you have could be helpful. I don't believe it was my friend. You have an alibi. Anything I can give to the police." I was pleading.

"When I called him to set up the appointment, I heard a man in the background. Older, I think. He came in and started shouting at Jon Ray while he was on the call with me. I don't know who it was, but I heard that voice again. When I was on the bed, taking those shots. I was out of it. I'm sure he drugged me. I heard that man's voice again. They were shouting again. I'm drugged and barely functioning, and they're screaming at each other." She chuckled, but I thought it might be from nerves more than anything.

"Thank you for letting me know about the mystery man." I had a feeling the mystery man might have been a disgruntled business partner.

"Do you want to know what they were saying?" Delinda Love asked me.

"I didn't think you'd remember in your condition at the time."

"They were fighting about money. The man told him he didn't have any more. He couldn't pay him what he owed."

"Hmmm." I noted that on my notepad.

"The rest is a bit fuzzy."

"When was this?"

"About a year ago. I never fully got over it. It still keeps me up at night. But I'm doing better. Working again at least."

"I'm sorry you didn't get the resolution you needed, but I am glad to hear it's getting better. Can I ask if you've ever met any of the other models or their families?"

"Why?"

"I'm wondering if there are other stories worth noting."

"So you can accuse them?" she asked coyly.

"No. All I really want is to prove he was an ass." I was tired of explaining this, and maybe I needed to change my delivery.

"I'm half teasing you, though you need to change your approach. It feels like you're accusing all of us."

I've been accused of that before.

"I didn't mean to accuse. Yes, I'm trying to help my client at the same time, because the wrong person shouldn't be blamed."

"I get that. I've talked to a lot of the other models in the course of all of this. My lawyer tried to have several victims speak to the police on my behalf. But the police still dropped the charges. A lot of us are hurt." She sighed heavily. "I'm sorry for your client, but there's nothing else I can tell you. I tried to get him legally, and I lost."

"Thank you for the information. I appreciate it."

"I'm sorry it wasn't much help," Delinda said.

"You gave me a little more to prove he was an ass. So, thanks."

Delinda Love ended the call.

There were more victims, I was sure of that, and I was more than sure they were on his model list. And yet, I wasn't any closer to finding that person.

I called for a pizza when I realized Will would be home soon, added a sandwich for Julia and noticed Andy calling me.

"Hello," I said.

"You need to back off from investigating Jon Jaime Ray. I just got off a call from Ericka Mason's family. Allan Mason said you're harassing him and wants to file a complaint against you." Andy's anger oozed through the phone.

"All I did was confirm with him that Jon Jaime Ray had a history of abuse toward his models. Penelope isn't the only one who had an issue with him. He took advantage of several of his models, and I think you're too focused on just her." My heart pounded as my gut twisted and burned.

"Butt out. You're not the police."

"Then do your job so I don't have to."

"Nikki. If I have to, I'll arrest you for compromising an investigation. Leave it to the police. We are doing our damn job."

He ended the call before I could reply. I put my phone down, shaking as I thought of his anger.

"Nikki. What's wrong?" I hadn't heard Will enter. He came to me, wrapped his arms around me. "You're trembling."

"Andy called. Threatening me with arrest if I didn't drop the investigation. One of the families complained about me."

I wrapped my arms around him and let myself be comforted. For the first time in many years, I didn't have to handle everything alone.

"Can I get you something?" Will asked.

I pulled away and wiped the few tears that I couldn't stop. "No. I have pizza coming." I leaned into him, so close I could feel his heartbeat.

He kissed my forehead. "That sounds great. I know I can't convince you to stay away from the investigation, so I'll remind you to be very careful. Andy's watching you now."

"I will. I suspect the answer won't come from questioning any more models. The ones I have spoken to say the same thing. They were abused by Jon Jaime Ray. They also say they never signed the model release form and were surprised to be taking nude pictures."

Will looked surprised. "They were drugged?"

"That's the assumption I'm going with. I don't have any proof though. The model I just spoke to said she was out of it when she was taking pictures."

"More than one person hinted at it, though?"

I nodded. "I'll stay away from the other models for now and concentrate on his other business dealings. Especially between him and Ethan Grater. Ethan wasn't happy I found a business connection."

"Why did you confront him?" Will asked. I thought he might have been angry that I had.

I knew I shouldn't have. I felt that after I dropped the articles of incorporation on his desk, but I left it there because I needed to know what he knew. "I knew I shouldn't have confronted him, but I needed to know what he knew."

His face softened. Will always seemed to forgive me for my indiscretions and the trouble I caused. I leaned into him. "I'm sorry I keep putting you into these positions. I don't want you to worry about me."

He wrapped me tighter in his arms. "I'll always be concerned for you. But you're looking for a murderer. I want you to be safe." He kissed my neck.

"I promise. I'll be careful. I just feel so guilty I got Penelope in this mess. I shouldn't have called her in the first place."

I heard him chuckle behind me, and felt his body shudder when he did.

"Your heart's in the right place. The timing of the letter was coincidental and bad timing."

"I hope so. I've gone through a hundred of the models. There're lawsuits, a suicide. Maybe I can run some queries. I've got all of the information printed. I'll write a report and send it to the police. Wash my hands of it. Hopefully it will be enough to save Penelope."

"Go ahead and start your query list and when the pizza comes, we'll eat. Also, if I'm moving in, we should pick a date to make that official so I can change all those important things like billing addresses and driver's licenses."

"Are you going to sell your house or keep it?"

"I think I'll sell it. But I think we need to talk about the future."

He looked serious; my heart pounded as I looked at his face. It was expectant.

"Marriage," I said.

"I think we need to be clear on that. And how we'll split the expenses and…"

I touched my finger to his lips. "We split expenses except for the kids. And marriage. I'm ready, but are you?"

"I am."

I kissed his lips and felt him watch me as I walked away to set up my queries and change into something more comfortable.

***

It was well past midnight, and I couldn't sleep. Queries had been running all evening and after the final one hundred were finished, I found four additional lawsuits against Jon Jaime Ray by four different models. One was tossed in his favor, one settled away from court, awarded to a model named Tiffany Breton, no amount specified. A third was settled in favor of a model named Daphne Finkel who won $125,000 judgment against him. The final lawsuit, still ongoing, was brought to court by a model named Nina Banks. If anything, I would think the photographer would have done harm to the two models who won against him. But the first model Tiffani Breton would have motive. I looked her up online. Her page three girl spread was just as the others, uncomfortable to view.

As I searched through the website, I found that sign in link and hovered the pointer over it. For a minute, I thought I'd create an account, but did I want to?

No.

I searched the website looking for the "About Us" tab and found the company information. The legal entity owned by Ethan was EG Enterprises; a subsidiary of JJR Entertainment, and it was on the website.

It was clearly an entertainment company, something Ethan would have known about. But did he know what Jon Jaime Ray was doing with the company? He would have if he did his research, or at the very least, looked at the damn website.

Again, I searched for lawsuits against both JJR Entertainment and EG Enterprises. I knew Ethan was suing Jon Jaime Ray but who was suing the two men? I dug in and learned there were ten lawsuits against Ethan and Jon Jaime Ray as dual defendants. Three were models which I verified from the list. The other seven were a result of bad business dealings; failure to pay, theft, breach of contract. I was shocked that Ethan, a seemingly upstanding lawyer was responsible for all of that. How had he hidden all of this?

I saved the names of the models: Cindy Baker, Lorena Simpson, and Jane Cooley, but I didn't think it was about them.

Again, I hovered my pointer over the sign in link. No.

I glanced at the clock. It was after one.

"It's late. What are you doing?" Will said with sleep in his voice.

"I couldn't sleep. Doing some research."

I saved all of my findings.

Will sat up. "Find anything?"

"Ethan lied when he told me he didn't know what Jon Jaime Ray was doing with their business. They've been sued numerous times. He also lied about the type of company. It's not a real estate company, it's an entertainment company."

"You think he's responsible for the murder?"

"I can't get it out of my head. Why lie to me when this is all public information?"

"Why does anyone lie about things like this? Did you save everything?"

"Yeah, why?"

"We both have to be up in a few hours, and you're doing all you can."

I added the new data to the email for Penelope's lawyer and sent it off. I put my computer away and snuggled close to Will as he put his arms around me. "I'd marry you without question. But I worry you're rushing in," I said in the darkness.

"I'd marry you without question. I'm ready."

"I love you," I whispered.

"I love you, Nikki."

I felt myself blissfully falling into sleep.

***

Morning slog. Will and I readied for work. He left earlier than me, and I left fifteen minutes before the partners would start. I realized I didn't have anything to do, so why show up if they weren't there to assign me anything?

When I arrived, the partners were not in, Carey was surprised to see me so late.

"Good morning, Nikki. Is everything okay?"

"All's well. I haven't had much to do, so I came in a little later. I'm sure it'll pick up soon."

I entered my office, turned on the light, and the computer and sat at my desk.

There was a small list of clients waiting for me in my email, and I took the first and worked my way through the documents; adding, editing, rewriting. Samuel knocked on my door.

"Hi, Nikki. How's the work coming?" he asked with a wide smile.

"It's good. I finished the first document, working through the second. I'll send them your way as I finish."

"Good. Good." He walked away without another word.

I looked at the document again. It was standard entertainment agreement for an actor and a new role in a local production. Just standard, and not much to add or change. I was more than regretting taking this position. Especially after finishing the last of the documents by 10:30 that morning.

Even with the stress and emotions of family law, I felt as though I was helping a family at their most vulnerable of times. Here I was not.

Another document hit my email and as I downloaded it and read, rewording a few excerpts, I heard footsteps coming toward my office.

"How's the investigation coming along?" Ethan asked.

"I've been ordered to not investigate it any longer. Per the police."

"That's a shame," Ethan said, though his jaw relaxed as if that was good news. But for who?

"I'm not sure who I was helping. I think I was causing more trouble," I admitted.

Ethan looked tired. I wondered if Jon Jaime Ray's murder kept him awake too. "Maybe you ought to drop the whole thing. I think you're investigating the wrong people."

He dropped several folders on my desk and stormed away.

I sighed and pulled the first one from the pile and began to read through the document, my stomach churning. Regardless of Ethan's displeasure at what I had dug up or Andy's warning, I was determined to make sure the correct person was sent to jail for the murder of Jon Jaime Ray, however I had to do it.

***

After completing the rest of the documents Ethan had left for me, several I had already finished yesterday, I walked them to the partners' office. Samuel was alone. He smiled picked up the first and looked inside. His smile turned to a grimace.

"Why did you redo this? Your work is exceptional. They needed no changes."

It was my turn to be shocked. "Ethan gave them to me with notes. I assumed that meant he wanted changes."

"I'm sorry. They were fine. Send me the versions from yesterday. We'll use your last drafts."

"Ok. I'll go and do that," I said confused.

"Is everything okay?" Samuel asked.

"Everything is fine. I think I'm still trying to find my footing here. This is just a weird incident. I'll go and fix it." I turned to leave.

"Wait."

He walked me to my office and closed the door behind us.

"I know you're bored here. I can see it in your face and mannerisms. But I want you to know we're grateful you're here."

"Thank you."

"I saw that you sent the letter to the clients who had no balance and hadn't used us in at least two years. I have the newest letter for clients with balances, who we're still working with. That should go out today. Review the letter and make sure it sounds okay before you do."

I grabbed a notebook and made a note. "I'll start that after I send you the last versions of the documents."

"What's really wrong, Nikki?"

And there was the reason we were behind closed doors. "I've been investigating Jon Jaime Ray's murder and much of what Ethan told me about his relationship with him is just not truthful."

Samuel didn't match my gaze, preferring to look out the small window behind my desk. I took that to mean what I said meant something.

He finally looked at me. "I've known Ethan for a very long time. We met in law school. Stayed friends working for other law firms until we decided to join together. He knows my family; I know his."

"Could he have kept some of his life private?"

"He could have been hiding part of his life. All I know is, he's a good man. I suppose he had a reason to not share the truth with a new employee."

I suppose that was a reasonable explanation from Samuel, but I wasn't buying it, because it's easy enough to find the information I found on the internet. And no one knew?

"Did you know Ethan had an entertainment business with Jon Jaime Ray?"

Samuel's eyes widened in shock. I expected him to know about it. I stared at my work bag where I kept the folders containing information about Ethan's business.

"I know Ethan's been dabbling in outside interests. An entertainment company is a good niche for him. Especially since Mara wanted to be an actress. That might have been his intention," he said coolly and walked away.

It was unsettling Ethan lived two lives, one that even his closest friend knew nothing about. I wondered if joining Jon Jaime Ray in business was more nefarious than helping Mara with her career.

CHAPTER 13

So, boys, that all sounds terrific. I can see my slimeball landlord choking on this." Myles Landry slapped his hands together, a wide smile on his face. While he was the same person, today he was in khakis and a blue blazer, a far different look than Lola. I almost couldn't picture him any other way.

I had been scribbling notes from our meeting. My hand was cramped, and I shook it out. Myles winked at me when I caught his glance. I shrugged, and he seemed to find that amusing. I found myself drawn to Myles, even Lola, for this person had an ease and confidence about himself, and I wanted to be in his presence. And besides, Myles was far more interesting and less stressful to be around than Samuel and Ethan.

I know I was partially responsible for Ethan's demeanor toward me, having outed his business dealings, if only to him, but Samuel, an astute attorney, sensed the tension between us and tried to make up for it by being overly generous with his compliments and smiles. I could see through them, though, he was upset about something; I feared it had to do with me.

I focused on Myles, because everything else, I seemed to have made a mess of in such a short time.

"We're glad you're pleased," Samuel said. He tidied up the filing and all pertinent exhibits, placing them inside the envelope. "We'll file the lawsuit in the morning. So don't fret. Your landlord kicked you out without cause, and is holding your property hostage. We have evidence against him, and the lawsuit will force him to answer for his actions." Samuel's voice was gentle and kind as he explained it all again to Myles. It seemed like overkill, but it also felt like a mask for Ethan's inattentiveness. He said nothing as he doodled on his pad.

"What's your next project?" I asked as I put my notes in the Landry file.

Myles's eyes widened in excitement, and he beamed.

"I'll be taking on a new role. It's a vaudeville review. A little of this, a little of that." He was purposely being coy as he wiggle waggled his hands. He offered no other information about the show, but I couldn't wait to see it.

I knew Myles sensed the tension in the room, and he stood. "Okay, gentlemen. If you don't need me for anything else, I'll be heading out. Between Ethan's sulkiness and Samuel's overcompensation for it, I'm ready for a nap. Nikki, will you be a dear and walk me out?"

I looked at the partners as if I needed permission when I really didn't. Ethan busied himself with a folder, fumbling with the pages, and Samuel smiled again. His actions felt so very Stepford Wives in contrast to Ethan's lack of care.

Myles shrugged when I looked at him. "Thank you again. I appreciate all of this and look forward to getting my things back."

"I'll be happy to walk you out." I, like Myles, needed a break from the oddness and led him outside to his car parked in the small, tight lot. "It's good to see you again." I reached for a familiar hug, and he enveloped me in a bear hug.

When he let go, he widened his arms and asked, "How do you like my true self?"

I liked him in whatever version of himself he arrived in. "Hmmm. Is that really your true self or are all the sides of you simply part of a whole?" I asked him.

His blue eyes twinkled, his smile wide at that question. "Now that is a good question. I suppose you're correct. One side or the other isn't my true self. Each side is just a side and together I am one complex and spectacular individual."

With Myles it was easy to laugh. Easy to be comfortable even in my skin.

"So, tell me Nikki, what's going on with Ethan today?"

He leaned against his car as he studied me.

For a moment, I felt some panic. Truth was, I didn't know Myles well enough to divulge, but he was a character who understood people. I couldn't exactly lie. "I suppose it has to do with me learning something about him and as a result, he's unhappy about what I discovered."

"And what did you learn?"

I debated how much I should tell him, if I should even tell him anything at all. But that was my job in a nutshell; parsing information without divulging anything at all. I bit my lip as I thought about it. "I can't tell you much. But in the course of investigating Jon Jaime Ray's murder, I discovered some disturbing business dealings that are of public record."

Myles looked unphased by the news and nodded. "Ethan and Jon Jaime Ray were in business together," he said, not as a question.

"How did you know? Samuel wasn't aware of it."

Myles chuckled. "I worked with Jon. I saw Ethan with him on occasion. And before you ask, Ethan begged me to not tell anyone about his business with Jon Jaime Ray."

"It's an entertainment company and fits with his legal specialty. Which makes me wonder why he would he ask you to keep that connection a secret, unless he was doing something he shouldn't be doing. Am I close?"

Myles nodded. "Jon Jaime Ray operated … shall we say, just below the law. Ethan knew this. He had to have known what Jon was doing when they went into business together. If not then, he would have found out soon enough. I don't know for sure what went on between them but I did hear them argue once." Myles nervously glanced at the office.

I turned. Ethan was staring at us through the window beside the door. As soon as our attention turned to him, he left the window.

"He's angry at you, but it makes sense now. You discovered his secret."

I was confused. If his only secret was, he was a partner with the murder victim, albeit, an abusive ass of a victim, it was a matter of public record.

"That wasn't much of a secret. I found it online," I said.

Myles looked at me with all seriousness. "Very few people knew about this business. You found it. Which means you can learn about what really went on between the two of them. That must scare him."

"Do you think there are secrets between them worth looking for?" I'm not sure why I asked that question because

I believed Myles was right. Ethan knew I could find out what really happened between the partners, especially with the pending lawsuit.

"I think there is, from my dealings with them. Remember, I heard them fight. There was animosity between them."

"What was the fight about?"

"Mara. Ethan's niece."

I nodded. "I heard she knew Jon and had some business with him. Modeling, I think."

"Mara wanted to be an actress. Ethan created the company to legally represent her as an agent and book her gigs. Acting, singing. I came into the conversation late, didn't catch much of it, but they were fighting about a video shoot. Or a video that was just recorded. It was definitely about something Mara had made and Ethan's role in that video."

"Ethan produced something untoward?"

Myles laughed. "I can't tell you that for certain. But you are on to something. Porn isn't too far off of what Jon Jaime Ray produced. May I ask how you're investigating Ray's murder?"

I nodded. "I've been reviewing the list of models from his website. I've been looking for anything that looks odd in their lives; lawsuits, murders, suicides. There are several lawsuits, one suicide. I just think the police haven't been looking at all of the possible suspects. Only a very convenient one."

Myles put his hand on my shoulder. "I think if you want to find the killer you need to expand beyond the list of models. I think you haven't reached the tip of the iceberg where Jon Jaime Ray is concerned. A lot of people hated him," Myles said.

"Including you?"

"I didn't kill him. I haven't had business with him in two years. He was an ass, he was crooked, he probably abused his models. I got away from him when I realized who he really was. He had nothing on me, and I had no beef with him after that. At least nothing I chose to engage in. I walked away. I was lucky. I'm sure others were not."

"The police told me to butt out. Ethan suggested I leave it alone."

"Are you going to leave it alone?"

"I gave my friend's lawyer everything I found. I'm not sure what else I can do." I felt myself tense as I crossed my arms against my chest.

"You don't strike me as the type of person to give up." Myles continued to observe me and seemed to understand me better than I understood myself, though I'm not sure how he knew that. But I disliked throwing in the towel when I knew something was wrong. In this case however, I wasn't sure what was wrong.

"You don't know much about me, but you sound sure about that."

Myles laughed. "Consider me a good judge of charac-ter. I even believe the murder isn't the only thing bothering you."

I raised my eyebrows. "No, it's not. It's the job. I feel like I'm not in the right place, and it has me on edge."

"Sometimes parts of life are off kilter. You're here for now. It doesn't mean it's permanent. You'll find your way. Just put yourself first once and awhile. Take time to recharge."

He climbed into his car.

"Thank you," I said to him.

"Any time."

I watched him drive away and reluctantly walked back inside to see what awaited me.

***

The lawyers left at three as I was working through the merge print on the letters to clients explaining the closing of the law firm and what Samuel and Ethan would still be doing for them. As the letters printed, my phone rang.

"This is Nikki Page," I said, though I knew who was on the other end.

"Ms. Page, it's Allan Mason."

"How can I help you, Mr. Mason?" I worked to keep the chill from my voice, but it was hard after he filed an official complaint with the police.

"The police are looking at me for Jon Jaime Ray's murder. This is your fault!" he shouted.

"Actually, Mr. Mason, I didn't give your information to or make any accusations about you to the police. All I told the police was they needed to expand their list of suspects. I think your complaint to the police, against me, started this."

He was silent for a moment. I waited patiently for him to say something or hopefully hang up.

"I…I'm sorry. I'm angry I'm being investigated in that asshole's murder. I'm angry Jon Jaime Ray got away with killing my sister, and I'm angry other women won't get justice for what he did to them."

He was pained and possibly not thinking rationally. And still I was angry at him for reporting me. "I'm sorry for your loss. I'm sorry you have to go through this. But the police have to go through the list of suspects and investigate all possibilities."

"Meaning me."

"Did you kill him?"

"No. I didn't. I'm glad the man is dead, but I didn't do it. He raped Ericka, and she was going to the police. He killed her to silence her." He was heaving and clearly upset. I wasn't sure at this point why he had called me.

"Did you tell the police your suspicions?"

"Yes. And now they think I'm a possible suspect."

"They're doing their due diligence," I said though I didn't want to defend the police right now. Not after Andy yelled at me and told me to butt out.

"They ruled it suicide. The police never asked us why we knew it wasn't suicide. I don't trust them," he said. "It was awful. And I'm sorry I called the police on you. I was so pissed you were calling and accusing me."

"I ... I wasn't accusing you."

"I know. I know. But it's all fresh again. It's all right there, everything that happened. How she changed, got hooked on drugs, lost her ambition." He was crying as he explained it all to me. I felt for him and his family. I couldn't imagine losing someone like that.

In this moment, it was this type of case, and the people who were at their most vulnerable that broke my heart and tested my resolve. But all in all, I knew I needed to see it through. Regardless of who actually killed the photographer.

"Do you have the police report?" I asked when Allan calmed.

He sniffled. "Yes. I can send it to you. Maybe you'll see something the police ignored."

"I can look at the report. But I can't promise I'll see anything the police missed. I'm guessing there won't be enough in the report to tell us what happened."

"But you won't give up? You'll keep finding out what happened?" he asked cautiously.

I thought about Myles and his assessment of me. "I'm determined to see this through, but if you call the police on me, they'll arrest me. I've already been warned."

"I'm sorry I called the police. I just want justice for Ericka. I want the world to know what that asshole did to her."

"I will keep working on it. I want to know what happened to all of his victims and get them justice too."

"Thank you, Mrs. Page. And thank you for sticking with it."

After we hung up, Allan Mason sent me the police report, and I printed it off. I read through the scant report and noted the suicide note, the bottle of pills beside her dead body.

Based on the scene, I could understand why the police ruled it suicide. It wouldn't help the family grieve and move on, but if they really believed she was murdered, someone did a great job covering it up.

CHAPTER 14

Cutting through the darkness, my phone rang out with "Uptown Funk." I flew up from sleep, my heart pounding, my hands shaking. I worried something had happened to one of the kids. It took me a moment to realize it was summer vacation, and the kids were asleep down the hall.

"Who's calling at 2:17 a.m." I murmured at the phone number flashing on the screen.

"This is Nikki Page," I said with a dry mouth and roiling stomach.

"Mrs. Page, this is Leonard Price; Penelope Pinkerton's lawyer. She's been brought to the police station for questioning. She's asking for you."

"Crap." I looked at my phone again. "Why did they bring her in at two in the morning?"

"They're convinced she killed Jon Jaime Ray. I think this is a powerplay, merely to force a confession."

"Did they find new evidence?"

He sighed loudly. "Mrs. Page. It's early in the morning. Penelope is asking for you. Could you please come here so we can resolve this, and I can get my client home?" He sounded irritated and a little angry, but I still didn't know why he needed me, even if Penelope asked for me.

"I'm not sure how I can help you or her. Beyond the notes I sent off to you. Did you receive them?" I asked as I tried to clear the cobwebs in my still sleepy brain.

"Yes. They were thorough and much appreciated. But she's asking to speak with you," he reiterated.

"Why? I don't have anything else. What could I possibly do tonight?" I didn't want to leave the warmth of my bed, or leave Will's protective embrace.

"Who is it?" Will murmured.

"Penelope's being questioned. She asked for me," I whispered.

"I know it's an extremely bad time, Mrs. Page, but I'd like you to come in. We can use your help."

I had invested so much time already, so I swung my feet to the floor.

"Fine. I'm on my way." I hung up the phone and climbed out of bed.

"Does she have a lawyer?" Will asked as he stood at the closet door.

"That's who called." I slipped on a sweater and jeans. "I'm not sure why she wants me. They have my notes. I was going to send them my updates in the morning."

"It is morning," Will said bitterly. "You need to stop running around for people who aren't paying you. It's two in the morning." Will wasn't shouting, but his voice was angry.

It was the first time in thirty years Will had ever took that tone with me.

"What should I have said? Her lawyer called me."

He placed his hands on my arms. "I love you. I see that you're unhappy at this new job, and you're searching for that right thing. But you're running yourself ragged."

I sighed heavily. "I know. I'm sorry. I'm so sorry."

I leaned against him. He rubbed my hair. Kissed my temple. "Don't apologize. I worry about you. Do you want me to go with you?"

I shook my head. "Go back to bed." I reached up and kissed him. "I'll be back as soon as I can."

***

The parking lot was nearly empty, as I parked my car under the closest street lamp and ran into the building. The reception desk was empty at 3:05 a.m. which was odd but I knew where

I was going. I had been here on many occasions and turned left down an empty hallway toward the interrogation and viewing rooms.

"Ma'am. What are you doing here?"

I jumped at the officer's voice and turned toward him. He was young, barely old enough to shave. His uniform was pressed and clean, his eyes wide and awake unlike myself who could drop any minute.

"I'm Nikki Page. Leonard Price called me and asked me to come in. He's here with Penelope Pinkerton."

"I need to see your ID."

I rolled my eyes, pulled my wallet from my purse and handed him my driver's license.

He glanced at the picture and then to me before handing it back. "Follow me." He led me to the viewing room door and escorted me in.

"Mr. Price asked to see me. I need to get in there." I pointed to the mirror.

"Please wait here," the officer ordered.

I watched through one-sided window, as Leonard sat beside Penelope. Her face was ashen, as Andy's was red, as he was yelling at her. Across the table, Gary, sat stunned if I had to guess. And yet, he didn't do anything to stop Andy's tirade.

I turned on the speaker, horrified.

"You had buyer's remorse. Regretted signing that contract. He gave your lawyer the contract with your signature. The one you claimed you didn't sign. You went back there, killed him and came back later to call it in so you could appear innocent. That's how it went down."

"Detective Butcher. Stop harassing my client. You've asked her this before. You've seen the recording. She was terrified when she came out of his office. If you don't have anything else to ask, either arrest her or let her go."

Penelope shook. Leonard held her hand.

The officer who escorted me into the viewing room, entered interrogation and whispered to Andy. He glanced directly at me though he couldn't see through the one-way mirror. I shut down the speaker.

Andy stood, knocked the chair into the table and left the room. He entered the viewing room.

"What are you doing here?" Andy growled.

"Leonard Price asked me to come," I said without looking at him. Leonard was whispering to Penelope who looked as though she was fighting tears.

Gary stood and left the interrogation room, his exhaustion written all over his face.

"Why did you have to do this now at two in the morning? Did you get new evidence? Or are you trying to intimidate her to get her to confess to a crime she didn't commit?" I finally looked at Andy. He didn't appear any happier to be here than Gary did.

"I don't have to tell you what evidence we have, or why we brought her in this morning." He began to pace, his face scrunched tightly. "Go home, Nikki. This isn't your case. You don't belong here."

"Are you even looking at anyone else? Or did you take the easy way because of the letter on the victim's desk?" I asked. Gary joined us in the small room. He looked at me with a pained expression. Again, he didn't intervene.

Andy walked past me, clipped my shoulder as he reached for a coffee pot and poured himself a mug. "Go home, Nikki." He took a sip of the coffee.

"Leonard Price asked her here. You can come with me," Gary said and motioned me to join him.

Andy growled as the door shut behind me, and Gary let me into interrogation.

I sat across from Penelope.

When Gary left us alone, I asked, "Why am I here?"

"I needed help. You promised me you'd help me," Penelope screeched. "Look at how well that went!"

I was already wallowing in guilt. I didn't need Penelope to hammer that home. I kept repeating that moment when I interfered, the day I first saw her, upset and crying in the café. If I hadn't reached out that day, she probably wouldn't be here now. I should have left it alone.

"You have a lawyer to help you," I said.

"I didn't do this. They're gonna charge me because of the letter you wrote."

I couldn't escape the consequences of my actions that day. I screwed it up by calling her, asking if she needed help. I pushed for the letter requesting the signed contract. It was just another plan gone awry. While I knew this was about Penelope, and the other models, and even Jon Jaime Ray, I couldn't help but ask, why me? My stomach churned.

"Penelope. Nikki's correct. That letter was your only option at the time," Leonard said.

My breath hitched.

"But it got me in this mess!"

Rage boiled inside. Maybe it was the lack of sleep or the blame game. "You still say you didn't sign it. Have you had the signature authenticated yet?" I looked directly at Leonard.

"It's still inconclusive. Which means they can't prove it's her signature just as much as they can't prove it wasn't."

"That's something. And you need to realize they're using that one piece of evidence as an excuse to harass you," I told her. I thought of Andy and his determination to go after Penelope, of Gary's reluctance to join him in his actions, and I had a thought that maybe Andy was taking his anger toward me out on Penelope. That would be a problem. I took a deep breath.

I shouldn't be here.

"Why? Why?" Penelope pleaded.

Leonard squeezed Penelope's hand. "They have nothing. And they won't find anything. You're the only lead they will milk as long as they can."

"Having said that, what's the new evidence they used to drag her in here tonight? Why the hell are they bringing her in at two in the morning?"

"It's all circumstantial. They found the murder weapon. It's been confirmed to be the weapon," Leonard said.

"And who does the gun belong to?" I asked as I looked at Leonard Price.

"It's unregistered," Leonard said.

"Did they do a gunshot residue test the day you were brought in?" I asked her.

She nodded. "Yes. It was negative."

"I'm confused then. Why the hell did they bring her in?"

"First the unregistered gun. They're looking for the owner. Going through all the gun shops in the area. But this is what they're stuck on. They've calculated the estimated height of the killer. It matches Penelope's height at 5'8"."

Leonard pulled out the computer and set up the recording. I watched the recording again and focused on the image of an indiscriminate figure as he or she entered and then left the JJR Productions office. While this recording was slightly higher quality than the first one I viewed, it was still unclear as to the sex of the murderer.

The baggy clothes were worn on purpose to hide the actual frame size of the person, or whether or not they had the hips of a woman. But even if the hunched person stood tall, the height was not tall, not short.

I watched the gait of the walk as I tried to make out the hips. For me, that was key. In the baggy clothes, I was unable to determine sex. And I most definitely couldn't see hips. But that gait. It read male to me.

"You can't tell who that is, man, woman, young or old. But the way they're walking, it looks like a man. I know the clothes are oversized on purpose, but I expect hips from a woman. I can't determine any."

"That's my thought as well. But because it's still undetermined, I'd like to have this eliminated as evidence. It doesn't prove or disprove guilt or innocence for that matter."

"So why do they think this is Penelope?"

"Very simply, the height. And this."

Leonard pulled out his copy of the evidence and pushed several documents to me. I was staring at phone records with Penelope's phone number highlighted. I noted the dates and shuffled through each page. "You called Jon Jaime Ray eleven times in a week and a half. Why?"

"I begged him not to publish the pictures. He laughed and said he had my permission. Each time I called, he laughed at me." She was crying and wiped her cheeks.

Did Jon Jaime Ray forge her signature, drug her to get the pictures, and ignore the fraudulent approval? Was that enough to make someone commit murder?

I was still stuck on how they determined it was Penelope on the recording. I pulled the computer closer, made the picture a little larger and stared at the murderer, slightly bent as he or she walked away. I watched Penelope as she entered the office and left minutes later, I touched the computer and froze the screen. "Did you have Penelope recreate the video? If you look at the torso of the murderer, he looks very long wasted. And then look at Penelope. She's short waisted with long legs. Even if they're the same height, the proportions are off." I looked at Leonard. He smiled.

"I can have measurements taken. The other issue is Penelope coming out of the office. She's clearly upset as she dials the police. The police claim it looks real because she's an actress, so she must be acting."

"Not evidence," I said. "Is there any other physical evidence?"

"Finger prints, a hair sample. The killer was wearing a knitted cap. Penelope was not. I suspect that's the hair sample they found. We're waiting for the results," Leonard said.

"Penelope went in to speak to him and found him dead. If you look at the video again, the killer was wearing gloves. Entering and exiting."

Leonard nodded. "Now you're caught up. The killer was covered up. Most likely the evidence will point to Penelope who went in uncovered. I called you here because I'd like to officially hire investigate the murder. I'm hoping you might have other names or scenarios that can help get attention away from Penelope."

I had left the house with the list and pulled it from my bag. "Here are the latest names I've come across. Several models sued Jon Jaime Ray. Some lost their lawsuits, some won. If they lost, I would figure that would be a strong motive to kill him. I've spoken to Allan Mason, brother of Ericka Mason and a former model, Delinda Love. Either could have been angry enough, but I have no other evidence."

I slid the folder to him. He opened it up and glanced through it and smiled. "Thanks for this."

"There's one last thing. My boss is in business with Jon Jaime Ray and was suing him. I spoke with a witness who heard them fighting. He said something about videos but wasn't able to make out what it was. I put that information in there as well."

Leonard raised his eyebrows. "Seriously?"

I nodded. "I think the videos refer to videos shot through Jon Jaime Ray's company. I have a feeling it's about pornography."

Leonard raised his eyebrows. "That makes your boss a suspect."

"Yes, it does. I hope it helps. The more I discover, the less I know."

"Isn't that always how it goes," Leonard said.

"Nikki. I'm sorry I got so angry. I can't believe this is happening to me," Penelope said.

"I can't imagine being in your position. Don't worry about me." I glanced at my phone. "I need to go. When I find out anything else, I'll let you know."

I struggled to pull myself upstairs and to bed. It was after four when I got home. I lay on top of the blankets. Will pulled me close. "Do they have more on Penelope?"

"They have physical evidence, but they're waiting for a match. I gave Leonard the rest of my research. He wants to hire me to keep digging."

"Good. You shouldn't do so much work for nothing. You're too good for that. And all this work, you deserve pay."

I leaned against him as I tried to fall asleep. I didn't think it would come because I had a strong feeling the fingerprints and hair would come back to Penelope because as we already determined, the murderer was covered from head to toe.

CHAPTER 15

Jon Jaime Ray left a trail of abuse and heartbreak behind him. The pain grew exponentially, reaching out like tentacles, attaching to anyone who had met, heard of, or had dealings with him, ever.

I had never met him and even I felt the pain left behind.

It oozed out at my workplace as Ethan avoided me as much as possible during the day. It was the most uncomfortable I had ever been in a job since I started working at twenty-two years old. I had the distinct feeling he regretted hiring me as much as I regretted taking the job.

The lawyers had filed the lawsuit on behalf of Myles Landry that morning. I was filing his case file in the cabinet and I thought of Myles, a man who seemed to be a new friend, whose company I enjoyed. If it wasn't for this job or for Jon

Jaime Ray's murder, I wouldn't have met him. I'm glad I had. Maybe it would be a wash.

But then again, every time Ethan and I were in the same proximity, he would glare at me, so maybe not. Against my better judgement, I decided to stay on at the law firm, partially to honor my commitment to the new job while I looked for another one and partially, I might learn something about Jon Jamie Ray's murder. Was it conflict of interest? Probably.

He glared at me as I walked past the partners' office.

I took a moment in my car before pulling away. I pushed meandering thoughts to the back of my head, and by the time I reached the house, I needed to put the week behind me. The kids were out with friends enjoying another summer evening. I glanced at my phone. Will wouldn't be home for some time as he was working on a client's file he needed to finish for the morning.

Restless and nowhere close to being hungry, I grabbed my keys and purse and got back in the car. I wasn't sure where I was heading.

"Penelope didn't do this," I said to myself and tapped my fingers on the steering wheel. The restlessness was overwhelming. "How do I figure out who did this?"

All the evidence discovered up to this point was inconclusive and yet, none of it stopped the police, or more specifically, Andy, from taking that to mean Penelope killed

Jon Jaime Ray. Unless they were withholding evidence, which they couldn't have been. Not with her lawyer pressuring them for all of the evidence. In the fervor to find something, and not finding anything that seemed useful to Penelope, I was left with the idea that something shifted in the suspect list. Someone was able to hide in the myriad of possible suspects merely because the list was so large. There were too many. "The police checked the office. I'm sure they checked his house. But it's easier to hide something at home."

Finding Jon Jaime Ray's home address, I did a legal U-turn and followed the directions to a rather innocuous neighborhood of family homes with bicycles, swing sets, and two cars in each driveway. I followed the winding road, surprised I only saw two neighbors out on this summer night; one walking a fluffy white dog, the other running.

I parked across the street from Jon Jaime Ray's house and took in the older home. The split-level house was light tan with dark brown trim. Overgrown bushes flanked either side of the front door, pansies grew in patches under the front window. There was nothing flashy about the house, nothing that shouted an entertainment photographer/producer had lived here.

The house was completely dark inside, police caution tape still hung across the front door. It was eerie staring at the house knowing its owner would never step inside again.

I had the sense I shouldn't be here.

"What the hell am I doing?"

I hadn't noticed I was tapping my hands on the steering wheel again. I stopped, stared at the house.

"Do I dare?"

While it was early evening, it was still somewhat light outside, though the shadows were growing darker and longer. Without contemplating it, I exited the car and ran for the house. As I trekked up the small hill and around to the backyard, my phone buzzed. Will texted me.

I'll be home in two hours. Last meeting. I promise.

No worries. I love you.

I love you. He texted back.

I felt guilty not sharing my location or the idiotic plan that formed in my head, but I didn't want him to worry, and I did promise I wouldn't get into trouble.

But the police were being narrowminded in their investigation, and I knew the answer was somewhere in the office or in the house. It usually was.

When I reached the back of the house, I knelt beside the basement window and glanced inside, but the windows weren't just dark, some sort of material was blocking the window.

"Hmmm."

I stood, walked toward the sliding door. I turned on the flashlight on my phone and peered inside. From what I could see, it was neat and tidy, if not a little out of date in the design. It wasn't what I was expecting, though I didn't realize I was expecting anything.

I slipped my sleeve over my hand and touched the door handle. It slid open easily; someone had forgotten to lock the door.

Glancing around, I was almost sure no one could see me as I stepped inside the kitchen. The deafening silence wrapped around me and nearly suffocated me. "I need to leave," I murmured to myself. In hindsight, I should have taken my own advice, but my curiosity got the better of me as I wandered the kitchen. I touched nothing as I moved my flashlight across the envelope piles that lined the counter. Again, covering my hands I spread the mail out and found the same bills that I had in my stack at home. I placed them back in a neat pile and continued to walk the space.

What I noticed as I walked through the rooms, was an impeccably clean and minimalist home that seemed staged and that there was nothing in here that said Jon Jaime Ray was the occupant who lived here. There were no trinkets, no photos, no artwork on the walls. Nothing to show the life he had led.

I continued down the hallway finding myself in the bedroom area. Bedroom four, the smallest of the bedrooms was fitted as a home office. I opened the drawers, each folder neatly labeled with the type of bills they contained or the subject matter of the documents inside. The folders however, were empty. In the closet, clothes were hung evenly, pants with pants, shirts with shirts, separated by color.

In the primary bedroom, I saw the same; clean, overly organized drawers with nothing out of place or seemingly missing. There was nothing useful here.

I continued back to the stairs and walked down, finding a family room and the door to the garage. One quick peak in the garage showed me two cars, a shelving unit with tubs of stuff, oil cans, old rags. Otherwise, it was neat and clean.

Back at the stairs, I noticed a door with the handle hanging down, the door ajar. I pulled it open, found the light and turned it on.

At the bottom, a basement. But not any basement. I was staring at Jon Jaime Ray's studio. At the center, a raised stage with a bed on top. Three cameras were lined along the perimeter of the stage, lights hung from the ceiling.

In the far corner, was a small sound proof room with a mix board inside.

I wandered.

A door to my left opened to a large closet. Racks of skimpy dresses, skirts and pants hung by color and type. Shelves held collections of high heeled boots and strappy sandals. I shuddered and closed the door and opened another. This one was filled with baskets containing, whips, chains, handcuffs. I felt my hands shake as I exited.

At the center of room, I stood and slowly spun, taking in each angle. Being here made me want a long, hot shower.

I knew I should leave; I had no legal right to be here, but I walked the perimeter and entered the larger room again. The walls, the floor, the proportion of each seemed, off. I couldn't pinpoint why the dimensions of the room seemed to be wrong and confusing me. I stepped on the stage. My eyes wandered across the room; the walls, the floors. The walls! They seemed too thick for a house in the suburbs.

I climbed down from the stage and walked to the panel covered walls and gently pushed against them feeling for hollow spaces. They were... spongy?

When one of the panels rattled, I pushed, and it slid open. I could feel my jaw open after I revealed a hiding space filled with boxes. Boxes were filled with folders, loose papers. I pulled out one of the boxes, pulled up the lid. My jaw fell open again. I was staring at hundreds of loose photos of models in various stages of undress.

My head spun with the possibilities, and I put the pictures back in the box and the box back in its hiding spot, leaving the wall open. I continued along the wall finding another loose panel, and slid it open. More of the same; folders with pictures. Leaving that door open, I pressed against the wall, finding a third door. And there I saw it.

A ledger. I pulled it from the shelf and skimmed through it. There are initials, numbers, and dates, but on their own, without studying it, I had no idea what they meant. If I had to guess, it looked like a code of some kind. I pulled out my phone and began to take pictures of the pages.

When I was almost finished, I heard footsteps above me. My heart pounded, and I knew there was no escape. Someone advised the police I was here. Or maybe I missed a camera or motion sensors alerting them to my presence. It was too late for me. I glanced at the ledger in my hand and tossed it back into its hiding spot. I left the hidey holes exposed to whoever was on their way down here. Not only did I want the police to realize what they had missed the first time in the house, I wanted them to see the evidence when they arrested me, so they could use what I had discovered.

I stood as though I belonged there, as the footsteps descended the stairs.

When Andy and Gary reached the bottom of the staircase, they glanced at me; I'm not sure which of us were more surprised by my presence.

Andy stormed over, turned me around and put the handcuffs around my wrists. "I told you to butt out," he growled in my ear. I shuddered and wished it was Gary arresting me instead.

"You're under arrest for breaking and entering, hindering an active investigation," he said as he yanked on my arms and nearly dragged me toward the stairs. I should have felt fear, but I only felt exhilaration as Andy pushed me up the stairs.

I glanced at Andy. "I didn't break in. Someone left the door unlocked."

***

Andy left me alone in the interrogation room for thirty minutes. I didn't have a chance to ask for my call, though the thought of calling Will about this made me tremble. He was already upset by my recent actions, and I hoped that what I had done wouldn't be the thing that made him second guess our relationship.

It had been reckless and stupid, and I wasn't feeling any better when Andy, followed by a sheepish Gary, stepped inside the room.

"What the hell were you thinking?" Andy said.

I ignored him and stared at Gary. He couldn't look me in the eye. I had a feeling Andy was keeping him from me.

"Nikki, answer me," Andy said, his voice raised, his face red.

"Penelope didn't kill Jon Jaime Ray. I'd like my lawyer now," I said.

"Nikki, stop. Just answer the question. What were you doing in that basement?" Andy asked.

"I've asked for a lawyer." I placed my phone on the table. Gary motioned for Andy to leave the room.

"Nikki," Will said when he picked up. "Where are you?"

"Lake Zurich police station."

He was silent for a moment. "Why?"

"I was arrested. Caught in Jon Jaime Ray's basement."

"Nikki. Andy's after you. Why the hell did you go and do that?" Will's anger was palpable and my hands shook.

"I'm sorry. If you can't come, can you recommend someone to come and get me out of here."

"I'll be there in ten minutes." Resigned, he sighed and hung up.

I knocked on the viewing window, sat back down, and waited for Andy and Gary to return. Gary entered alone.

"What were you thinking?" he asked as he sat.

What was I thinking? I was thinking I'm lost, and not sure which direction to go with my career. Which seemed odd as usually that was the only thing in my life that made sense.

I looked at Gary. His question was legitimate, and I knew I was in real trouble. But the boring job, the idea of Penelope as a murderer, it all added to my discontent.

"How did the police miss those hiding spots?" I asked him.

"That's not the point, Nikki. You're in a lot of trouble."

"I realize that. But I'm frustrated. You're looking at one person only, and there are hundreds of suspects."

"We have evidence, and we're following all leads. Though what you found is quite interesting and disturbing."

"Can you use it?"

"Yes. We can. We arrested you in a home you didn't belong in and consequently the evidence was in our sight. That was smart of you."

"I'm not an idiot. I do know the law."

Gary grimaced. "You need to let us do our jobs."

"Then do a better job at it," I hissed. "You're not looking at anyone else."

The door squeaked open. Will was shown the interrogation room and the air turned chilly. I watched Gary stand and leave and Will sat. His jaw clenched. The tension in the room was thick and all my fault.

"I'll post your bail, and you'll be able to come home."

I nodded. "Thanks. I am sorry I got caught." And when I thought about it, I changed my mind. "Actually, I'm not sorry. I found them the evidence they need to pursue other suspects."

"What's going on with you," he whispered to me.

"The job. This case. Being a paralegal was so much of who I was and that part of me feels dead. I should be happier. The kids are great, Jack's been less of a hassle, and… you." I looked at him, wiped tears from my eyes.

He touched my cheek. "I'll post bail, and then we'll get out of here."

I nodded and watched him walk away to spring me from jail.

***

The car ride was uncomfortably silent. Will parked behind my car, and I got out. I stared at Jon Jaime Ray's house with some disgust, got into my car and followed Will home.

I let myself cry as I pulled into the garage beside Will's car. I would have stayed there had he not been waiting for me to come inside.

He noticed the tears but said nothing as we made our way upstairs. I was exhausted and frustrated. For some reason, Myles Landry popped into my head. I had been so impressed with how effortlessly he moved through his life. With the exception of his lawsuit against his landlord, he was confident, sure of himself and didn't question how he lived his life.

Why was I having so much trouble centering myself?

"Why did you break in," Will asked as I slipped off my shirt and put on my pajamas.

"The job, and the regrets I have over taking it. I feel like I'm drowning in the weeds. I needed to find the connection between Jon Jaime Ray and his murderer. It's in those books or on that website. I'm sure of that. And now I've pissed you off. I feel sick."

"I'm not happy about what happened tonight, but I love you, Nikki. Even though I'm pissed as hell that you did that. How could you risk everything? How could…" He backed away, turned and faced the other way. "You need to be more careful. It's not like you to be so careless." He turned back and faced me.

"I'm restless and directionless. It's been one week, and I can tell I made a mistake with this job. But I need money, I need the insurance." I was drenched in tears. I felt as though I deserved to be this miserable. Especially after tonight.

I walked to him and put my arms around him. He was trembling, and he didn't immediately put his arms around me.

"I am so in love with you. Hopelessly, in fact. And everything was perfect until this job. Until I reached out to help Penelope."

His arms found their way around me, and he held me tight.

"You will find your way. I'm here with you, and I'll support you any way I can. I just don't want to pick you up from the police station again."

"I'm so sorry I let this happen."

He reached down and kissed me. I felt as though I was clinging onto him and that if I let go, I would spin out of control and land in the waste land of nothingness. I needed to change that. I needed to change the course of my career, and I needed to fix what I broke between Will and I before I lost everything I treasured.

CHAPTER 16

The silence in the house was deafening. The kids finally had their day with Jack and Brayden, spending it at the zoo. While I was glad their relationship with their father was better, I was waiting for the other shoe to fall and the next big conflict to arise. For now, I restlessly paced the house as I waited for Will to finish his work for the day.

I thought he was purposely evading me for the stunt I pulled last night. I couldn't blame him for still being angry. It had been stupid to enter Jon Jaime Ray's house without permission. Remembering it and reliving my arrest kept me up most of the night.

Will worked inside the sunroom, a computer on his lap, a legal pad beside him on the sofa. I had started the morning fetching items for him, being as accommodating as I could. I even tried flirting, but the attempt was cringeworthy at best and now my stomach ached when I looked at him.

I anxiously sat in the den, looking through the glass French doors, worried that I had irreparably screwed things up between us. I glanced back at my book, but it was taking me more than several readings to finish the paragraph, and I still had no idea what I had just read.

"NO, Janelle!" Will's harsh voice startled me, and I looked up through the French doors. He was pacing. His computer and notes on the sofa as he stopped, rubbed his hands through his short hair. He paced along the glass doors.

"You need to stop calling me."

My annoyance only added to the stress he was already feeling and my guilt worsened. I stood and opened the door, stepped inside the warm room, only cooled by the fan and open windows. Will turned and looked at me. For the first time since he bailed me out of jail, his face softened. He reached his arm out for me, and I took his hand.

"No more. The divorce is final. We're over. I'm not coming over there to talk. Don't call me again." He gently hung up the phone.

"What?" I started to ask.

He shook his head.

"She heard I'm moving in with you," he said and leaned against the sofa staring out into the back yard.

"I'm sorry I've added to your stress," I said, still holding his hand.

"Last night definitely didn't help." He closed his eyes. "I understand why you did what you did. I'm irritated, but I know what you were hoping to accomplish. You accomplished it. For now, the police are leaving Penelope alone."

"Really?"

He nodded. "Leonard called and told me."

"He didn't call me." I tried not to seem dejected. It was just odd.

"He wants you to continue doing what you're doing. The change in focus for the police doesn't change that. He thinks you're a good detective."

I grimaced. "Good to know I'm doing something right."

He wrapped me in his arms. "You do a lot right. This thing though. Breaking into Jon Jaime Ray's house, that was stupid. But productive. When you get your PI license, please don't do that."

I looked up at him. "I promise. I'll be careful. And know I'm sorry you had to get me out of jail. I never meant to add more stress to your life. Especially with Janelle lurking about." I glanced at his pile. "How much more work?"

"I'm done. I'm drained. And it looks like the youngins are home." He pointed out the window, they were running up the deck toward the sunroom door.

"Hi, Mom, Will," Jacob said as he ran into the house.

Julia ran in next, turned toward me. "I never want babies, ever."

"Good to know since you're fourteen. It'll get better as he gets older."

She rolled her eyes and headed through the den.

I watched Emily say goodbye to her little brother, cooing and then hugging her father. She waved goodbye and then came inside. "Dad wants to talk to you," she said and looked at Will. "Fire pit if you want to do s'mores."

"That's the best offer I've had all day. I'll go get it built," Will said.

Emily followed her siblings inside.

"Want me to join you with Jack?"

I shook my head. "No. I've got this."

By the time I got to the driveway, Jack had the baby inside his car seat, and he was standing by the open door.

"What can I help you with?"

"Is everything okay?" Jack asked.

I shrugged. "Everything's fine."

"I heard you were arrested."

I was surprised the kids mentioned it, though Jack was an officer of the court and had his ways of learning things.

"All part of the investigation," I said coolly.

"You're being careful?"

"Jack, what do you want?"

"I want you to be happy. I want you to be careful and not get into any more scrapes. I was worried when I heard you were arrested."

"Breaking well, more like entering without permission. I handed the police a whole lot of evidence in a murder case. It's all good."

"The Jon Jaime Ray murder case?"

Why was I was surprised he knew about that too? He didn't live in the area any longer. But then he knew a lot of lawyers.

"Yeah. There're a lot of suspects, and the police were ignoring that fact. Now they have more. But that's not what you really want to know. Please don't worry. I won't end up in jail."

"Nikki. I know I've been an ass, but I'm really trying to make it up to everyone for what I did."

The baby started to fuss in his car seat. Jack turned and looked inside.

"I should go," he said.

"Don't worry about making it up to me, just worry about the kids."

He nodded and then said, "About that Jon Jaime Ray murder investigation. I had a client sue him. Ray falsified documents. Used my client's logo on a document, doctored it. I almost didn't win the case for my client. An expert was finally able to prove the forgery. There're a lot of people out there who would have liked to see that man dead."

I didn't bother to ask which lawsuit it was. Attorney client privilege. If I really wanted to know, I could look that up based on what he told me.

"What I can tell you is, before my deposition with Jon Jaime Ray, I overheard him talking on the phone. He was discussing a large sum of money. While I was only catching half the conversation, he was discussing the purchase of a large piece of property somewhere in the suburbs. I suggest you look for property owned by him."

"When was this?"

"About six months ago."

"Thanks. I hadn't even thought to look for property. Though it's ironic. My boss was his business partner. He claimed he thought it was a real estate business, when in fact it was an entertainment production business. But maybe there was more."

The baby fussed again.

"Jon Jaime Ray was a disgusting human being, and I'm guessing so were his friends. Please be careful."

"I will."

Jack climbed into the car and backed down the driveway. By the time I got to the backyard, the kids and Will were sitting around a nicely built fire laughing at something, all comfortable with each other.

I headed to the fire pit.

"They had a dino exhibit across the zoo. With butt holes in each dino," Julia said and cracked herself up. Emily rolled her eyes, while Jacob held his marshmallow above the fire.

"We were supposed to go to dinner. But she called him back home," Jacob groused.

"Was the day good otherwise?" Will asked.

"Yeah. It was. I still get mad at him sometimes," Jacob admitted.

"You'll get mad. But as long as it gets better," Will said.

A few months ago, listening to their conversations about their father would have caused me a serious stomach ache. Tonight, not so much. Jack seemed to be making it up to them.

I caught Emily's gaze. She nodded and walked away from the fire pit. It seemed like an odd thing for her to do.

"Dad wants to come over for lunch tomorrow if that's okay?" Jacob asked.

I shrugged. "Thanks for the head's up. And as long as he's not coming to ask you all to move in with him, I'm okay," I tried to joke.

"Mom. Ugh. Amber, remember?" Jacob said.

I chuckled lightly because of all else, I didn't want to lose my kids. It had taken me so long to get us right again. I didn't want to disrupt that.

Emily emerged from the house carrying something. I looked at her, felt my eyebrows raise, curious about the item and why she went in to get it.

She came back to our circle, moved her chair beside me and sat down.

"How's Penelope doing?"

"For now, the police are backing off."

I noticed Will grimace and then busy himself with a marshmallow.

"So, what do you have?"

"There's something weird. I kept thinking I remembered something, but couldn't pull it out of my brain, and then when we were at the zoo, it just popped in my head."

She held out a photo album. I was surprised she still had one. The page was opened to a volleyball picture. It was Emily, her freshman year of high school, standing with older girls, their arms around each other smiling for the camera.

"What am I looking at?" I asked.

"We always had a really big practice weekend. The freshman, JV, and Varsity and then the big picnic afterward. I remember, Penelope came to it one year because she had been on the team in high school. That's how I got interested."

I looked at her and nodded, but didn't see where that was going.

"You work for Ethan Grater, right?"

I nodded but still didn't see a connection.

"This is his niece. Mara Grater. She was on the Varsity team my freshman year. She was like my 'buddy,' helping me acclimate to the team. I wasn't really friends with her, but thinking about Penelope and your boss and the whole thing." She pointed to the picture. "This guy here, it's her uncle. He used to come to practices and games. It was creepy."

I pulled the book closer and stared at a picture of my daughter and her friends and Ethan Grater in the background. It did seem creepy. I still wasn't sure where this was going.

"Did you know she recently died?" I asked.

Emily nodded. "I had heard from Coach Peterson. I couldn't go to the funeral, and I didn't know her well. I hadn't talked to her since she graduated. It was about three years ago."

I handed the picture back to Emily. "I'm not sure why you wanted me to see that."

"Mara sent me a message about a year ago. Telling me she had a great opportunity for me to make a little extra money. It was out of the blue, but I went to meet her at the café. Her uncle was sitting there, at another table. It was really creepy, Mom."

I heard the words and my stomach churned. "Oh…" I bent over feeling the explosion of understanding. Mara Grater had tried to recruit my daughter. My teenage daughter.

"Mom?" Emily asked, worry in her voice.

I stood. "I'm sorry." I pulled her close. "I'm sorry. I know what they were trying to recruit you for."

Emily pulled herself away. "Mom. I got out of there so fast. I blocked Mara on everything. Phone, social media, email. It was so weird."

"Why didn't you say anything?" I touched her cheek, smoothed her hair.

"I was embarrassed I even went to see her. But it all came back to me so clearly. There was something weird in their relationship. Really weird." Emily handed me the picture. "You need to be careful."

I glanced at Will. He was worried. I was worried and now so was Jack and Emily. What had I stumbled into?

***

While I wasn't nauseated when Jack came over for lunch on Sunday, I preferred not to be in the same room as him. He ate lunch with the kids on the back deck. I hung inside reading.

"You don't have to hide from me too," Will said.

I glanced up from the book. He no longer seemed angry with me, and yet, I supposed I was hiding from him as well, still embarrassed by my arrest.

"Giving you space."

He sat down on the edge of the sofa opposite of me, seemingly unable to relax.

"I appreciate that, but it's unnecessary. If we're going to make this work, we need to keep talking."

I nodded. "I know. That communication thing. I guess I'm embarrassed and the fact they haven't charged me with unlawful entry is making me nervous. Like they're building a case against me."

As if on cue, the doorbell rang. Will and I glanced at each other, I shrugged and walked to the door, mostly to get away from our awkward conversation.

I was surprised to see Gary alone at my door.

"Uh, hi," I said.

"Can I come in?"

"Sure." I motioned for him to join me in the front room. "What's up?"

"The police aren't pressing charges against you considering you gave us a wealth of evidence we didn't have before."

I smiled. "Found any new suspects to harass?"

"You know that's not how it works. Right now, the timeline fits one theory. We're working on it."

"Yeah, well thanks for not pushing the illegal entry. I know I shouldn't have done it, but I was sure the answers were in his home. I just had to find them."

"We were able to clear the Mason family. The ledger

you found gave us a healthy list of people to interview and investigate."

"Glad I could help."

"Please don't interfere any more. It's making Andy cranky, and you don't belong on the case. Let us do our jobs."

"Leonard Price hired me to investigate."

Gary grimaced. "I see."

"I promise I won't make your life any more difficult than I already have," I said.

Gary touched my arm. "You're really good at what you do, but you're too close to the case because of your former relationship with Penelope. And your boss. It's a conflict of interest. Just stay out." Gary stood to leave.

"My boss, Ethan Grater's niece Mara Grater died several months ago. She worked with Jon Jaime Ray and tried to recruit Emily to work for them."

Gary's eyes widened.

"Oh, Nikki. I'm so sorry. Did he hurt her?"

I shook my head. "No. She got out of the meeting before anything happened. I just wanted to let you know that yes, this is personal for me. I'm not sure if I can drop it."

Gary grimaced. He knew that because I was hired by the person of interest, I was on the case and he couldn't stop me. "Just be careful and don't do anything reckless or stupid."

I walked him to the front door.

"I'm glad you and Suz are talking again. She really missed you."

"I missed her too."

He kissed my forehead, waved goodbye to Will, and let himself out.

I turned. Jack was watching me.

"They're letting you off," he said.

"Yes. Go be with the kids."

"I came here to spend time with them and make sure you're okay. I still can't believe you're working at Grater and Ross."

"I needed money. That meant a job. I'm fine."

"Nikki, you need to be careful. There are a lot of angry people who don't want the police to find out who killed Jon Jaime Ray. Let the police do their job."

"Don't tell me what to do. Please, Jack, drop it."

Will stepped up. "Jack, Nikki has everything all under control."

Jack eyed Will suspiciously. "I have no ulterior motives in this. You have to believe me. I want to make sure you're okay. I fucked up big time, but I still care about you. There's a lot of history between us."

I observed Jack. His sentimentality surprised me.

"Yes, we do." I could have been snarky or angry. I decided not to be. "Thank you." I reached out to him, offered a side hug.

It was his turn to be confused. "I… have we just turned the corner?" He offered a cheeky smile, the kind he used to give me when we first started dating. At his age, it wasn't as cute.

"Don't press your luck," I said as I pointed my finger into his chest.

With a smile, he turned and walked back to the kids.

"I think you did," Will said.

"Funny, he doesn't bother me nearly as much as he did last week," I said with a shrug.

CHAPTER 17

I arrived at work on Monday, my usual early time. It was nice to see Carey there pulling out her work for the day.

"Good morning, Nikki. Have a good weekend?"

"I did. How about you?"

"It was great. A lot of running around, getting things done, but it was good."

I nodded and headed to my office, unsure of what I'd be doing today. I logged in and pulled up email. There was nothing new from the partners. I checked the other file folders, still nothing. I had no voicemails, no other messages.

I sat back, took out the photos from the ledger I had taken and reviewed them but still couldn't make heads or tails of the notations.

As I worked my way through what I thought were initials, I compared them to the model list I had created. When Carey came into my office, I hadn't heard her until she cleared her throat. I glanced up. She appeared worried, complete with wringing her hands together.

"What's the matter?"

"Ethan's ill. He's not coming in."

I stood but stayed behind my desk, my thoughts racing with what might be wrong.

"Is it odd for him to call in sick?" I asked, confused why Carey was so worried.

"He never calls out. I've worked here three years. Never."

"Oh." I still didn't understand her worry until Samuel walked over.

His jaw was tightly clenched, his arms against his chest. "Everyone time to go home. Bring whatever work you have today. Set up the main line recording." He looked from Carey to me, and I understood Carey's worry. Something wasn't right.

"Samuel, what the matter?" I asked.

"I don't know. We'll pay you for today, consider it a national holiday or something," he said as he shuffled away, his shoulders slumped. Carey and I glanced at each other before separating and preparing to leave.

Off on this summer afternoon felt like playing hooky. I stood in the middle of the front flower bed, picking weeds. I glanced up, closed my eyes and sniffed the air. It smelled fragrant like the flowers surrounding me.

In that moment, I think I had an answer to my work problem, now that I realized it really was in my control to change it. My PI classes were starting next week. I had a healthy amount of my severance left. I could do it. Couldn't I?

I sat in the grass, pulling another tough clump of weeds, as a car came down the street and up my driveway. I knew it was Gary's car.

He parked and came out, wearing his usual jeans, collared shirt, and comfortable slip-on shoes. He made it to me in a few quick strides and sat across from me.

"Twice in two days. I should either be honored or worried."

He nodded. "Worried. Andy thinks it was Penelope. I don't. I'm concerned Andy's going after her because you're friends with her." He grimaced.

"That's highly unethical."

"It is."

He was holding tightly to a folder but didn't offer an explanation. He didn't offer much as we sat in the grass.

"I've been going through that model list. I've talked to more disgruntled or scared victims than I ever had for a murder case. They're all cleared of the crime."

"And none of them fit the build of the killer?"

"Based on the recording, we've put the killer as a slim person around 5'6"-5'9". Male or female. We still can't tell."

He finally handed the folder to me. The top document was the suspect list. I read through several lines of notes as he cleared each witness. They all had something to say about the photographer. None of it good.

I looked at him. "Jack told me he had a client who sued Jon Jaime Ray for forgery. He used someone else's logo and created false documents. I haven't looked up the lawsuit, but I think there's a good chance it was someone else not on this model list."

"There are definitely a lot of people who could have done it. We've gone through the other lawsuits, interviewed those who lost their case in court, the others who settled, the women who won. They all have alibis. Penelope doesn't have an alibi."

"We have a shitty murder victim who exploited others. And none of these models look good other than Penelope?"

Gary motioned to the folder. I shuffled through the papers and found a crime scene photo. I held it up.

"It's a hiking boot Men's size eleven, women's size nine."

I couldn't picture Ethan in hiking boots but he was slim, possibly 5'9". Maybe he wore the shoes to hide his identity.

"Penelope is that height and wears a size nine women's shoe," Gary said.

"My boss is that height as well."

I glanced back at the folder. Shuffled through more pictures. I found Jon Jaime Ray's phone records with Penelope's phone number highlighted.

"There's no other phone numbers that are repeated multiple times?" I asked.

"There is one."

I looked through the list and the notes. It was Mara Grater's phone number. "Mara Grater died about six months ago. It was ruled a suicide."

"Other models claimed she wouldn't have killed herself," Gary said.

"Oh."

"We've gone through the phone records. I will admit what we could salvage from voicemail, Mara's calls to Jon Jaime Ray were a bit eye opening. There was something sexual about them. She did threaten to kill him on several occasions. I'm wondering if we should reopen her death case."

"I think it would be worth more than a look. Not just at that connection. Ethan was business partners with Jon Jaime Ray."

"We're investigating that too. The man had a lot of businesses. None of them good. But there's this."

Gary clicked on his phone. "Listen to this." He played a message that I assumed he found on Jon Jaime Ray's voicemail. "If you don't give me back ALL of the negatives and copies of those pictures, I'll kill you!" It was clearly Penelope's voice on that message. But then who hadn't made threats that were never followed through.

"A threat isn't proof she killed him. Are there any other messages or emails?" I asked.

"Please then. Tell me what other options you have. She's the strongest."

"Ethan was suing him. Read the lawsuit. And those pages from the ledger. I'm fairly certain they're initials and dates. Not to mention, Ethan's the right build. He's slim, about 5'9"."

Gary pulled out copies of pages from the ledger he had in the bag beside him. "Don't tell anyone I'm giving this to you."

I raised my eyebrows, confused that Gary was sharing what the police had.

"Why? If Penelope's the strongest suspect you have…"

"I still don't think she did it."

I looked at the pages from the ledger. I had only had time to take about five pages worth of pictures. He handed me copies of the entire journal.

"Without a formal request from the suspect's lawyer, this is illegal," I said.

"It's not if we hire you as a consultant," Gary said.

"I'm already working for Penelope's lawyer."

Gary stared at the pages he just gave me biting his lips as if thinking of his next move. I held the pile out to him. He shook his head.

"Her lawyer asked to see the evidence we have. I had to give those to him. If you're working for him, I'm sure they'd give them to you."

I looked at the pages: the entire ledger book that I had found.

"You're smart and you can figure out what this means. We're at a loss and have someone already working on it. Just tell me who killed the man."

CHAPTER 18

Gary's request sat heavy in my gut as I surrounded myself in ledger pages, my computer open on my lap. I wasn't alone; Will sat beside me, his nose in his computer, working on one of his client files. I had no idea how long we had sat there in our own work, until he broke the silence.

"How's it going?" he asked.

My eyes were blurry, and I was ready for a break.

"Well, if I'm reading the ledger correctly, I matched several initials to names on the list, including the lawsuit plaintiffs, and business associates."

Will rested his chin on my shoulder; our previous disagreement slowly fading into the past. "That's impressive and most probably correct. Any likely suspects?"

"Boiling it down to what's in the ledger, there might be fifteen names Jon Jaime Ray might have been blackmailing. I'm guessing based on the numbers beside the initials. Small enough to be monthly," I said. "And your work. Are you almost done?"

"Yeah. I just signed off on the document. I'd help you, but it's not my case."

"Thanks for the almost offer, but I'm ready to be done." I pulled piles together and clipped them into a large book. I tossed my work on the chair.

"Have you found any videos or pictures that would explain why they were being blackmailed?" Will asked.

"I have a theory." I looked at him and grimaced.

"Which is?"

I pulled up the JJR Productions website and turned my computer screen to him. My mouse hovered over the log in link.

"You want me to get the account?" Will asked.

"No. I have an email address I use for things like this."

"For porn?"

I chuckled. "No. Just for work-related things where I really don't want emails coming into my in box."

Will clicked on the link, and I entered my throw away email address and my not real personal data, effectively opening an account on the site. The website let me in immediately. But as

I noticed, I needed to pay per each video. "I'm not sure I want to pay for these things."

Will pointed to the names under each video. "I'm guessing the names are fake."

I looked at the video descriptions. "Probably. I really don't want to use my credit card."

He chuckled. "Want mine?"

"No. It's a little ick."

He wrapped his arm around me. "So, what now?"

"I'll send this new shortened list and see if that helps narrow a killer. There're just so many."

I put my computer away and something on the first sheet of the ledger caught my attention. EG. But not just EG, I also found ML. Would that be Myles Landry? I knew they had all known each other in some way. Even Jack knew the man.

"Is everything okay?"

"Give me a sec." I continued to scan the page and then the next. I found what looked like log in credentials. I sat back on my bed with the computer, logging in, now as I assumed, to be Jon Jaime Ray.

"Jon Jaime Ray gave you what you needed. Nice of him," Will said.

I shrugged as the credentials let me in to the back end of the website. I clicked the subscriber list. "Okay. He's got 10,000 subscribers. I'm guessing this list will prove fruitless.

Why would the subscribers have any reason to kill the man who owns the website?"

"Business associates, an angry model, yes," Will said. "I'm sure it's one of the victims, models, blackmail victims. Someone he recorded."

"Here's the list of videos, no names."

Will handed me the list of initials. I compared them to initials on the website. "Why keep a physical ledger when you have it all here?"

"That's a good question."

I clicked the video labeled EG and held my breath as the video loaded.

It was most definitely Ethan but not how I expected.

"You can't quit. We had a deal," Ethan sneered.

"Uncle Ethan. I don't want to do this anymore. Jon Jaime Ray is dangerous. He's hurting them. Don't make me do this anymore," Mara pleaded.

"I have no choice. I have to give him models or he'll kill me," Ethan said. He was so close to Mara, and she inched away as far as she could from her seated position.

She shook her head as she cried. "No. No more." Her voice was barely audible, just enough to make out the words.

"You will get me another model. Do it." Ethan slapped Mara's cheek. She held her hand across her cheek and ran away crying.

My stomach roiled and my hands shook as I clicked out of the video.

"Ethan owed Jon Jaime Ray money because he was being blackmailed by the photographer. Part of his payment was to recruit models. He used Mara to do it."

"He had a lot to lose if this came out," Will said.

My phone rang. I saw the number, and my heart sank. "This is Nikki."

"Mrs. Page, this is Leonard Price. Penelope's just been formally charged in the death of Jon Jaime Ray."

"I have something for you, and I'm on my way."

"Penelope's been formally charged," I told Will.

"I'll drive."

***

I rushed inside with the ledger pages, highlighting the login. I ran for the front desk. "I need to speak with Leonard Price."

Penelope's lawyer walked out of the conference room when he saw us. "What the hell happened?" I screeched.

He held up his hands. "They're going after her hard. They're convinced she did it. Most of the evidence doesn't hold up. Unfortunately, they now have a witness that claims he saw them together the evening before Jon Jaime Ray died. I'm demanding bail be set. But I'm hoping you have something."

"Who's the witness?"

"Allan Mason," Leonard said.

I couldn't hide my surprise. Even though many of the models seemed to know each other and possibly their families, it seemed to be convenient that all of a sudden, Allen had information. He could have said something when I talked to him. Why didn't he?

"Where did he see them?" I felt anger, confusion, and disbelief. This didn't make sense.

"He claims he saw Penelope at a restaurant near the studio at nine p.m. with Jon Jaime Ray. We're trying to get a hold of the video recordings from outside that restaurant. The servers can't confirm or deny she was there with him."

"Did they confirm Allan was there?" I could feel my face flush. I was getting angrier.

"No."

"That's bullshit. He's the brother of one of the models who killed herself. Only he claims Jon Jaime Ray killed her because she was going to the police after the he raped her. There's no way Allan saw anything unless he was following Jon Jaime Ray."

"There's nothing on the video surveillance at the office saying he left to meet anyone. There is a back door, but it was locked, and no key was found."

"And they arrested her for that? It's all circumstantial and false testimony by a 'witness,'" I said.

"Nikki. She'll be out tomorrow on bail. She's not a flight risk. I'm just hoping you have something else for me."

I handed him my marked-up pages. "This was part of a ledger found at Jon Jaime Ray's home. See here." I pointed to the sheet. "The victim was blackmailing several people. Here." I pointed again. "This is a login to the back end of his website. It's all there as well. And…" I took a breath as my body shook. "My boss claimed he had business dealings with the deceased, but he was suing him. He was also being blackmailed by the deceased. Because there's a video on the back end of the site with my boss and his niece."

Penelope's lawyer took the sheets of paper. "Oh. I see." He looked at me, visibly shaken. "I know Ethan Grater. I knew his family, including Mara. Are you sure it was him on the video?"

I nodded. "It was unmistakable."

"Thank you, Nikki. For all of this. It's a big job to get through that list. There are apparently a lot of potential suspects. You've made my job easier."

Leonard touched my hand and offered a thin smile.

A door slammed. Will stepped closer to me, his arm around my shoulder. I glanced up as Andy stomped toward me.

"What the hell are you doing here?" he growled.

"Mrs. Page is working for me. I asked her to come in," Leonard said.

Andy glared. "Go home. You don't belong here."

"Why are you going after Penelope? There are so many other people out there who could have done it. Suspects with more to lose than Penelope!" My voice rose as my anger bubbled to the surface. I could have slapped him, but I balled my fists tightly.

"We have enough on her. Motive, and means. So, leave, Mrs. Page. You don't belong here."

"The phone call is circumstantial. The timing circumstantial. If you're going after her because of me, your whole case is unethical. You are still missing other suspects!"

"You're not the police. You're not a part of this. Go!"

"You are a jackass. A narrowminded jackass!" I stormed away from him, tears blinding me. I felt Will's hand on my back as he led me outside. Still in the entry of the police station, I could hear Leonard advising Andy that he will request the original ledger to examine. I smiled slightly, but it didn't stop the sinking feeling in my belly.

Outside, I paced. Anger, fear overwhelming me. "Nikki. Please stop. You did more for Penelope than the police. Her lawyer will get her off and get her out of there." Will tried to remain calm, but I think he was reacting to my hysterics.

The door to the police station opened. Andy walked out and found me still pacing near the front door. "You're out of line, Mrs...Nikki. Stop investigating this case, or I'll be forced to arrest you for obstruction."

I stared at him, met his gaze and kept eye contact.

"Obstruction? Obstruction! I've given you all of your evidence!" I screeched. "I'm so glad you ghosted me. You're an asshole, and frankly, I wouldn't trust you to investigate anything for me ever!"

Andy jumped at my admission. Rather than hearing more, he ran back inside the police station.

I stormed off.

Will jogged to match my gait. "He's angry you're besting him."

We reached his car, and Will opened the door for me. I sat.

Both of us inside, he started the car.

"What was I supposed to do? Ignore it. Not help her. This is bullshit."

I wrapped my arms around myself and let myself cry. I was overwhelmed knowing there were more suspects out there, and Detective Andy Butcher, didn't care because he was still angry at me because I showed him up in his last case and figured out who the killer really was. To further anger him, I solved a twenty-year-old murder case that no one knew was murder.

We were silent for the remainder of the short trip home.

"They have enough circumstantial evidence to launch an investigation. I don't think the DA will move forward with what they have," Will said when he pulled into the driveway.

"I hope not. If she did it, if the evidence clearly proved her guilt, I'd drop it and walk away. But I'm not seeing that."

"I'm not either. I'm pretty sure the DA won't as well."

I got out of the car. Will walked with me inside the house. The kids were hanging at the kitchen island, worry on their faces.

"Mom. What happened? You flew out of here so fast," Jacob asked.

I studied my kids. Each face was worried, each relying on me to be the parent there for them. Every day, all day. I risked that when I went to Jon Jaime Ray's house, and I seemed to be doing that by continuing with this investigation.

Oftentimes as a full-time working mom, I felt that guilt, but this was different. Working for a law firm wasn't dangerous. This was. I was debating the whole PI decision.

"Penelope was arrested, and the police won't listen to any other possible suspects. I'm sorry. I'm in a crappy mood."

"It's okay. Go upstairs and try to relax. You look like you're about to explode," Julia said. I couldn't help but chuckle.

"Thanks. I will. I promise. I wanted to tell you I'm sorry I let this thing with Penelope get in the way of time with you.

I'm trying to stay out of trouble with the police, but I feel like I'm messing everything up."

"You're not messing up. You saw a problem and tried to fix it. The police don't always get it right," Jacob said. "That's why we need lawyers." He smirked at Will.

"We're fine. Do what you need to do," Emily chimed in.

"Thanks. I've been ordered to stay out of it."

"Yeah. Like you'll do that," Julia said.

"I have to be careful. The police think I'm interfering."

"Even though you gave them their best leads," Will said. His phone rang. He grimaced and declined the call.

"Who was that?" I asked, though I was pretty sure I knew.

"I'll deal with it later. What do you think your next step is?"

It should have been to rest and relax with Will, but that's not what I did. I reached for my computer.

"Jacob, order pizza for dinner. I need to take care of something."

Jacob nodded; Will followed me upstairs.

"What are you looking for?" Will asked.

I pulled up my databases and typed in Ethan Grater.

"Lawsuits, legal actions against Ethan."

It didn't take long for the database to churn out the answer. "Ethan filed bankruptcy about a week before Mara was killed."

Will read the screen, took the computer and shuffled through the bankruptcy filing until he found what he was looking for.

"Jon Jaime Ray actually filed for compensation from the bankruptcy. Ethan owed him about $1.3 million dollars.

"That's a lot of money."

I pulled up Jon Jamie Ray's website and signed into the back end of it, pulling up the blackmail list. "Jon Jaime Ray was taking him for $5000 dollars a month. Also, a lot of money."

I scrolled again. "Ethan was behind, by a lot. So, did Jon Jaime Ray threaten to kill Mara to make him pay or did he kill Mara to force Ethan to pay? It's retribution," I said.

"That's a strong motive. You did say Ethan was suing Jon Jaime Ray?"

"He was. And Ethan filed bankruptcy, and Jon Jaime Ray was a creditor. What a mess."

Will called Leonard and gave him the new information about Ethan. I could hear Leonard through the phone, his voice speaking fast. "Okay. I'll let Nikki know. Thanks." He turned toward me. "He's grateful. He thinks that will be enough to convince Gary to let Penelope go."

"I hope so. It's about time the police listen to reason."

CHAPTER 19

Nikki, be careful today," Will said as he packed his lunch in his bag.

"I'll be fine. Ethan doesn't know what I know."

He kissed me, his gaze lingered on me when he pulled away. "I'm serious. If the police start poking around Ethan, he'll know, and that'll make him dangerous."

I nodded. "I'm going to quit." I slid my letter of resignation toward him. "I can't stay on. Not when I know what I know. Should I just call out sick?"

He took a deep breath, and let it out slowly. He seemed to be giving that some thought. "Give them the requisite two weeks. The police didn't have time to sort through what you gave them yet." His hand lingered on my cheek. "Just be careful."

"I'll call you at lunch."

He nodded, kept his gaze on me before heading out.

It didn't calm or settle me, but I had to at least give my letter of resignation and get my personal things. Will was right. We gave Leonard the information last night.

Last night. It felt like years.

My phone rang.

"Hi, Gary."

"Are you on your way to work?" he asked without greetings. My hands shook. Something was breaking. My head was spinning.

"What's the matter?" I managed to ask.

"Leonard gave me the website information you found. How much did you see?" Gary asked. There was contempt in his voice harsh and angry, but it wasn't directed at me.

"I saw enough. Have you contacted Ethan Grater yet?"

My heart pounded. I didn't like where this was going. Especially after Will's worry.

"No. I wanted to talk to you first. There are several videos with his niece. Did he talk to you about Mara?"

Thinking back to my early conversations with Ethan, two weeks ago hit me. Those two weeks felt like two years.

"When I first started, he caught me looking into Jon Jaime Ray's murder on Penelope's behalf," I started. My thoughts were jumbled in my head, and I thought back to that first conversation. "Initially, Ethan told me he had worked with Jon Jaime Ray before. He implied it wasn't a good relationship. He didn't mention Mara at first."

"When did you find out Mara was involved?"

"I dug around. I work with an admin who was friends with Mara. Emily knew Mara through volleyball." I shuddered at the thought of what Emily had told me, of how close she came to possibly becoming another victim.

"How well did Emily know Mara?"

"Not well." My voice squeaked. "Emily told me that Ethan was always at games and practice. I've seen pictures."

"Nikki, we're investigating right now, and won't be going after him yet. But you work there. Please be careful."

"You're the second person to say that to me today. Should I not go in this morning?" Anxiety was starting to grip me, and I was dizzy.

"Go in. Don't let him think something is off or wrong. Like I said, Penelope is still in jail. She'll be released later today. And we won't be going after Ethan yet. But we're close."

Even knowing that, I still couldn't stop shaking.

"Are you finding all the connections?" I asked.

"We're finding them. Your list helped us link the initials to all of the suspects. Who they belong to, all of the models, the business associates."

"Jon Jaime Ray and Ethan Grater were business partners," I said nervously. I was thinking I should quit on the spot, but Gary was right, I couldn't tip Ethan off to anything out of the ordinary.

"We found that on our own before I got your notes."

That didn't surprise me. But now I was fishing for information.

"And you saw Ethan's bankruptcy, and Ethan's lawsuit against Jon Jaime Ray?"

"Yes. You found much more than we did because you widened your investigation for Penelope's sake. The evidence is a messy web of information. Thank you for sticking with it."

"And what does Andy have to say about this?"

"Nikki." Gary sighed. "He liked you very much and in his warped mind you showed him up. He's not the right man for you, which was painfully obvious, but he's not handling this well at all. He feels like you did it again. I say I'm glad you're concerned and smart and capable, and I feel awful that I let Andy lead us in this direction for so long."

I let out stale air. "Thanks, Gary. I never meant to piss him off. I feel like he's got it out for me and not seeing things clearly."

"You're welcome. I think Andy will be taking a leave of absence. He needs it. And I think you need to watch your back. Call if you have any issues."

My hands shook as I fumbled with my phone, ending my call with Gary. If he thought this phone call would ease my anxiety, he was wrong. I was a mess, but if I didn't go in, I could tip Ethan to the fact something was coming. But now the police knew Penelope was innocent. The rest of the case was disturbing and after spending time in Jon Jaime Ray's world, I always felt the need to shower. I was ready to move on with my PI studies.

Not wanting to tip my hand, I shoved my research under my bed. I slung my lightened bag over my shoulder and left for the office knowing this would be my last day.

***

When I arrived, I was alone in the parking lot. With two warnings to be careful, all before eight, I remained in my car, the doors locked, the music on low.

My stomach roiled, and each time a car drove past the parking lot, I breathed a little easier. I couldn't live like this. It went so bad so very fast.

And I couldn't sit in my car any longer.

I looked around, I was still alone and left my car. Running for the front door with my keys in hand, I opened the door, locked it behind me and grabbed the letter.

The office was dark, and I switched on each light as I passed the switch, finally entering the partners' office and dropped the letter on Samuel's side of the desk.

I stared at that letter for several minutes as I debated whether or not this was the right thing to do. Would that tip the partners off to the fact that things were changing? I reached for the letter, but I heard a car drive through the parking lot and left without taking it with me.

I rushed to log into my computer, and make it seem like everything was fine.

Footsteps climbed the wooden stairs to the front door and the door opened, the bell jingling alerting me to the fact I wasn't alone.

I pulled up my email, not expecting anything new, and I was right. Nothing new since yesterday. They were retiring, and they were dumping clients. There wouldn't be much work left, long before their two-year timeline.

The footsteps stopped, and I glanced up. Ethan was glaring at me.

I felt a fear that I had never felt before. My heart pounded, and my knee shook uncontrollably.

"Ethan. I wasn't expecting you so soon. Are you feeling better?"

He didn't say anything as he glanced at my desk, searching for something maybe.

"Is there anything you need right away?" I tried to remain calm; my voice betrayed me. I grabbed my notepad, and a pen and stood.

"Are you okay, Nikki? I suspect your extra work to help your friend is clearly not benefiting your job here." His voice was cool, unemotional.

"Oh. I'm fine. I'm not working on that anymore. There wasn't much I could do, and the police have it well at hand."

"Do they have any more suspects?"

I shook my head. "Not that I'm aware. They don't keep me apprised of their investigation." I leaned against my desk to steady myself.

"You seem distracted. We can't have that."

"I'm not distracted. I didn't sleep well. My friend was arrested. But I know she's innocent. I'm sure the police will figure it out soon."

"I hope for your friend's sake, if she's really innocent, the police will make it right. But I'm sure the police know what they're doing." Ethan smiled, and I held onto the desk top as my knees buckled. I glanced at the clock on my computer. Carey would be here soon.

"Who do you suppose killed Jon Jaime Ray?" Ethan asked as he stepped inside my office.

"I don't know. I never found any definitive answers. It does appear Jon Jaime Ray was blackmailing multiple people."

I watched Ethan carefully. He flinched slightly by that revelation. "Do you know who he was blackmailing? That I'm sure would be helpful to the police."

"The list is coded."

Ethan seemed to relax, smile almost.

"I'm sure the police have experts who can work through all of that," Ethan said.

My mind raced as I realized telling him that was wrong. If I had dug my own hole, should I confront him? Should I tell him about the videos I had found? Or should I just run? The only exit out of my office was behind Ethan. Even with his age, I didn't think I could run past him.

"Nikki. You seem conflicted. Is there something I can help you with?" he sneered.

"No. No. I'm fine. If you have work for me, that's all I need."

He nodded. "Hang tight. I have something for you."

I sat down and breathed a sigh of relief when he left. He stormed back moments later, holding my letter.

"What's the meaning of this?" Ethan ran into my office, waving the letter at me.

"I…" I hadn't expected this reaction.

His face was red. I thought he might explode.

"We gave you this job. You can't quit without notice. We can ruin you."

"I don't think there's enough here for me. You can handle the load without me. The first two letters were sent out. There not much left. You'll be fine."

He leaned over the desk, his face level with mine. He was feeling the heat, his face was red and sweat poured from his forehead. "You know. You know!" he screamed. He began pacing the small office which wasn't easy with two chairs and the desk.

"I don't know anything. Really, I don't."

He came around my desk, yanked me up from the chair. "How do you know?" he growled.

"Know what?"

"Mara was my everything," he said in an angry whisper. "You shouldn't have found what Jon Jaime Ray had done."

"I didn't find out anything that wasn't already online. And you worked with him. You did more than work with him. Didn't you?"

Ethan, still holding my shoulders began to tremble. "You don't understand. I loved her."

"You used your niece. You acted as her pimp to recruit models. He recorded it all. He was blackmailing you."

He pushed me down into the chair, and it slid backward.

"Why did you even tell me you knew about Jon Jaime Ray? Were you trying to get ahead of the eventuality that I'd find out about you and him? Deflect the attention away from yourself?"

"It was perfect. Your friend being accused. *Was perfect.* I hoped they'd have enough. I didn't figure you were smart enough to figure out the rest."

He backed away. I waited to see if he would make a move, leave me alone in my office so I could go home. When he left me enough room to leave, I grabbed my bag and walked away.

CHAPTER 20

Fuzzy images called out to me from the abyss. I couldn't make out the shapes or sounds, it was all jumbled inside. I was just beyond the threshold of those images and the nothingness and wherever I was.

Damp, stale air filled my lungs as my body slowly came awake.

My fingers scratched the ground I found myself on. It was chilled, damp, musty, and covered in silky dirt.

As my body woke, pain ran through my head, and down the right side of my body. It pulled me from my haze. My eyes opened to darkness.

Where am I?

The kids!

Panic engulfed me. I rolled over, my eyes darted across

the darkness until I found that sliver of light. It seemed miles away from where I was.

Fully awake with pains where I didn't know pain could be, my head began to clear. And like hitting a brick wall, I felt it.

Where am I?

I sat up. "Ow. Shit!" I bent from the waist after hitting a low ceiling.

Where am I?

I turned toward the sliver of light.

My phone.

I patted my pockets, it was gone.

What happened?

I tried to draw the memories of where I had been. How I had gotten here. The last thing I remembered…

No, it couldn't have been.

Memories raced back to me. I remembered the office. With Ethan.

Ethan!

He had guessed I knew everything.

Terror raced through me. My only thoughts were escaping for my kids.

On hands and knees, I crawled toward the sliver of light. It was just enough to know there was a way out.

Gary and Will had both thought I had time, and I thought they were right. But Ethan, he knew. I should have kept my mouth shut. I shouldn't have said anything. But he knew and he goaded me.

This was all my fault.

I cried. Tears ran down my dusty face, and dropped to the floor of what felt like a large crawl space under a house.

With each step forward, my hands scratched against the cement floor, my knees bruised from bumping against the ground. It took all I could to keep moving forward as my head spun from being hit by something.

Minutes, or it could have been hours since I was in this prison.

How did Ethan get me here? And I felt it. My back and arms felt scratched and sore. I still couldn't figure out how he got me in here and across the space.

It didn't matter. I needed to get out of here.

I finally reached the small door. It was thin, and flimsy as I pushed against it. The door wouldn't budge.

"No. No. No." I pounded on the door.

I rested my head on the flimsy wood and took a breath. I need to get out of here! I couldn't wallow in this predicament.

I sat in the silty dirt. My butt burned from being dragged across cement, and my arms ached. I felt at the door, found the edges, bits of wood, a nail, and what felt like a lock.

Shit!

I pushed against the wood. It bent but didn't break as I put pressure on the door.

Maybe...

I rolled to my back, feeling the hard floor against the bruises and cuts. Trying to stop the flow of tears, I focused on my escape. I pulled my legs to my chest and breathed through the pain of movement. When I was ready, I held my breath and pushed against the wood door. The feeble wood cracked but the lock held the door in place. I pulled my legs back again and kicked. And kicked again. Each fruitless attempt frustrated me, and I let the tears flow.

I thought of Will. I had broken my promise to him. I hadn't been careful. My kids. My kids. I needed to get back to them.

I kicked again, and again, and again, and I didn't stop until the wood gave way.

"Ugh!" I shouted with one last kick until my shoe had broken completely through the door.

I yanked it from the hole in the door and rolled to my stomach, sucking in air as the pain in my head exploded.

Just a little longer.

I look through the opening at the dark basement I didn't recognize and pulled at the wood, ignoring the splinters in my fingers and palms as I created a hole large enough for me to squeeze through.

I needed to get out.

I climbed through the hole and dropped myself to the ground.

With few windows, the basement was nearly dark. I wondered how long I had been here. It didn't matter, I needed to get out alive.

I crouched low, and held out my hands searching for furniture and other items in my way. I found a sofa, chair, a low table. Even as my eyes adjusted to the low light, I stumbled, my arms flailing as I fell over what felt like an ottoman. On the floor, pain flew from my toe to my hip. I pushed myself back up. Shapes of objects, boxes, and more furniture became clearer. I scanned my location. When I found my path, I saw the stairs a short distance from me and ran for them.

"Where are you going?" Ethan sneered. "You'll never get out."

I turned. He was illuminated by light coming from a small room. I could see the knife gleaming in his hand.

I ran up the stairs. But Ethan, for an older man was quite nimble, and he lunged for my legs, tripping me and pulling me down.

"Get off of me!" I kicked at him.

He squeezed my ankle as he pulled. "It'll be over soon, Nikki. Don't fight it."

"Let go!" I yanked on my foot. His grip was tight, and I felt trapped.

"You can't go to the police. You can't tell them of my involvement," he said, so calmly I was frightened by him.

"You killed Jon Jaime Ray. Why?"

I stopped pulling on my leg. Absently, Ethan eased his hold as he considered his answer.

"I didn't kill him! He wasn't worth it." His voice was frenzied, quick and high pitched.

"He was blackmailing you," I said as calmly as I could. The more I spoke, the lighter the grip Ethan had on me.

Keep him talking, I told myself.

"Yes, he was. I had so much on him and yet, I had more to lose." He was barely holding on to my ankle. "I had a plan," Ethan continued.

Keep him talking.

"Killing him wasn't the plan. I wanted him to suffer as I suffered." As if he remembered what he was doing there, he grabbed my leg, squeezing tightly.

I was losing him.

"He was blackmailing you. Why?"

"I don't know. I did nothing wrong. I loved her."

"She was your niece, and you used her. It was abuse. He knew it. He recorded you," I said.

When I kept his focus on me, he let off the pressure. I felt the grip on my foot lessen again.

"He knew I loved her; he wanted her out of the way. It was getting in the way of business, so he killed her," Ethan snarled.

"Jon Jaime Ray killed Mara?" I asked. If the victim's families were correct, Jon Jaime Ray killed at least two.

"He was horrible. A horrible man." Ethan began to cry, and I pulled myself forward. Ethan grabbed at my leg. I bounced on the stair as he dragged me down. His nails dug into my skin as he yanked.

"Ethan, the police already figured it out. Killing me will only make things worse for you. Confess, and they'll make it easier."

"NO!" he screamed and let go of my leg.

In a quick motion, I crawled up until I could run to the basement door.

"No!" Ethan screamed.

I reached the door. It was stuck or locked. I pulled on the handle and pushed on the door. Ethan grabbed me, wrapped his arms tightly around me, squeezing. I couldn't breathe.

Stay awake. Think.

I turned my head, could feel his triceps against my lips. I bit down hard on his hand.

"Damn it!" he shouted.

I turned and pushed at him.

Even in the darkness, I could see everything. It was like slow motion as he fell backward. He flailed his arms, as he lost his balance on the step. I watched in horror as he slid down the stairs and his head smacked against the cement floor. It bounced up and back down. I heard his skull crack, and my stomach churned.

I rushed down to him, felt for a pulse. It was so weak. "Oh no. Ethan, hang on."

I raced upstairs. In my horror, I forgot, the door was locked. I pounded on the door in frustration. "Think, Nikki. Think!"

I looked down the stairs, Ethan's motionless body lay in lump.

"He locked us down here. There has to be a key."

I raced back to Ethan, searching his pockets. Finding a key, I pulled it out. I touched Ethan's neck. His pulse was barely there.

My legs shook as I held the railing making my way up the stairs.

I fumbled with key in the lock.

"Focus. Focus!" Finally getting the key in the lock I turned, pushed on the door. I had no idea where I was when I made it to the darkened kitchen.

Turning on the light switch, I searched for a phone, and for any piece of mail that would tell me where I was.

When I found my location, I picked up the receiver and dialed 911.

***

The thin blanket from the EMT was doing little to keep me warm. I held it close around me, but I could stop the violent shaking, as the police began to cross the house in their search for evidence. By their movements and the number of bags they left the house with, it appeared there was much evidence to find.

I watched in horror as the medical examiner wheeled Ethan's lifeless body from the basement, across the living room where I sat next to Gary.

Andy walked into the house, stared at me, his face softer than the last time I saw him. I looked away.

"You don't remember leaving the law office?" Gary asked. I turned back to him. "No, I don't. I came in early. Ethan cornered me. And then he backed away. I saw it as my chance, and I grabbed my bag. That's the last thing I remember."

"And you woke up here?"

I nodded. "Don't ask me the time. I don't know how much time passed from the time I was at the office to the time I broke out of the basement. I called as soon as I got to a phone."

"It's three o'clock. Carey began to worry as soon as she arrived since your car was in the lot and your bag was on the floor. You were nowhere to be found. Samuel knew something was wrong. We went to Ethan's house first but obviously, you weren't there. We didn't know about this place," Gary said.

"Where are we?"

"This is a real estate deal Ethan had. It was hard to find," Gary said. He watched as the police continued to bring items from the house.

My head was finally clear enough and my only thought was Will and the kids.

"Do you have a phone?"

As I asked, Will rushed through the door. I began to cry, relieved that I was out of the basement, relieved Will was here. Grateful that the right murderer was discovered.

"Nikki," Will said as he wrapped his arms around me and kissed my cheek. "They called me at ten to tell me you were missing. We looked everywhere. I'm so glad…" He stopped talking. I looked at him, there were tears in his eyes too.

I held onto Will and could see Andy look at us and turn away. Coming through the door was Samuel Ross. Relief washed over his face.

"Nikki. I'm so glad you're okay. We were so worried. Carey cried when the police found you."

I pulled away from Will. Samuel sat beside me. "I suspected Ethan was into something. But I had no idea about any of this. About Mara and the website." Samuel visibly shuddered.

"And Nikki. We were so worried. Your car was there. You weren't." He held my hand. "I'm so sorry. I've decided to close the office now. You can stay or you can go." He pulled out my resignation letter. "Let me know by the end of the week what you wish to do."

I nodded and offered a weak smile. I simply didn't have it in me to think about anything.

"Such a coincidence. You started at the office at the same time as your friend needing help and Ethan." He shook his head and stood. "I need to deal with Ethan. I'm very sorry, Nikki."

I watched Samuel exit the house hunched over and saddened by the events.

"Ethan said he didn't kill Jon Jaime Ray," I said softly.

Gary turned back to me. "There's evidence."

"That was the last thing he said. I'm just relaying what he told me." I wasn't in the mood to go into any more details. "When can I go?" I asked. I suddenly realized how parched my throat was, and I coughed.

"The police aren't holding you for questioning, but the EMTs are concerned," Gary said.

"Nikki. You were hit hard. The EMTs will be taking you to the hospital for observation," Will said.

"Mrs. Page, we're ready to take you to the hospital," a nice young, female EMT said to me.

I nodded.

Will helped me stand. I gave Gary a hug, and I let the EMT load me into the ambulance.

CHAPTER 21

"Mom!" Emily screeched as the kids ran into my hospital room and to my bed. Though they stopped short when they saw the tubes hooked from me to the monitors that beeped and flashed.

Except for the concussion and the pain, I was fine. Ethan had hit me pretty hard on the head. For now, the hospital wanted to monitor me, and I was okay with that.

"We're so glad you're okay." Jacob choked up. Wiped his cheek. "Will told us what was happening. We called you, and we helped search."

I nodded, but the motion made me dizzy. I lay back against the bed.

Jack stepped inside the room. Relief on his face. "Nikki," he said.

"Hi, Jack."

"I'm so relieved. The kids were worried. I was worried."

"Where will you be staying tonight?" I asked the kids, knowing they couldn't go with Jack. They didn't look at him; they looked at Will.

"I can stay with the kids. They'll be happier at home," Jack said.

"No. Dad, it's fine. Will lives there. And Emily's nineteen. I think we'll be fine," Jacob said.

I watched Jack as Jacob said that. His jaw clenched. I wasn't sure if that was jealousy or the realization of what he had lost and how much work he still had to do. I wasn't going to worry about that now.

"That makes sense," Jack said.

"I'll come home in a few hours. I want to make sure your mom's good," Will said. "They'll be fine, Jack."

Jack nodded. "Nikki, call me anytime if you need anything. Thanks for taking care of things, Will."

I watched him leave, his shoulders hunched, slightly dejected. I'd keep saying it. What transpired was his doing. If the kids rather have Will with them, Jack would have to work through it and make the necessary changes in his relationship with them. It was better, still not great. Thinking of it made my head hurt more.

Julia climbed on the bed beside me. I wrapped my arms around her, and she rested her head on my shoulders. "We were so scared, Mom."

She shuddered and cried softly.

"I'm so sorry. I was trying to heed everyone's warnings and be careful. To stay out of danger. But Ethan, he… I thought I had time to get out of there. Before he knew the police were looking at him."

I kissed Julia's soft hair.

"We're just so glad they found you. You just have a way of getting into trouble. You need to work on that," Emily said and sniffled.

I chuckled, and it hurt a bit. "All I could do was think about you. I just wanted to be with all of you." I reached for my phone that Will had brought with him. I glanced at the time. "Okay. It's seven. I think you go home; get some rest, and I'll be home tomorrow. We'll all rest and watch movies or something. But go. You don't need to stay. I only want to sleep."

"We want to stay," Emily said.

"We'll go. Let's go and take care of everything so Mom can come home tomorrow to a clean house." Jacob raised his eyebrows. I wondered what they had gotten up to while I was gone.

Each of them hugged me and kissed my cheek. Julia took her time to climb off the bed. She didn't want to go. I watched them leave, saddened that I sent them away, but I really needed sleep. It had been the longest of weeks.

After the kids were gone, Will climbed on the bed, and wrapped his arms around me.

"I'm sorry I got us into this," I said.

"You wanted to help, and you saw there was something there. You chased it to the end. That's who you are."

"I'm so out of sorts. I'm not myself." I lay on the bed and closed my eyes. "Everything seems so good in my life except for the work. And it's completely upended me."

"I love you. Our lives are good. The kids and I get along. I don't want to be anywhere else than with you." He kissed me again. I turned toward him, not wanting this moment to end.

"I'll be back tomorrow morning. I wanna get back to the house. See if the kids need anything. They were upset." He had a pained look on his face, and couldn't look me in the eyes. "Maybe I shouldn't have told them you were missing."

His voice trembled and I assumed he was feeling some guilt for telling the kids what was going on. Or maybe I was reading too much into his expression.

"They're old enough to know. They needed to know there was a problem. Thank you for being there for them."

"I'm quite fond of them."

I kissed him. "I'm quite fond of you."

"I love you, Nikki."

Past ten that night, I was unable to sleep even though I was exhausted. The kids texted for a while, keeping me apprised of what they were doing that evening. I think it made them feel less anxious, though it made me feel so guilty for putting myself into this position.

Even at night, the hospital had unmistakable sounds that surrounded sick people; beeping machines, squeaking footsteps across the floors, the murmur of voices discussing patients. Remembering Ethan as he fell down the stairs replayed in my head, over and over as I tossed and turned on the hard hospital bed.

Not able to settle, I texted Myles Landry. I had liked the man and even though I knew he had been blackmailed by Jon Jaime Ray; I didn't let that stop me from contacting him. I wanted to let him know I wouldn't be working on his case any longer, and I wished him luck.

My phone rang.

"Hi, Myles. You didn't have to call back. I wanted to let you know what was going on."

"It's late, Nikki. I figured it was something serious for you to text me after ten. Tell me, what happened?"

My stomach roiled but it could have been the concussion. "I had a run in with Ethan. He tried to kill me."

There was silence on the other end.

"I killed him trying to get away from him."

The tears came, but I didn't want to cry again. It was draining, but I couldn't stop it. I let them fall.

"He killed Jon Jaime Ray, didn't he?"

"That's the plot line for the moment, though, before he died, he claimed he didn't kill him. Jon Jaime Ray was blackmailing him. He was blackmailing you too."

"He was. He was horrendous. I was working on a way to get him to stop. Almost had it, and now he's dead," Myles said without much emotion in his voice.

"Yes. Ethan and Jon Jaime Ray are dead." I didn't know what else to say.

"Will Samuel close the office?"

"That's what he said. I think he's ready to leave it behind. And after finding about Ethan, he doesn't have it in him to keep at it."

"I'll be sad to see you go. You sure you can't stay until the end?" Myles asked.

"Honestly, Samuel asked. I'm not sure if I should. The job had me on edge since I started. I don't seem to have the same ease and confidence you do when I'm in difficult situations. I don't know how you do it."

He laughed. "I have wonderful friends, family, and a supportive partner. I'm happy and comfortable in my skin. I did sense you weren't happy at the job. And so soon after you started."

It was my turn to laugh. "You're observant. I've been having trouble finding the right job, and I took the first job that was offered. I have kids that need feeding, homing, and the other life things."

"Kids do need to eat."

We were silent for a moment when he said, "What do you want from your career?"

"I want to be settled in my job. Comfortable in it. Have work to do so I'm not bored. I'm going to study for the Private Investigator license, so I can add it to my repertoire."

"That sounds like an excellent idea. Follow your dreams, never let them go. You have older children, yes?"

"I do."

"Well then. It's a good time to live your life for you now. Do what makes you happy. Remember you have all the control."

"Thanks, Myles. I will definitely consider that." After we said goodbye, and I hung up, I felt a little surer about my situation than I had in months. He was right, I still had the control, something I kept forgetting.

***

Ethan's dead body lay on the slab in the morgue. I spent the night thinking of what I had done to him. Seeing him didn't erase my guilt, but at least I knew he couldn't come at me again.

"I'm sorry."

I turned.

Andy was there, his face pained. "I was awful to you. I took my anger out on your friend. I didn't do my job," he said.

"Apology accepted." I didn't want to get into an argument with him. I was already upset and still reeling from what I had done. Andy didn't seem any better than I did; he appeared anxious as he joined me at the window looking at Ethan's body on the table.

"I'm still very sorry." His voice was soft, scratchy. His hair was messy, his shirt untucked, his tie missing. It looked like he had a rough night.

"Listen. You weren't great, but you investigated. You were just stuck on the one person. Have you ever killed someone?" I asked.

"You did what you had to do to escape him," Andy said. He reached out to me and put his hand on my shoulder. I didn't flinch, and let him offer me support and kindness.

"It still feels unreal and crappy," I admitted.

"Most police officers never unload a gun on suspects or have ever taken a life. I was trained for it, and it didn't feel great when it happened to me. I can't imagine being a civilian…" his voice trailed off as he dropped his hand beside him.

After several uncomfortable minutes, I looked at Andy. He'd aged in several days. "Are you okay?"

"No. I've been suspended."

"I'm sorry if I put you in a bad position," I said though I knew I had nothing directly to do with the position he was in. I was surprised by the suspension though. I thought it was supposed to be a leave of absence. Less punishment, same result.

"It was me. All me. I was jealous of you and your ability to solve the cases I was stuck on. I was an ass to you because you're really smart and really good at what you do. I couldn't just be happy with us."

I faced him as morgue technician covered Ethan with a sheet.

"Is it because I'm a woman, your date, or both?" I asked. I tried to keep it lighthearted, but it was accusatory.

"Both. I guess I'm misogynistic, and I didn't realize how much so. Hurting you was an eye opener. The suspension is fitting."

"You're a good detective. Don't forget that."

Andy grimaced. "Thanks. I'm not so sure that's true anymore."

I reached out to him and wrapped him in a hug. "As long as you learn something at the end of the day." I pulled away. "What will you do now?"

Andy sighed. "I'm required to complete therapy. When I'm off suspension, I'll be on desk duty. I should have my badge back in six months if I don't slip up in that time."

"I'm sure you'll handle it fine." This time when I smiled, he smiled back.

"And you. Are you happy?" he asked.

It was all about perspective. "I am. I might frustrate Will at times, when I get it in my head to help someone. But he trusts me, and he loves me. He's my partner, and he's happy for my success."

"I'm happy for your success too. You deserve it. I just wish I felt that way before all this happened. I regret not seeing that."

I looked away, back into the morgue as the staff wheeled Ethan back to one of the freezers.

"I apologized to Penelope. She's still angry. I understand that."

"As long as you're taking care to fix things."

He leaned against the window as the staff closed the drapes. "There's something else I need to tell you."

"That doesn't sound good." Suddenly I felt flushed and held onto the wall for support.

"The evidence is back. The hair sample, the DNA found on Jon Jaime Ray's body. It's not a match to Ethan."

I felt my knees buckle. My head swam with the news.

"He didn't do it." Ethan told me as much. I thought he might have been lying to save face.

Andy walked me to the chairs in the waiting area. I sat. My breath quickened. "Who killed him?"

"There're no matches in the system. We don't know. If you had to guess, who do you think killed him?"

"I never found anyone that felt definite. All I can say is look at the list. I only talked to a few people. When I talked to Allan Mason early on, he was angry, wouldn't tell me where he was the night of the murder. He claimed he didn't do it. But the fact that Allan has come forward now; to claim he saw Penelope with Jon Jaime Ray the night he died, seems odd at best and very suspicious."

"You think he was lying."

"I do. Why was he there? It's too convenient. Leonard was supposed to get the security recordings from the restaurant and from JJR Productions office. I don't know if that panned out."

Andy pulled out his notebook and scratched away some notes. "We pulled the warrant for that this morning." He looked at me. "Motive?"

"He claims Jon Jaime Ray killed his sister. She didn't die by suicide. The family could be angry enough."

"Anything else I should know?"

"Look at the list. I'd start with the women who lost their

lawsuits against Jon Jaime Ray and work on the people he blackmailed. They had the most to gain by killing him."

He made his notes and stopped. He looked at me. "You're amazing. I really screwed up."

I tried to smile. "Thank you for saying so."

He hugged me again. The awkwardness seemed to have disappeared between us. "I can't say I'm sorry enough, Nikki. Believe me when I say good luck with the next career change. I really do wish you the best."

I watched him walk away and felt a shift in my life, as if I went from standing still to moving forward and I was ready to explore the possibilities.

***

I was on the couch wrapped in a blanket. The kids brought me drinks, chips, and cookies all day. I was stuffed and feeling slightly overindulged. It was nice.

"Hi, Nikki," Penelope said as she entered the den.

"Penelope, hi." She was carrying flowers and handed them to me.

"I wanted to thank you for your help. If it wasn't for you, I'd still be in jail. I wanted you to know I'm very grateful for the help."

"You're welcome. Can you sit and stay?"

Penelope sat beside me. "How are you feeling?"

"Tired and achy, but good, otherwise. And you're welcome. I felt bad at first, thinking if I hadn't butted in originally, none of that would have happened. Thankfully, I could help fix it."

She glanced around the familiar room. Not much changed since she babysat here.

"I always liked working for you. The kids were great, and you always had the best snacks."

She looked at her hands but not at me. I waited for her to say what she wanted to say. "I'm so embarrassed. I believed he'd make me rich and famous. How could I be so stupid?"

I reached out and touched the hand she couldn't stop looking at. "Not stupid. Wishful and he offered what you thought you wanted. He played on your feelings and took what he wanted," I said. *He was predator, pure and simple,* I thought.

"He was awful. Scummy and horrible. I think I learned my lesson." She looked at me and smiled.

"It takes a lot to figure things out. Do you know what you'll do next?"

She nodded. "I'm going back to school. I've always been interested in fashion design and merchandising."

"That's great. I'm so happy for you."

I glanced at my former babysitter. She seemed happy sitting there. Content in her next decision. I hope I'd be that happy when I started my PI classes.

"What about you? What will you do next? It's not like you really have a job anymore," she said cheekily.

"Well, I kinda still do. But I'll be taking classes so I can sit for the private investigator's exam. And then after that, we'll see."

She hugged me. "I should go. I have a dinner with family tonight to celebrate. Thank you again, Nikki."

***

After Penelope left, my mother, Jack, and Suzie visited. While I felt good seeing most of them, it ended up being less relaxing. I enjoyed my time with Will on the sofa, watching tv, wrapped in his arms. For the time being, the kids were perfectly happy to sit beside us watching movies. We were all confused when the doorbell rang.

"I'll get it," I said and stood before anyone else. "It'll probably be for me anyway."

I opened the door, surprised Samuel stood on the stoop. He had been crying. I motioned for him to come in.

"What happened?" I asked as I led him to the dining room table.

"I didn't know what he was into. They, the police. They brought me in for questioning. I watched the videos. I didn't know."

"He hid it from everyone."

"I'm ashamed I didn't know."

I touched his shaky hands. "He fooled everyone. It's your job to accept that there was nothing you could have done. He hid that part of his life on purpose," I said to him.

Samuel hung his head. "I should have known. I could have done something."

"No. You couldn't have. He made his choices, and now he's gone. And Jon Jaime Ray is gone. They can't hurt anyone else ever again."

Samuel nodded. He pulled out my resignation letter and slid it to me. "Please stay. Help me clean up the office. I need it cleaned out. Records stored. I'll pay you more."

He seemed so sad. Disheartened. I hadn't made the decision until this moment. "I'll stay. We'll work on it."

"Thank you. Thank you. I've taken up too much time."

I walked him to the door and gave him a hug. "You will get through this, and you will find a way to move on."

"Thank you. Rest for now, and I'll see you on Wednesday."

"Thanks."

I watched him walk to his car and get inside, a broken man. When he pulled away, I returned to the den. The kids were still sitting, looking on expectantly.

"Everything okay?" Will asked.

"I'm going to stay on and help Samuel close the office. And then who knows."

I sat beside Will and curled against him. He put his arm around me.

"When do you start the classes?" Jacob asked.

"The PI classes start tomorrow. I'm looking forward to it."

"Can I add one more thing to your already overpacked schedule?" he asked.

I glanced at him. Intrigued. "That depends on what it is."

Will pulled out a velvet box from his shirt pocket, opened the lid. "Marry me?" he asked.

I glanced at the ring, and then to Will, and I turned to the kids when I heard snickering. They were smiling widely. I think I had been left out of the joke.

"Yes. A big resounding yes."

I kissed Will, and in that moment, I knew everything would change for the better. Oh, what a year it had turned out to be.

CHAPTER 22

After resting for two days, and the constant care of the kids, but mostly Will, going back to work didn't seem like a bad option. I wasn't sure what to expect when I got there, but I wasn't surprised by the somber mood when I entered the office. Carey was already there, a pile of folders on her desk, and yet she was engrossed in sending a text. I was surprised.

She looked up when I entered.

"Hi, Carey."

"Nikki. What a few weeks." She held a folder like the many strewn across her desk.

"It has been." I looked down at the table. "I feel like I should apologize for what happened."

"You mean if you hadn't looked into the case or even came here to work, none of this would have happened?"

It was exactly what I was thinking, though I couldn't help but wonder if this would have come out even if I hadn't become involved.

"Nikki. Ethan was being blackmailed. It was only a matter of time before it caught up to him," Carey said. "He built a house of cards. You were the final card, and it all came crashing down around him and everyone else. It's not your fault."

Carey looked at the folder she held and tossed it on one of the many piles. Picking up a second. I thought she was dismissing me, possibly angry for what went down.

"I am sorry. I'm sorry you lost a job, and your world is crashing down."

She tossed another folder on a pile. She smiled when she looked at me. "Nikki. It's not all that bad. I'll find something else."

She tossed the rest of the folders on the pile. "I can't help thinking of Mara. Of what she had done. How Ethan used her. It's gross."

I nodded. There wasn't anything I could add to that summation.

Carey leaned against her desk; her arms wrapped around herself. "I don't think Mara killed herself."

I studied Carey. She was the second family member or friend of someone who committed suicide, who didn't believe they killed themselves.

"I've heard that before. I suspect you're correct."

"How do we find that out?" Carey asked earnestly.

"I can request her death file. Review it for anything odd."

"You can do that?"

"I can. Since you're not the only one suspicious of the death, a pattern begins. I'm investigating on behalf of a friend's lawyer and that gives me some access. I think it's possible Jon Jaime Ray killed some of the models who were fighting back."

Carey visibly shuddered. "If there's anything I can do, please tell me."

I smiled and headed to my office. Stepping inside no longer had the awkward air about it now that I had an official end of business and had clear responsibilities. And no Ethan. I entered my office, turned on the computer and pulled up the email from Samuel detailing my duties for the rest of my time here.

And then I went to work on the emails that needed sent.

Thirty minutes later, I looked up when Samuel knocked on my door.

"Hi, Nikki."

Samuel was tired. His eyes were ringed in darks circles, his hair, which was normally neat and in place was disheveled. Even his clothes were out of the norm for him, though he seemed confident in his jeans and collared shirt.

"Hi, Samuel." I rose and walked to him giving him a hug. "How are you feeling?"

He stepped inside the office and took a seat in the chair. I sat beside him.

"It's been a shock. It's been horrible. The family... the family went from denial to horrified within several hours. They feel... awful for what you experienced."

"I'm sorry for your loss. I know you were close to Ethan."

"Not as close as I thought." He leaned back in the chair. "We're still processing what we've learned. Carey said you could look into Mara's suicide. No one believed she killed herself. She had so much to live for. But the videos..."

I reached out and touched his hand. I didn't have the words.

"I'm sorry. I shouldn't bring this here," he murmured.

"It's okay. It's a lot. Let me see what I can do about Mara's death. We'll keep it quiet unless I learn something."

Samuel nodded. "I'm glad you're here. I saw you sent another email list out this morning. Is there any problem with the second?"

"I'll send it next, unless you have something else for me."

He shook his head. "Go ahead and send the list. When that's done, pull all clients with ongoing cases. The files can be pulled and stored in one drawer. The rest, can be boxed up for storage I've just arranged. Paper records need to be retained for five years before I can have them destroyed."

"I'll use the lists I created and pull the ongoing cases, and move those where Carey suggests. I see the boxes out in the waiting area, and I'll start filling those with transfers."

He sighed. "Thank you. You're a lifesaver." He gently rose and ambled out, and I began to pull the lists.

***

After sending my second email list to the clients, and loading up the first box of client files for the storage unit, I contacted the Lake Zurich police department and requested Mara Grater's death investigation file.

I was expecting to pick it up on my way home from work but in a twist, Andy brought it to the office.

"Surprised to see me?" he asked.

"Kinda, yeah. I thought you were suspended."

"I am except for Jon Jaime Ray. And this." He held up the folder. "I'm making amends for my past behavior. I saw your request, I thought I'd drive it to you."

He looked embarrassed as he handed me the folder. He held his lips together as if trying not to vomit.

As he stood by my desk, Carey and Samuel entered my office and sat in the chairs.

"Mara Grater was ruled a suicide. But after Nikki found the connection to Jon Jaime Ray and with Ethan in the mix, we are taking another look at Mara's case. The family is devastated, but before Nikki requested the file, the family requested that Mara be exhumed and the post mortem be re-done. The request was made on Monday. The exhumation will be tomorrow. Full drug panels, and another look at how she was killed. I'm sorry for the loss of your friend and sorry the police didn't look at her death from a different angle."

"Why wasn't more done before she was buried?" Samuel asked.

Andy's jaw clenched. He swallowed and didn't respond directly to the question. After taking a breath and letting it out, he said, "The suicide note. The scant notes in the file that highlight the days leading to her death. While it appeared, she may have been depressed and was pulling away from friends and family, those who knew her were adamant she didn't kill herself. It could have been looked at more carefully."

As Andy explained police reasoning, I glanced at the items in the file. That's exactly what the notes said.

"With what we know now, we believe we need to re-open the investigation," Andy said.

As I shuffled through the folder, I noticed newly printed phone records from Mara's phone to Jon Jaime Ray and to

Ethan. A lot of phone calls. I began to count. I was already at twenty and not done with the list.

"Were there any voicemails on her phone?" I asked Andy.

"There were, but we took another look. There was a recorded call." He took out his phone and hit play.

"I'm going to the police," a young girl said.

"You can't. Mara. He'll kill me. We just have to get through this and it will be over. Don't call the police," Ethan pleaded.

"You let him drug me. You let him abuse me!"

"Mara. I didn't know he did that. I can get him to stop but you need to give me time."

"You owed him money and pimped me out to him. I hate you! I hate you! I hate you!"

The call ended and Samuel and Carey were left in a stunned silence. I pretty much expected something like that.

"She was going to the police. Ethan killed her," Carey said softly.

"We don't know for sure. Allan Mason claimed Jon Jaime Ray killed his sister. Maybe he also killed Mara as a way to control Ethan," I suggested. Either way, both of the men were dead and wouldn't pay for what they had done.

"We'll pursue the investigation to ensure we know what actually happened to Mara. And for Ericka Mason, we've reopened her death investigation as well. We want to know how she died. The family said she wouldn't have killed herself," Andy said. He pulled another folder from his bag and handed it to me. "Again, Nikki, you've inserted yourself into some cold cases. Not so old this time, but still." He pointed to the folder. "If you see something we haven't seen yet, please let us know. If either ends up as a suicide, at least the family can have closure."

"Are you sure about this?" I asked as I took the folder.

"I'm sure. I'm strictly on Jon Jaime Ray's murder and nothing else. I suggested you for this, and my Lieutenant agreed. There's a contract in there for you to sign and instructions for what to do. You'll officially be working on the case with the police department behind you."

"I don't know what to say. Thank you for suggesting me."

He nodded. "I know you'll figure it out." Andy let himself out.

"What do you think Nikki?" Samuel asked me after hearing Andy close the door behind him.

"I think people looked at these deaths with tunnel vision. It might not lead to anything; it might be just as it was ruled, but it might not. Unless you have something pressing for me, I'll start on these folders this afternoon."

Samuel nodded. "Myles's lawsuit was filed on Monday. We have nothing pressing for now. Let me know if you need something from me," Samuel said. He stood and shuffled to his office. He looked as though he aged by decades in the last five days.

Carey stood. "Thanks for pursuing this. If you didn't, we wouldn't have answers or closure."

I watched her walk away before sitting down and reviewing the cases that had once been determined to be nothing.

***

"They're exhuming her body?" Julia grimaced. "Eww."

"A crime might have been committed. The police want to make sure," I said as I cleared the rest of the plates from the table.

"This is still Penelope's deal?" Jacob asked.

"Indirectly. In the course of the investigation, this came up," Will explained to him.

"Do you know who killed that bad guy?" Julia asked. She was trying to understand the pieces and parts of the investigation. I think she was still confused.

"The police cleared the person they thought killed him. They're still looking," I said as I washed the pot with rice stuck to it. I pulled my hand out, my new engagement ring was still on my finger. It sparkled with water and soap, and I moved to the countertop and took it off, leaving it in a clean bowl. I still couldn't believe we were engaged.

"How do they find the killer?" Julia asked.

301

"The medical examiner will go back to the body and look for any physical evidence that might have been missed since it was ruled a suicide. The police will review the witness testimony and most likely re-interview some people. They think the person who killed the photographer is on a list I had given them a few weeks ago. They'll see if there's anything new to find," I said as I scraped away the rice.

"And how does this relate to Mara?" Emily asked.

There had been so many intersections and theories that led to Mara's death, to Ericka's death. So many bad decisions and illegal behavior. Two young women died because of another person's mistakes and wrong choices.

Will looked at me, I looked at my expectant kids. "Ethan Grater tried to kill me. I think it's because I knew too much. I knew what he had done. But the family doesn't think Mara killed herself. Another family thinks their loved one was murdered as well. Both claimed it was Jon Jaime Ray. That would make the suicides related to the murder investigation."

It didn't clear the confusion.

"But Penelope's free?" Emily asked.

"She's free. Going back to school."

"They still need to find out who killed that photographer," Emily said.

"Yes. That's still priority though Mara will be exhumed tomorrow and the other suicide victim will be exhumed the day after. Like I said, the police think the cases are related."

I finished washing the pot, and let it dry on a towel across the counter. I joined the family at the kitchen table.

"People do bad things for a lot of reasons. This case was weird from the beginning. Hopefully soon, three deaths will be resolved."

They weren't resolved soon enough.

CHAPTER 23

Samuel asked me to join him at the cemetery the day of Mara's exhumation. It was a chilly summer morning as I stood beside him; he held my hand as if it were a lifeline. Mara's father, Michael Grater stood on Samuel's other side. After expressing my condolences, we stood in silence watching the back hoe remove layers of dirt. Beside Mara's grave, a growing mountain of dark brown dirt.

When the hoe hit the casket, Michael Grater went rigid, his jaw tightened, and he worked it back and forth. Two cemetery employees dropped into the grave to remove the remaining dirt around the casket.

"If he wasn't already dead, I'd kill him myself," Michael said under his breath.

Samuel squeezed his hand.

"I'm sorry my brother hurt you," Michael said to me as bands were placed around the casket to lift it from the hole.

"That's not something you should worry about now," I said.

"He wasn't right. We didn't know," Michael said.

I glanced at him. He was focused on the casket he and his wife had so lovingly chose for their dead daughter. It surely wasn't an easy time for the family, and I couldn't imagine planning my child's funeral.

"Ethan hid it. There was nothing you could have done," I said, but the words were hollow. They didn't see what Ethan had been doing to their daughter, and they would have to live with that for the rest of their lives.

When the casket was free from the ground, it swung over to the waiting stretcher and was secured into place. From there, we followed it to the coroner's van. Michael cried as Mara's body was driven away.

"What now?" Michael asked.

"They'll do a thorough examination of Mara's remains, and they'll try to determine if she was drugged and how she died. I'm so sorry, Michael," Samuel said.

"Thank you for your support. I hope they find who killed my girl."

I watched the heartbreaking walk of a father who lost his daughter in the most horrific way. He got into the car, started it and peeled away.

"I'm going to meet him at the house with the rest of the family. You'll go to the morgue?" Samuel asked.

"I'm on my way now." I didn't relish time in the morgue for this, but Samuel had asked.

He walked me to my car and waited for me to leave. He looked almost as heartbroken as Michael Grater had. As I drove to the morgue, I wondered if I'd make it through this new autopsy or would it break me too?

***

I wasn't required to watch the autopsy from inside the room and was grateful. The smell might be too much to bear.

Instead, I stood outside the autopsy room, viewing the proceedings through the large window that separated autopsy from the waiting room.

After gently placing Mara on the table, the medical examiner, Dr. Sharon Emmanuel, began to remove the smart suit Mara had been buried in. One button at a time, until the she rolled Mara on her side to release the jacket. She repeated the motions with the blouse, bra, skirt and underwear until all that was left was Mara's naked body under the harsh lights.

It was a meticulous process as Dr. Emanuel began by parting Mara's long, brown hair. It cascaded around her bare shoulders and even after six months, she only looked like she was asleep.

SHERYL STEINES

After her death, she had been cleaned and made up, any physical clues would have been washed away or so I thought.

Dr. Emanuel began with Mara's hair, gently combing through it, looking for anything that might have been missed. After each pass, she tapped her comb on a white sheet of paper. From where I stood, I couldn't tell what she had found. I'd have to wait like everyone else.

When she finished with Mara's hair, she used a magnifying glass to examine her skin, her face, behind the ears, along her neck, down her shoulders, arms, and hands. Any place on her body that could hide a puncture wound.

Now that the police weren't convinced it was a suicide, I thought.

After examining and shooting pictures of her work, Dr. Emanuel cut a 'Y' shaped incision from her clavicles down to her belly. I grimaced. While I had seen this done before, it didn't get any easier to watch, and yet, I couldn't look away.

"How's it going?" Andy asked as he pulled a chair to my left, and Gary pulled another to my right.

"I thought you weren't supposed to be here?" I asked Andy.

"Special compensation as they think my murder victim may have killed her." He took a seat and watched like I did.

"Well, Dr. Emanuel combed Mara's hair and tapped it on the paper, but I didn't see anything. If she was murdered, I'm guessing poison taken internally."

308

"I'm inclined to agree with you," Gary said. The three of us sat in a row watching intently as Mara's organs were removed and weighed. As Dr. Emanuel stared at the inside of Mara's body, she seemed paralyzed or stunned. She glanced at us with confusion on her face and waved us in to join her.

I followed Andy and Gary into the room, placing Vicks under my nose to mask the smell. Dr. Emanuel took pictures of the esophagus as we settled around the table. "There's an ulcer on the esophagus. She must have ingested something that burned through the tissue," she said.

Dr. Emanuel put the camera down, pulled out a scalpel and began to cut out the ulcerated tissue. She placed it in a plastic container.

"Poison?" Gary asked.

"Possibly. Toxicology won't tell us anything, since she's been dead six months. But I also noticed this." She pulled on Mara's lips; you could see a faint bruising and teeth marks along the inside of her lips.

"If I had to guess, she was forced to ingest something, and a hand was placed against her mouth to keep her from spitting it out."

She moved from the esophagus to the stomach and opened it up. "Whoa," she said.

Andy and Gary leaned in and offered me a space beside them. I shook my head. "You can tell me."

"We assumed she had ingested pills. There was an empty bottle beside her. But she still has several, possibly fifty or so pills in her stomach," Gary said.

"With the bruising on her mouth, you think it's possible she was murdered?" I asked.

"I think it's a strong possibility. I do see some scratches on her fingers. The nails had been trimmed for the funeral. I'll take samples in case something is there."

We watched as she snapped photos of the stomach contents and Mara's fingers. She took samples. "I'll send these out today. Hopefully there's enough to prove murder and who did it."

"Thanks, Dr. Emanuel. Let us know as soon as you know," Andy said.

I was thankful when I followed them out, but I had a feeling in my gut that they wouldn't find much that could be used.

***

The next day was a repeat of the day before, though I hadn't been at the cemetery for Ericka Mason's exhumation. But I was at the medical examiner's office sitting where I had sat the day before, watching Dr. Emanuel complete an autopsy on a woman whose death was also ruled suicide.

Both had worked with Jon Jaime Ray; both ended up dead.

Without saying anything, Andy handed me a folder and sat down beside me. I perused the contents as Dr. Emanuel began her 'Y' incision in Ericka's chest.

I was staring at copies of emails, several Mara Grater to Ericka Mason. Each one, friendly letters, engaging communications between two women who appeared to be friends. After several weeks of writing, Mara asked to meet with Ericka about an amazing business opportunity. One that would make all of her dreams of being a model and actress come true.

"Mara was the recruiter. She went after Emily."

I looked away from the folder as Ericka's heart had been cut out and now being weighed.

"Emily didn't…"

I shook my head. "No. She said it was creepy and didn't pursue it. I can't tell you how grateful and nauseated I am by this."

"I'm sorry, Nikki. For all of this case."

I turned toward Andy. He seemed genuinely upset, or maybe it was because his suspension was about to start.

"No more apologies. Let's find out who killed who and move on with life. Okay?"

He nodded.

Gary joined us, sitting himself on the other side of me. Just like the day before.

I continued to read the emails; there were a lot of them. They started so innocently and became more forceful as Mara worked her way into Ericka's dreams and fantasies, playing on those, ready to pounce and strike when Ericka was most vulnerable. It worked. Ericka agreed to meet and within days, Mara emailed her the modeling contract, plus a model release. The same one Penelope claimed she didn't sign.

"Mara as the recruiter brought all these girls to Jon Jaime Ray. They all took semi-nude photos and, in some cases, videos. I can only assume she was killed based on her desire to leave the position. She didn't want to do this anymore. She was good at what she did, I can see why they wanted her to stay, but why kill her?" I asked as I churned the information over in my head.

It didn't make sense. Did Jon Jaime Ray kill them both because they knew too much or to threaten and scare Ethan?

"I was able to get the outfit Mara was wearing when she died. The family put it in a paper bag and then into a garbage bag. They've been holding on to it for six months hoping an investigation would be open," Gary said.

"It's at the lab now?" I asked.

Gary nodded. "We're not going to get much from these autopsies, but I'm hoping we'll get something from her clothing."

"I don't think Ethan would have killed Mara. He loved her and needed her in his own little creepy way," I said.

"Unless she was going to the police," Andy said.

There was nothing to argue with his point. I thought that could be a reason why Ethan might have killed her. But I did say, "Unless Jon Jaime Ray killed her to teach Ethan a lesson."

Andy didn't argue that point with me. "We're looking at that as well."

It felt odd to be working so closely with Andy on this. He seemed resigned and accepted me as a team member. Maybe he was changing.

"Mara tried to recruit Carey, the receptionist at Grater and Ross. She also felt Jon Jaime Ray was disturbing, and she never went to her interview with him."

"It was a good thing for her," Gary said.

We grew quiet as Dr. Emanuel stared at the same body part that had stumped her on Mara Grater's autopsy. She waved us inside.

"Same thing. Same lesions on the esophagus. Without toxicology, I can't determine if she was poisoned but by the looks of this and her stomach, and the inside of her mouth…" she motioned with her hand how someone had held their hand over her mouth. "I'll say we're looking at similar circumstances in how each young woman died."

"Possible murder," Andy said.

"I would say yes. I found something in her hair and it might be enough, but I don't think we'll ever have a definite if she was murdered. I'll keep working on her body though."

"Thanks, Doc. When you have your report, pass it along to Gary," Andy said.

We left the room together.

"We'll be bringing in Allan Mason for questioning in the next few days if you'd like to watch," Gary said.

"Keep me posted. I'd like to if I can. Make sure he explains how he happened to be at that restaurant at that time. It's odd," I said.

"We think so too," Andy said and he left the basement floor for a cleaner locale.

Gary and I followed walking up the stairs to the lobby.

"You truly are amazing. You brought us what we needed to get on the right path. When do you start the classes?" Gary asked.

"I had the first one two days ago. I'm hoping it all works out."

"I'm sure it will be great," Gary said as he turned toward the detectives' room.

I headed home believing everything would fall into place. I didn't know how wrong that was.

CHAPTER 24

We had heard from several former clients of Samuel and Ethan requesting names of lawyers to take their future business to. I shot off letters to those clients, boxed up their files, and stored them in the waiting area.

I moved on to clients that were no longer alive, or had already moved on to other legal firms. Those would be stored for the requisite five years.

"I'm tired," I said to Carey as we moved the last of the boxes for the day.

Samuel came in, looked at what we had done and said, "Go on home. I think you've done enough for the day."

"I have no complaints with that," Carey said.

I followed suit, shutting down the computer and putting my bag over my shoulder. "I think I just want to sleep," I said.

"The autopsy?" Samuel asked cautiously.

"There're some things that looked odd. But they're not sure the body is going to tell them much. I'm sorry." I touched his hand. He held mine.

"Thank you for sitting through it. If there's anything to find, I'm sure the medical examiner will find it."

He nodded and closed himself in his office. I couldn't imagine what was going through his mind.

"See you tomorrow," Carey said as she sprang from the door and into the glorious late afternoon.

I followed and reached for my phone when it rang. I sat in the car and stared at the building as I answered Gary's call.

"Results so soon?" I asked without saying hi.

"Actually, yes. And I need to know what you know about Allan Mason?"

"I don't know much. Did you find something about Allan?"

"Nikki. He's the right height, and the CSI team found hair on Jon Jaime Ray. A small sample in his hand. It's Allan's coloring and texture. We're waiting for the warrant to get his DNA."

"He was angry that I called him. Even as I explained why I was calling, he accused me of accusing him. He told me to not call again. And then…" I stopped. Gary already knew what had happened next.

"He reported you. Took the attention away from himself and then claimed he saw Penelope and Jon together before the murder."

"He was lying about that," I said.

"I think he was."

"What's next?" I asked.

"Be careful. You've already been kidnapped over this, and now we're closing in on the murderer."

"I will. Thanks for letting me know."

I stayed in my car staring at the office for a moment as I processed the call from Gary. I could see a silhouette moving through the building as Samuel appeared to wander aimlessly. After everything that had happened in the last two weeks, I could understand that restlessness.

As I started my car, Samuel opened the door, and stared in my direction though he seemed to be looking through me.

After a few moments, I backed out of the lot and headed home.

***

Allan Mason, thirty-year old male, college educated as an engineer. Everything I could find on him was he was a decent, hardworking man. As I reviewed his social media, I could tell he clearly loved his family and his sister Ericka. From his posts after she died, he clearly blamed Jon Jaime Ray. I was surprised Jon Jaime Ray hadn't sued him for libel.

I found Ericka Mason's social media. She was beautiful, and I understood how she would fall into modeling as a career. Her personal life appeared full; she had a lot of friends, a successful career, that is, until Jon Jaime Ray came into her life. I continued to scroll through the pictures, and then I saw something odd. A face I recognized.

Where?

I pulled up JJR Productions website and searched the pictures of the models until I found the familiar face. Delinda Love. I had spoken to her, she told me about a conversation she overheard at Jon Jaime Ray's studio while she was high from drugs. She had admitted to knowing some of the models, apparently Ericka Mason was one of them.

Did she know Allan Mason as well?

Back to Allan's social media, and I continued through his pictures, finally finding one with Delinda Love. They definitely knew each other and from what I could tell, they had known each other since *college*. Based on the pictures, they could have possibly dated.

Could they have both planned something together?

I saved the picture and sent it to Gary, explaining the connection between the Delinda and Allan. I didn't know if the connection was anything or if it would even help, but this time, my gut told me there was something there.

He responded immediately.

That's helpful. Thanks. He texted back.

Still unsettled, I pulled up Delinda Love and the police investigation. As with Penelope, there was a signed model release, and evidence that signature was fraudulent. How did the law suit get tossed out?

I found Delinda's photos on page three like the rest of the models, I found her credit scores, her debt. While she was now a fairly successful makeup artist, she was deep in debt, both her and her husband. It all seemed to happen after her photo shoot with Jon Jaime Ray. I went back into the back end of the website, and searched for something related to Delinda Love. I found her initials, clicked on the link and found documents attributed to her.

To get back at the photographer, Delinda Love or as her real name, Linda Johnson, was caught with her hand in the proverbial cookie jar as she stole money from a local charity where she had been volunteering. How Jon Jaime Ray discovered that, I would probably never know. But rather than having her arrested, he used what he knew about her and blackmailed her like a long list of others.

Well, that explained the debt.

I downloaded what I had found, continued to search through the website for anything else on Delinda Love and Linda Johnson. When I found nothing else on her, I sent Gary the documents.

The doorbell rang as I finished my searched. I thought it odd that the kids or Will would ring the doorbell, so I cautiously opened the door.

I was surprised by what I saw.

Will's ex-wife, Janelle Dixon Mann faced me. I hadn't seen her in years, and I was surprised by her appearance. She had lost more weight than she could spare, was rail thin and sickly if I had to describe her. Her red eyes were ringed with purple as if she hadn't slept in weeks. Her hands shook at her side. What struck me most was her face; it was angry, and it radiated off of her.

"Janelle. Hi," I said as I held the doorhandle tightly.

"Are you going to invite me in?" she asked.

I shook my head. "No. What are you doing here?"

"I've come to meet my replacement." She eyed me suspiciously and left me feeling vulnerable and anxious.

"You've already met me. Why are you here?" I asked again.

She smiled as she tried to walk inside. I stopped her. "Janelle, either tell me what you're doing here or leave. I'm not interested in having this discussion."

"Nikki, Nikki. We were friends. But I never believed you and Will. In all those years, you never had sex or dated. Come on, please. I don't believe it. I always thought that was a lie. And now…" She backed up a bit and looked at the house. "I don't understand. Why you? You're mousy, can't hold on to a husband. I've seen Jack's wife. She's hot, you know."

I held my breath as I tried to steady my shaking hands. Of all things, I thought of Myles Landry and his confidence or her confidence depending on the day. I let go of the door handle and walked on to the front stoop.

"Why are you here?"

"He's my husband. You can't have him," she said in all seriousness.

"And you came here to tell me that?"

"I want you to know I'm getting him back. And you'll be that poor pathetic Nikki whose husband traded up," she said in a mocking tone.

I held my left hand toward my neck as if I were scratching it, making sure my beautiful new engagement ring was visible to her. Janelle's eyes popped wide when she noticed it, as she recognized what was on my finger.

"If you think that's enough to hold him, you're mistaken." She turned and walked away.

I held my ground and watched as she stumbled down the brick path to her car. She wasn't drunk; I couldn't smell it on her, but I wondered if I should have pulled her out the car and kept her here. Before I could act on the thought, she turned on her car and backed down the driveway. As she drove away, she passed Will who stopped but started again, pulling up the driveway. I waited for him to get out of his car. He couldn't get to me fast enough.

"Why was Janelle here?" he asked. There was more worry in his voice than curiosity.

"To tell me I'm poor and pathetic, and I will lose you when she gets you back, and I'll always be poor and pathetic. Oh, and Jack traded up."

He reached for my hands, stared at the ring on my finger. "Did she see it?"

"Yes."

"I don't like that she came here."

I stepped into him and kissed him. "I'm fine, but she's officially a problem."

"Maybe. I think I'll file a restraining order against her just in case."

He wrapped his arm around my shoulders and walked me inside.

CHAPTER 25

I sat at my desk, Carey and Samuel sat in the visitor chairs. Gary set up a large monitor to his laptop and clicked a video link.

We watched in anticipation as the recording began to play.

Allan had come forward to say he saw Penelope with Jon Jaime Ray the night he was murdered. We watched the recording from the restaurant. Penelope was there. She wasn't alone.

"Penelope was down the block from his office that night," I said incredulously.

"She was. And you know who she was with," Gary said.

Neither one of us could mistake that face. She was on the website; she was a page three girl, and Delinda Love was clearly having a heated discussion with Penelope.

With rapt attention, we watched the two women arguing in the middle of the nearly empty restaurant. It was clear that Penelope didn't want to be having the discussion, and she mouthed "No!" and ran from the restaurant.

Immediately after, Delinda Love made a phone call and paced before leaving the restaurant.

"We're bringing in Penelope for a discussion about this. We've also pulled Delinda Love's phone records."

"Allan said he saw Penelope with Jon Jaime Ray, and he's clearly not at the restaurant and neither is Allan. I'm guessing you'll find Delinda made a call to Allan."

"Why did he incriminate Penelope?" Carey asked.

"To throw suspicion from himself," Samuel said.

"Ask Penelope why she chose not to be in on the plan to kill Jon Jaime Ray," I said.

Gary clicked out of the recording and pulled up another. "We're pulling phone records now." He glanced at his phone. "The police just took Penelope into custody as a witness and are on their way to the station. I have two more officers pulling in Delinda Love and Allan Mason. I could use your help," Gary said to me.

I glanced at Samuel, he nodded.

"Sure. And what's this next video?"

Gary clicked the video; one I had seen before. "We know this isn't Penelope. We believe it's Allan. The hair sample we found should prove that. But look at this." He let the recording run until Allan was almost out of the picture. He slowed it down.

"He looked up and nodded," I said as Gary sped up the recording and Allan ran away.

"If it is Allan, he killed Jon Jaime Ray because he believed the photographer killed his sister. Delinda was being blackmailed. Now if they tried to recruit Penelope as a third, why? What part did Delinda play? What part would Penelope play?" I asked.

"Let go find out," Gary said.

***

I sat in the observation as Gary entered with an angry Penelope sitting beside her very organized, yet annoyed lawyer.

"This is outrageous. Why is she here?" Leonard asked.

"We need Penelope to clear up something for us and possibly put a murderer or two behind bars."

Penelope was drumming her fingers against the table. When Gary didn't accuse her, and let her know she was only there to help them, the drumming of her fingers stopped.

I breathed a sigh of relief; the sound was getting to me.

"Okay. What do you need to know?" Leonard asked.

Gary slid a still shot of Penelope and Delinda in the restaurant. "The date should be familiar to you. It's the night

Jon Jaime Ray was murdered. Can you tell me who you're with?"

Penelope's eyes widen. "I … I don't…"

"You were having a rather animated conversation with this woman. It's all on the recording. I suggest you tell me what this is about."

Penelope slunk in the chair. "It's Delinda Love. Jon Jaime Ray was blackmailing her after her lawsuit was thrown out by the court. We were discussing options against him. I told her I had a plan. She laughed at me, argued that it wasn't going to work and told me he'd get away with it again. She asked me if I cared about Ericka Mason and all of the others he abused. I told her I trusted my lawyer that we'd get him this time."

Penelope began to cry.

"What did they want you to do?" Gary asked gently.

Penelope wiped her cheeks as she tried to calm herself. "They said we had to stop him. He needed to die. I told her no. I wasn't going to do that. There was a better way. She told me it was all worked out. All I needed to do was go in there and make it seem like there was a burglary. She and I would set the scene after it was done."

"Who is 'they'?" Gary asked.

"Allan Mason, Delinda, her husband Buster, and a few other girls."

Gary pushed a pad of paper and a pencil to Penelope. "Write it out, please. Names and dates."

"They'll know it's me," Penelope whined.

"Do you want to be arrested for obstruction?" Gary asked.

Penelope sighed and began to write out the list. Gary motioned for me to enter. I did as he asked, left the viewing room and entered interrogation.

"Why didn't you tell us immediately?" I asked when I entered.

Penelope's hands shook at the sound of my voice.

"I didn't know if they did it for sure. It wasn't supposed to go down that night, but they knew I had a lawyer send Jon Jaime Ray the request for the model release. They set me up." She was still crying as her head bowed, and her shoulders slumped.

"Allan was supposed to kill him and then what? You and Delinda would go in and make it look like a robbery gone wrong?" I asked. It seemed like a cliché plan concocted by upset young people who hadn't thought the whole thing through.

Leonard whispered something to Penelope, and she sat straighter and continued to write out her story.

A knock sounded on the door, and Gary answered, returning with a folder. He read as he walked and sat down across from Penelope. "What do you know about the gun used to kill Jon Jaime Ray?"

Penelope looked up. "If I agreed to the plan, that wasn't my part. Just to fake the robbery."

Gary showed me the report about the gun shot. Jon Jaime Ray was killed by a .38 special. There had also been a report ran about guns owned by the models and other suspects in this case. Two models owned a gun of that caliber; a Willa Convers and Delinda Love.

"Where do you think it is now?" I whispered.

"That's a good question."

When Penelope finished, she signed it and pushed the pad toward Gary. "That's everything. Am I in trouble?"

"You should have told us when we first questioned you. It could have saved us a lot of time and energy."

Gary nodded to Leonard and the lawyer and his client stood and walked from the interrogation room.

"The search warrants are being issued for Delinda Johnson's and Allan Mason's homes and offices. I'm guessing the gun is already gone, but we'll see what we find. Are you ready to come with me?"

"Where to?"

He smiled and motioned for me to follow him.

***

"Okay. Thanks. That helps a lot," Gary said as we sat outside Allan Mason's home. The police were inside, looking for evidence based on the warrant. Allan was outside, indignant as the search went on.

"You have no right. This is a travesty. I'm calling my lawyer!" Allan yelled as he was kept from re-entering his home.

He dialed his phone and yelled into it as he asked to speak to his lawyer.

Bags and bags of evidence came out of the house, some heavier than others as I assumed in one of the boxes was his computer.

As the box was being carted away, Allan broke free from the officer babysitting him and ran after the computer. "I need that for work. You can't have that." He reached for the box and pulled at it. A different officer tugged Allan away. He pushed and tried to yank his arm from him. When he freed himself, Allan pulled his arm back and punched the officer across the chin. A second officer tackled Allan to the ground.

I watched with some amusement as Allan was handcuffed, yanked to standing position and led away to one of the many police cars.

"He didn't help himself much, did he?" I asked when the car door was slammed with him inside.

"No, he didn't." Gary looked at his phone and answered. "Yeah. I'm watching the proceedings. I haven't gone in yet." He nodded as he listened.

I changed my focus to the search as another few boxes were removed. I glanced at my own phone. I had missed a call from Will. I'd call him back later.

"Okay. We'll go in now. Thanks." Gary turned to me. "We need to go inside."

That didn't sound good.

I followed Gary out of the car, up the sidewalk to the front stoop. The house was a small tri-level, and we walked the stairs to the front door. It was a charming cottage, white with window boxes filled with flowers, a light blue door. We walked inside.

The first floor consisted of a living room, dining room and smallish kitchen. I think it had been tidy before the police got here. Now there were open doors, drawers, cabinets, and closets. Items had been moved and tossed aside.

"This way," Gary said and he led me downstairs to a family room, a powder room and laundry area. Again, Gary turned to the left, and we descended a few stairs to a sub-basement. We entered a small room with a closet and two doors across from each other. The first door led to a mechanical room with a water heater and furnace.

The other room was storage. But as we entered the next room of the basement, we were met with piles of boxes covering the narrow room.

"Over here, Gary," shouted an officer in the corner.

I followed, and we stopped at an open box containing pictures. Inside, Ericka Mason smiled back at us. Hundreds of pictures of her in various stages of undress. Officer Stanley pulled them out and dug to the bottom.

"We found this," he said. Inside, pictures of Jon Jaime Ray. Entering his office, leaving after dark, at the restaurant, talking to models, business partners, Ethan. There were pictures of Ethan at his house, the house he took me to, pictures of me drugged and being driven into the garage.

I started to shake.

"All of these boxes seem to have more of the same. It appears he had been watching Jon Jaime Ray for weeks, if not months."

Gary picked up the picture of me in Ethan's car. I was clearly unconscious. I was still shaking knowing Allan Mason knew where I was and I was in trouble, and he did nothing to help me.

"He knew where I was," I said. My voice was dry, and I could barely speak.

"I'm not sure if he knew you were in trouble. We'll assess that when we talk to him. But if he knew, we can add compounding a crime." Gary put his arm around me and kissed my forehead. "Get these into evidence as soon as you can. I'm going to the station."

Gary gently led me from the basement, up the stairs, and out of the house.

When I was back in the car, I looked at him. "Now what?"

Gary looked at his phone. "Allan's at the station. Being charged with assaulting a cop. We'll talk to him. Delinda's there too. Do you want to come with?"

"Yes." My phone buzzed; I checked it. Again, it was Will. I answered. "Sorry. I missed your call. What's up?"

"Janelle. Have you seen her?" he asked. He was breathing heavily and voice was tinged with worry.

"No. What happened?"

"Be careful. She left me a letter. Just be careful." He hung up before I could answer.

"What's the matter?" Gary asked as he pulled away.

"Will asked if I've seen his ex. She sent him a letter, and he hung up."

"Is everything okay?"

"I'm not sure. I should get home and make sure the kids are safe."

Gary started toward home. "I can send over a police cruiser to watch the house if that makes you feel safer."

"Let's just get there. You can go to the station, and I'll just..." I could barely speak as I thought of Janelle, missing and out there, angry at me and Will because of our relationship. Something was going on with Janelle, and she was unpredictable.

My house seemed all in order as we pulled up. Both Emily and Jacob's cars were parked, but I flew from the car for the house without saying goodbye.

The kids were sitting around the television though they were reading, writing, or playing on their phones.

They glanced up at me, confused.

"What's the matter, Mom?" Emily asked.

"Janelle contacted Will and then went missing. I just wanted to make sure everything was okay here."

"Are we in danger?" Julia asked, worried.

Gary entered the house. "I have a police cruiser outside. He'll watch the house, Nikki, if you'd like to come with me."

"Are we okay, Uncle Gary?" Julia asked.

"We want to take precautions. Janelle is not acting herself," Gary said.

"We'll be fine, Mom. If the police are here, I'm sure they can stop something," Jacob said. I wasn't sure if he was trying to convince us or himself.

"Text Will or me if something happens."

"Go, Mom. Solve the case," Emily said.

Gary checked the doors and windows before walking me to the car. He waived to the police officer in the cruiser and backed away.

I watched the officer exit the car and walk around the

house, checking all entry points for an intruder. I wish I felt safer as we drove the short distance to the police station.

***

I stepped outside the car; the warm air and sun did little to ease my mind.

My eyes darted across the parking lot, now worried Janelle was following me, concerned she could hurt Will, myself, the kids. And while I should be home to protect them, I felt a strong need to stare Allan in the eyes and ask why.

"Are you okay, Nikki?"

"I just want to get this over with and get back home to the kids."

He nodded and led me toward the interrogation room.

My stomach churned as we neared the viewing room.

Gary was handed a packet; I assumed it was filled with pictures. He opened the door to the viewing room and let me inside. I took a seat and turned on the speaker.

"Hang tight," he said and he entered the interrogation room where Allan waited impatiently with his lawyer beside him.

CHAPTER 26

G ary tossed the pictures the police had found in Allan's basement, on the table, and slid them to Allan. Allan looked down. If he was shaken by what he saw, he didn't let on. He folded his hands on the table, staring up at Gary.

"Why were you following Ethan Grater and Jon Jaime Ray?"

Allan shrugged.

"You just decided to follow these two men, snap pictures of one of them kidnapping an incapacitated woman because you needed a hobby?"

Again, Allan shrugged, but his hands were shaking.

Gary pushed the picture of me toward Allan. "That's Nikki Page. You had spoken to her on the phone. You reported her to the police. I'm sure we'll find Nikki Page in your search history verifying you knew what she looked like. What were you planning on doing? Giving this to the police after Nikki was found dead."

Allan shrugged for a third time. My heart pounded in my chest. I could have beaten him myself if I had been in the room. It scared me, how close my kids were to losing me again. And Will. Will.

I stood and paced in the small viewing room.

Gary shuffled the photos on the table as I turned to walk the opposite direction.

"Jon Jaime Ray. Why were you following him? And don't shrug. Your DNA was found on his body. We also have emails between you, Delinda Love and several other models about taking him out."

I stopped and looked into the room. Gary had been reading his phone so he must have gotten word and not told me. I could feel myself trembling, knowing the police were putting together the pieces.

"So, tell me, why were you following these men?" Gary asked again.

Allan's lawyer, a man I didn't know whispered something in Allan's ear. Allan nodded.

"They killed my sister. I was looking for proof since you dunderheads chose to believe she killed herself."

Gary recoiled slightly after the accusation. He was about to toss down more photos when there was a knock on the interrogation room door. An officer entered with a folder. Gary opened it, and smiled.

He pulled out several pages, found the one he wanted and put it on the table. He slowly slid it to Allan.

Allan glanced at it and turned away. His leg shook, his foot tapped against the hard floor.

"Read the email out loud," Gary ordered.

Allan shook his head. Gary pulled it back and stared at it. "Allan. I think now is a good time. I think I can get Penelope Pinkerton to help us. She told me a lawyer wrote that asshole asking for the model release. She thinks that will help get the asshole arrested. LOL. We all know what's going to happen with that."

Gary put the email in the folder.

"Odd that you'd communicate that way. Even if you delete the emails, we can get them. Which is what we did. There're a lot of those emails, you and Mrs. Linda Johnson. Planning to kill Jon Jaime Ray and Ethan Grater."

Gary sat across from Allan. "The gun is Delinda's. From that email, she gave you the perfect timing to go after him. With that letter recently sent to Jon Jaime Ray, killing him would put Penelope at the top of the suspect list. But there was no other evidence to work with that theory. So, what did you do? You became a witness, claiming Penelope was with Jon Jaime Ray the night he died. But you forgot, there were

cameras. Penelope was there, because Delinda invited her."
Gary pulled out another email, from Delinda to Penelope.
"Would you like me to read it?"

Allan shook his head.

"You get Penelope there, to discuss the plan. She won't
go along with it, so you decide to use that meeting to further
accuse Penelope, take the attention off of yourself. Am I
close?"

Allan's lawyer whispered in his ear. Allan nodded.

"Jon Jaime Ray killed my sister. She didn't kill herself like
the police claimed. She was going to the police. She was going
to tell you she was recruited by Mara Grater on her uncle's
order because he was behind it all with Jon Jaime Ray."

"Did you also kill Mara?" Gary asked.

Allan sat straighter. "No. I had nothing to do with her
death. I think that asshole killed her too."

"Why do you say that?" Gary asked.

Allan took a deep breath as if he were not inclined to
help himself and reveal the truth of what he knew. "Ericka
told me she heard Mara fighting with her uncle, with Ethan
Grater. She didn't want to do recruit models anymore. She
didn't want to be in the business anymore. Ericka thought
she might have been abused and forced to work for them. I'm
not sure if that asshole had something on her as well, but she
didn't want to do it either."

"Where were you the night Jon Jaime Ray died? When Delinda was at the restaurant with Penelope."

He hung his head and cried.

The models had been abused and used, their lives ruined because of what Jon Jaime Ray and Ethan Grater had done. While I hoped somehow, they would all find peace, I knew it would take time. And for some of the models, it was too late. For Allen Mason, I didn't know where he would begin to find peace, knowing he'd be spending the rest of his life in jail.

Gary nodded for the police officer who handcuffed Allan and read him his rights, leading him to the jail cells. His lawyer followed him out.

Gary looked at me and shook his head, then visibly shuddered at all that had happened.

He didn't have much of a reprieve as the next suspect entered the interrogation room. Delinda 'Love' Johnson, once coiffed and put together was wearing sweats and a t-shirt, her hair disheveled, and her make up smeared down her face. She was followed by her lawyer, a heavyset man, with thick, bushy hair and a mustache.

Delinda glared at Gary, as the officer directed her to the chair. She tripped over her feet and fell to the table. Gary stood and helped her to the seat.

When they had settled in the chairs, Gary sat across from her, his hands folded on the table in front of him. "We've arrested Allan Mason for the murder of Jon Jaime Ray. We have you as an accessory. Care to tell me what happened, or would you like to go through the formal questions?"

Delinda sneered. "I didn't kill that asshole. You have nothing on me."

Gary sorted the evidence across the table. "I have emails between you and Allan, you and Penelope, and you and a host of other models discussing the murder. Planning it. Shall I read them for you?"

He took out one of the emails and slid it to Delinda. Her hands trembled as she picked it up and read what she had written. Her lawyer took the email. "I want a deal for my client. She'll tell you everything you want to know. For a lesser sentence. No jail time, five years' probation."

Gary laughed. "I can't make deals with you. You know that. Tell me what you know, and I'll advise the DA that you were helpful."

The lawyer whispered to Delinda and then nodded to Gary.

"He drugged me, took the pictures, forged my signature on the model release. He lied, and when I went to the police, you told me you couldn't do anything. So, I sued that bastard and lost. I lost everything. I was in debt from the legal fees, I was in debt because he found my other bills and somehow found out I had stolen the money from that charity. He blackmailed me with it because if it came out, I would lose the rest of what I had. I'm a business owner; I can't have my clients know."

Her voice was high and tight as she shuffled in her seat.

"I knew Allan from college, and we reconnected at Ericka's funeral. He told me what he thought really happened. I told him what happened to me. We talked. It was all in theory until Penelope had that letter written. We knew. We knew if we could connect her, give the police a reason, she'd get blamed, and we'd be clear."

"You set someone up to take the fall on top of all the other things you did. She was as much of a victim as you were," Gary said.

"It wasn't supposed to happen this way." Delinda hung her head.

"Did Allan Mason kill Jon Jaime Ray?" Gary asked.

"Yes."

"We never saw you enter after to fake the robbery, why?"

Delinda glanced up at Gary as she wiped her cheek.

"He found the letter. Made sure it was front and center. Penelope walked right into being framed."

Gary passed a pad of paper and pencil to Delinda. "Please write out what you know as well as your part in this."

Delinda looked at her lawyer. He nodded.

I paced as she wrote several pages of details about her role in Jon Jaime Ray's murder.

Gary motioned for the officer to arrest Delinda. She was read her Miranda rights and walked from the room. Gary sat, stunned by the day's events.

I left viewing and joined Gary in the interrogation room. "You got your murderer," I said and sat beside him.

"All that destruction of human lives. Two greedy, twisted men destroyed so much." He turned to me. "Thank you. For getting us on the right track."

I hugged my long-time friend. "I'm glad I could help. I was wondering. Both Ethan and Allan claimed Jon Jaime Ray killed Mara and Ericka. Any news on that?"

He moved his folders around. "I got a text while we were out and then was handed this. Both women had been poisoned. They couldn't do toxicology due to the length of time they've been deceased, but they took hair samples. It was gradual over a few weeks. But the evidence is there. We'll take another look at Ethan's house and at Jon Jaime Ray's and search for the poison. We have a bit more time since they're both dead. But the search is scheduled."

He held my hand. "Can I take you back home? It's been a long day, and I have reports to write."

I nodded and Gary, with his arm around my shoulders, put me in his car and drove me home.

I knew I could sleep for days if no more problems popped up. Boy, was I surprised.

"Hi, ma'am. I'm Officer Collins. I just wanted to let you know, everything's been quiet here. I'll be here until ten, and my replacement will sit in that same spot."

I really didn't think Janelle would hurt any of us. But I wasn't willing to take the chance. "Thanks officer. I appreciate the time."

"Yes ma'am," Officer Collins said. He sauntered back to his car, and I dragged myself inside.

I glanced around my suburban neighborhood. It was warm, hazy in the middle of summer. It felt too early for dinner, too late for a snack. Maybe a dip in the pool. I closed the garage, entered the cool house and dropped my purse by the door.

The kids had heeded my warning and stayed inside. They were lazily watching television. Maybe I'd do that instead of the pool.

"I was thinking of taking a dip in the pool. Any ideas for dinner?" I asked.

"Ice cream," Julia said.

"Funny. I was thinking leftovers if you had no new ideas. Anyone up for a dip in the pool?" I mentioned again. By the looks of the kids, they were done for the night, each in varying stages of sunburn and sleepiness.

"Is it safe?" Emily asked.

"The officer said everything was quiet. He's outside now. I think we're good for the pool," I said.

"It's creepy having the police sitting out there," Emily said softly, as she closed her eyes, hovering between wake and sleep.

"I'm sorry. Will was supposed to talk to Janelle today. I'm not sure if he ever found her." I glanced at the wall clock. "He should have been back by now."

"Are you worried?" Jacob asked.

I shook my head as I looked at the phone. "Not exactly. I don't think Janelle will hurt any of us, but it might have been an emotional conversation."

I sat beside the kids, pulled up my phone as it buzzed. It was Will. I took a deep breath and answered with shaky hands. "Hi, sweetie. The police are outside watching the house. How was your conversation with Janelle?"

"Janelle's dead."

I sat there stunned. "I…" I couldn't process that single sentence. I didn't know what to say. We knew something was going on with her, we all did, and yet Janelle's death surprised me and the realization of what may have happened. Did Will do something? "What do you mean, she's dead? Heart attack dead or suicide dead?"

I was trembling. The kids looked on, worry on their faces. It couldn't be possible. Janelle was just at the house making trouble. How did this happen?

"Murdered," he said quietly.

"Oh damn. What happened? Where are you?"

"I'm at the police station with my lawyer. We should have it sorted soon."

My stomach roiled. "Sorted? Soon? Have they arrested you?"

"No. There's no evidence that I had anything to do with it."

"Then why are you at the police station?" my voice rose, but I couldn't keep it calm. Why was he there?

"Nikki. Don't worry. I called it in. I found her dead."

My mind raced. "Will, what happened?"

"I filed the restraining order and went to see Janelle. I wanted to tell her in person. Get her to understand she needs help. I found her. The door was open. She was… she was lying there."

That didn't ease the anxiety and worry about to bubble over inside me.

"When… when was she murdered?" Words were difficult for me to execute. What happened?

"They estimate she was killed at eight in the morning. I was at the courthouse if that's why you're asking."

I had unknowingly stepped from the good to the bad, and the world was crashing down around us. It felt like I was moving and thinking in slow motion. We were standing on the precipice of our new life and now, this. I felt awful for Janelle, for her parents, her siblings. What had happened in Janelle's life that led to murder?

I knew from experience that things had a way of looking one way but might have been something entirely different.

I had this bad feeling that things were never going to be the same again.

Not the end. Continued on Page Four…. Coming Soon

www.ingramcontent.com/pod-product-compliance
Lightning Source LLC
Chambersburg PA
CBHW070842260626
47170CB00007B/2466